"Heartwarming, lyrical, soulful, and with just the right amount of humor: this book sparkles with authentic, layered characters and beautiful, thoughtful prose."

— Jodi Meadows, NYT bestselling co-author
of *My Lady Jane* and *My Plain Jane*

Praise for *Compulsion*

"Skillfully blends rich magic and folklore with adventure, sweeping romance, and hidden treasure....Impressive."

—*Publishers Weekly*

"Wonderful....Eight Beaufort is so swoon-worthy that it's ridiculous."

—*RT Book Reviews*, RT Editors' Best Books of the Year

"Certainly delivers a compelling mystery about feuding families and buried secrets, not to mention a steamy romance."

—*Booklist*

"Even the villains and not-likable characters were so engrossing. I have to say I've already put the sequel on my TBR shelf."

—*USA Today*

"Mixes dark spirits, romance, feuding families, and ancient curses into the perfect potion."

—*Justine Magazine*

"Darkly romantic and steeped in Southern Gothic charm, you'll be *compelled* to get lost in the Heirs of Watson Island series."

—#1 NYT bestselling author Jennifer L. Armentrout

"The perfect Southern family saga: charming and steamy on the surface, with cold-blooded secrets buried down deep."

—#1 *New York Times* bestselling author Kendare Blake

"Haunting, atmospheric, and absorbing."

—Claudia Gray, *New York Times* bestselling author

"Beautifully written, with vivid characters, a generations-old feud, and romance that leaps off the page, this Southern ghost story left me lingering over every word, and yet wanting to race to the compelling finish. Not to be missed."

—Megan Shepherd, *New York Times* bestselling author

Praise for *Lake of Destiny*

"Delightful, charming, and heartwarming!"
—*New York Times* bestselling author Wendy Higgins

"I adored every page....Beautifully written and perfectly paced, with delightful traces of magical realism."
—Award-winning author Erin Cashman

"Well-written, well-crafted, well-paced and full of heart....So much charm it's magical!"
—*BookGeek*

"Martina Boone's gorgeous storytelling enthralled me from start to finish. The plot is captivating, whimsical, and full of surprises that kept me turning the pages."
—*Sincerely KarenJo*

"I loved this!!! It reminds me of a Nora Roberts series, The Gallaghers of Ardmore...but a Scottish version with men in kilts!"
—*Two Chicks on Books*

"Outlander-Lite Meets Gilmore Girls in Scotland. This is a story that sucked me in from the start and didn't let go until I'd laughed, shed a few tears and worked up an appetite. Fast. Fun. Romantic. Read it!"
—*Jenuine Cupcakes*

"This book had it all, romance, fantasy, folklore, drama, and emotional family issues....A great story and I enjoyed every minute."
—Linda Rutland

"Full of myths, legends, and life. The plot is good, the characters are great, and I couldn't put it down. When is the next book?"
—Cheryl Bond"

"This was so good I'll be reading it again. A wonderful story...with a touch of the fantasy of Brigadoon. I had to read it in one sitting."
—Debra Chase

Love for Two Lifetimes

Also by Martina Boone

Young Adult Fiction:

Compulsion

Persuasion

Illusion

Adult Fiction:

Lake of Destiny: A Celtic Legends Novel

Bell of Eternity: A Celtic Legends Novel

Magic of Winter: A Celtic Legends Novel

Echo of Glory: A Celtic Legends Novel

Legend and Nonfiction:

Welcome Home: Historic Romance
of the Celtic Legends

Love for Two Lifetimes

Martina Boone

MAYFAIR
PUBLISHING

Love for Two Lifetimes is a work of fiction, and the characters, events, and places depicted in it are products of the author's imagination. Where actual events, places, organizations, or persons, living or dead, are included, they are used fictitiously and not intended to be taken otherwise.

MAYFAIR
PUBLISHING
712 H Street NE, Suite 1014
Washington, DC 20002
First Mayfair Publishing edition September 2018
Copyright © 2018 by Martina Boone

Jacket design by Kalen O'Donnell
Interior Illustrations by Martina Boone
Cartoon by iartservice

Summary: "Following clues in years of unsent love letters after her mother's death, Izzy steps into a world of English aristocracy in search of her father, a world of secrets, lies, and masquerades, and falls for the last person she should probably ever love. A magical story about two generations of love revealed in prose, love letters, and more."

Published in the United States of America

ISBN 978-1-946773-19-7 (hardback)
ISBN 978-1-946773-21-0 (paperback)
ISBN 978-1-946773-20-3 (ebook)

For all the dreamers,
and for
my wonderful husband,
who plots all our travels and adventures.

PART ONE

Izzy
Brittle Leaves

The music wakes me. Mom's piano is a constant in our house. She listens to her compositions while she sleeps, and she plays—even louder—when she's awake. I love the magic of it, but sometimes I feel as if her music has taken over my heartbeat, my breathing, my *life* as well as hers. Today, she's awake too early, which means she hasn't yet gone to bed.

> Text to Elli:
>
> Me: Higher Grounds?
>
> Elli: Twenty minutes!

I dress in a scowl and the pink Oscar Wilde T-shirt my mother hates. To be fair, Mom hates all my Oscar Wilde T-shirts. She claims there's no point wearing quotes that advocate independent thought when I insist on going to a public school that seems to discourage thinking altogether. I tell her that just makes the message even more important.

"A MAN WOMAN WHO DOES NOT
THINK FOR HIMSELF HERSELF
DOES NOT THINK AT ALL."
OSCAR WILDE

In the shadow of the moon that still clings to the sky outside my window, I make my bed and gather my books together. The envelope that murdered my future lurks on the corner of the desk, and I grab that, too, before I trudge downstairs.

Arpeggios

My mother is in the morning room, coffee cups strewn everywhere, sheet music sprawled on the grand piano and the bench beside her. Rough drafts pour from her fingers to the keyboard in ultra-fast arpeggios—wild, tumbling notes like leaves chased by wind. Four dry leaves flutter to rest with a pile of others along the wall, their sienna and burnt umber stark against the sapphire of the Turkish rug.

I don't bother checking the closed window where

the sheer white curtains hang unmoving. Beyond it, the trees are still and bare, their leaves only now beginning to bud. In the darkness, daffodils glow like yellow stars uncurling among the black mulch in our flower beds. It wasn't the season that called the leaves into being; it was the magic of my mother's music.

I pad across the carpet and stand beside her. She stops playing to scratch something onto a manuscript page, then repeats a passage she has played already. She's recording the session, too, but she likes the process of setting the notes on paper. That's the one artistic thing I've inherited from her. The words I type on my computer always trickle one at a time from inside my head, while those I write longhand seem to flow through me instead of from me.

Mom looks up and smiles, her eyes still a little music-drunk. "'Morning, *querida.*"

"Good night," I say, "considering it's still dark outside. Waking me up this early is practically child abuse."

"So report me," my mother counters in her faint Argentinian accent, and her gaze shifts down to take in what I'm wearing. "That T-shirt, Isabelle! Must you?"

"Definitely. Also, shouldn't you go to bed?"

"Soon." Her brows furrow and form a spiderweb of creases on her normally smooth, warm skin. "Are you going to go tell Elli this morning?"

"I wish I didn't have to."

"In that case, I forgive the T-shirt. Temporarily. But in future, write your own subversions instead of relying on someone else's." She studies me, sharp dark eyes registering all the things I haven't said. Her features soften. "What do you say we celebrate this weekend, you, me, and Elli? I'm sure you two will work things out, and my Concerto in E-flat Major is nearly finished. We could fly to Paris."

I smile, because the concerto that Mom's composing has been "nearly finished" these past two years. By this afternoon, she'll either be in despair once more or so far down the rabbit hole of creation she won't remember mentioning Paris.

"Sure," I tell her, and I'm typing as I turn away.

Text to Elli:

Me: Leaving now.

Elli: Caffeeeeeine!

"Hey!" Mom calls after me and taps her cheek. "You forgot something."

I bend down to kiss her. "Make good art, Mom."

"Make good stories, *mija*."

I cross to the door and glance back from the threshold. My mother's playing again already, immersed so deep in her music that the rest of the world has faded. Another speed-of-light arpeggio rustles through the room, and another brittle leaf shimmers into being above the piano's gleaming, swooping curves. One more small piece of my mother's magic.

Choices

Elli's waist-length hair is lavender, which I not-so-secretly envy. She doesn't have much of it, which I also envy. I have enough hair for three people, which is like wearing a space-heater when it's hot, and when it's humid I look like a Q-tip dipped in walnut furniture stain. This means that, thanks to climate change, I'm doomed to a lifetime of hair-suck. Here in Arlington, Virginia, it's either humid or raining or snowing about 350 days a year. Today being worse than usual, I slink into Higher Grounds wearing a hot-pink beanie to go with my T-shirt, red coat, and purple sneakers, and Elli gives me a bug-eyed grin. Her grins are *happy*. They stretch from ear to ear.

"I knew it was going to be a good day. See? We couldn't have planned this better." She gestures at her own pink and red outfit, delighted at our color-coordination. Backing up to stand beside me in front of the bakery display that's lit up to make every crumb of sugar glisten, she aims her phone, angling it down while she draws her cheeks in and pouts her mouth out and does something sparkling with her eyes.

The hand I raise in front of my face is a half-hearted gesture. My puffy-eyed morning-look doesn't matter much in the grand scheme of things, and though she be but little, Elli is unstoppably fierce. She wins—as usual—and the photo is up on social media before I've plucked my Caramelized Honey Latte from the counter.

Carrying the cup to an empty table, I inhale the perfection that is the smell of coffee and absorb the way the music of the grinder and the steam and the water trickling punctuate the indie pop music playing on the sound system. Coffee smells like heaven, but it tastes bitter as heck unless you fill it with de-heckifying additives. Coffee that costs more than the per capita daily income of India is theoretically against my principles. But still. *Caramelized. Honey. Latte.*

My principles are a work-in-progress.

Elli throws herself into a booth, pries the lid off her Macchiato, and blows down into the steam. She picks at her chocolate chunk muffin. About a million calories float toward me across the table and settle onto each of my thighs. Elli eats. I absorb. That's how our relationship works.

Between bites, she peers across the table. "You didn't call me back or text last night, so what's up with you? Did your mom finish the concerto? Were you celebrating?"

"Nearly almost."

I refrain from mentioning Paris and focus on

trying to pluck the right explanation out of the useless swirl of thoughts inside my head. For once,
words completely fail me. Then again, I don't need
words. Rummaging in my bag, I retrieve the acceptance packet from Princeton that just broke my online
waitlist impasse. We're both silent as I hand it over.
Elli's officially a Princeton reject. One *yes* and a *no*
should be an automatic pass. That's what we agreed.
But this is Princeton.

Princeton.

Elli unfolds the letter, runs her thumb over the logo
at the top of the page, and reads the first sentence.
"Izzy!" Her eyes go moist. "This is fantastic. You
have to go."

I shake my head. "We pinky swore."

"Pinkies have an unwritten Princeton exception.
Also there's less humidity in New Jersey."

"I'm not picking a school based on hair-suck.
Columbia is great. Or Chicago. And we're both still
waiting at Yale. Anyway, since they rejected you, I
have to question Princeton's judgment. Which makes
me question the quality of their education. So, who
wants them?"

"*You* do. Princeton was your first word out of
the womb, just about. And your mom already took
the teaching job up there on the presumption that
we'd all be together."

"I'm resilient, and Mom doesn't have the patience

for teaching anyway—and since she's a literal diva, no one will think less of her for quitting. Really, I'm doing all her would-be students a public service. Think of the fragile young egos I'll be saving."

"It's my parents I blame for this." Elli plops her elbows down on the table and buries her chin in her hands and heaves a dramatic sigh. "If only they did something useful for a living! The Ivies are already drowning in doctor's kids, which makes me the last thing they need. But you? You have the whole Marcella-Cavalera-as-a-mother thing going for you. You're a trophy kid. Everyone has to take you."

"Hey! Watch it!"

"Oh, fine." Elli's hands surrender for her. "You know I don't mean that. You earned Princeton, and I got that stupid C in Freshman English. But seriously, what kind of a fascist teacher hates Toni Morrison? Or trees. Toni Morrison's trees. It was a darn good essay."

"It wasn't a D essay," I concede.

"Right? A solid B. B- tops." Elli pauses. Leans forward. Looks all serious. "But you know you have to go, don't you? No arguing, because I'll never forgive you if you don't go."

I'm not sure I will either, but college without Elli was never in the plan. Apart from Mom, Elli's all the family I've ever had. How can I possibly leave her?

—◆❈◆—

Izzy & Elli's Origin Story Version 3.5

Elli and I met in the hospital nursery eighteen years ago.

The way the story goes, her dad and my mom were both standing in the hall, staring at us through the glass like we were little aliens they didn't know what to do with. Dr. Andrew thought baby Elli was impossibly fragile compared to her brothers, who'd both been born looking like future football players. Mom had never held an actual infant and she'd never played with dolls. Even then it was probably obvious a baby was never supposed to be written into her concert program. Dr. A, being no dummy, took inventory of Mom's hospital gown and robe and asked if one of the babies belonged to her. Mom pointed to me in my pink beanie—baby pink back then, not the hot pink one I wear now—and asked which one was Dr. A's. He pointed to the bassinet next to mine.

The way the story goes, Elli and I were already looking at each other, and until the day we went home, we screamed whenever we were separated. I guess we got over that eventually. By then, though, Dr. Andrew and Dr. Eleanor had adopted both me and Mom, and Mom no longer held me like she was afraid to break me.

Elli and I never needed to adopt each other. We've always belonged, the same way Mom and I belong.

Other friends have come and gone, drifting around our periphery, shuffling with us through the usual series of linoleum-floored, locker-lined school halls and activity-overloaded summer camps. Elli and I are constant. She loves her family, but her messy, turbulent, sports-loving brothers are like alien beings, and she prefers the lack of stinky football cleats and the quiet of my house. I sometimes envy her the messy completeness of having both a mom and dad, not to mention siblings, so I like to borrow them all now and then. I live there, anyway, whenever school schedules don't let me tag along on Mom's foreign tours. But it's Mom and Elli and I who get along the best. Elli can cook *carbonado* and *empanadas* better than I can, and we both cook better than Mom, who burns a third of everything she tries to make and is more likely to give us *dulce de leche* on bread than something involving meat, veg, or actual nutrition.

The way our story was *supposed* to go, Elli and I would go off to Princeton in the fall. I would follow in the footsteps of F. Scott Fitzgerald, Eugene O'Neill, and Jonathan Safran Foer, and Elli would try to figure out why any reasonable human being—much less someone who calls themselves a scientist—could still fail to understand the dangers of climate change. Mom was going to drive up once a week to teach a class, and the three of us were all going to live together happily ever after. Or at least for four more years.

"The best laid schemes o' mice an' men
Gang aft a-gley."

Robert Burns

So. What am I supposed to choose? Mom and Princeton? Or Elli?

Man, I hate decisions.

The thing is, I know how lucky I am to even get to worry about all this. In the grand scheme of things, I have the best kind of problems. I have a mom I love more than Nutella chocolate tarts, a best friend who knows me better than I know myself, and some of the greatest schools in the world who are willing to teach me things. But no matter what I decide, someone I love gets hurt. Someone is going to lose. Something will change, and our three futures will diverge like that Robert Frost poem about the road not taken, which isn't about asserting individuality so much as it's about looking back and finding ways to justify the hardest choices. People always get that wrong.

I don't want to look back and have to justify.

Whispers

Final semester of senior year, not even the teachers care very much. Which explains why we're watching the travesty that is *The Scarlet Letter* with Demi Moore in AP English.

The door opens from the hall, admitting the sound of basketballs bouncing from the nearby gym and the hollow slam of a locker down the hall. I don't bother looking up from the pro/con lists I'm scribbling in my pocket notebook. Not until the rustle of heads turning and bodies unslumping penetrates my Princeton-induced depression.

For once, Principal Gupta isn't obnoxiously using the PA system or calling on the phone. Her long braid swings wildly as she duck-walks under the projection screen to Mrs. Murphy's desk in person. Both she and Mrs. Murphy are dressed in aggressively passive beige, and until this moment, I've never considered how similar they are in personality. I wonder if they are friends. Do they sit in the teacher's lounge together, sipping sludgy coffee and sharing complaints about over-involved or under-involved parents and bemoaning bygone days?

An imaginary conversation between them writes itself out in my head, but it's first draft, not even notebook-worthy. Frowning, I dig deeper, try to imagine the secrets they'd be desperate to keep the other from finding out, the secrets they've never told to anyone. Secrets are the key to every fictional character. Every interesting one, at least.

Elli pokes me in the shoulder.

"What?" I ask.

She nods toward the front of the room. Reaching over and taking my hand, she squeezes. Hard.

The whole class has lapsed into a nervous silence, and Mrs. Murphy and Principal Gupta have turned to look at me wearing those horrified, avid expressions that nice people get when something awful happens. I try to think of something I might have done to earn that look, but T-shirts and asking occasionally "challenging" questions are pretty much my main subversions. Neither one rates very high on the scale of offenses that would draw the principal's attention.

Still, Mom's going to say I told you so.

This is what I'm thinking.

Then Principal Gupta's hand is suddenly on my shoulder, and her voice is full of pity, and Elli's standing up to try to follow me, but Mrs. Murphy's shaking her head and bending to whisper in Elli's ear. I'm stumbling out into the hall where there are two police officers waiting, their shirts lumpy over Kevlar vests and their faces serious and sympathetic.

No-no-no-no-no-no-no.

This is what I'm thinking.

Because there's no possible *yes* in this situation.

There's only something horribly awful. There's only someone hurt.

And apart from Elli who was sitting beside me a second ago, I really only have one person in the entire world.

Just one.

And the police tell me there's been an accident.

Playlist

The police turn on the sirens as we drive to the hospital. That's how bad it is.

The patrol car stinks of sweat and vomit inadequately masked over with upholstery cleaner and pine-scented air freshener. We pass cars in blurred strands of brake lights.

Officer Tillman keeps turning to look at me, and I try not to hyperventilate, try not to picture my mother cut out of her car by firemen, hooked up to machines, lying in a hospital bed all alone despite a million doctors and nurses bustling around her.

Can she hear anything if she's brain dead?

She shouldn't die to the sound of hospital machines.

I start making a playlist of her favorite pieces on my phone— Liszt's "La Campanella," Prokofiev's "Concerto No. 3 in C Major," Beethoven's "Piano Concerto No. 5 in E-flat Major"—because it's something I can do.

I will never listen to these pieces again. How could I ever listen to them again? But Mom deserves to go out with what she loves.

Pausing to dry my phone against my jeans, I ignore the *ding* of Elli's zillionth text:

> Elli: ???? Izzy! Answer me! Please answer!
>
> Elli: Are you ok? Mom and Dad are coming. We're all coming.
>
> Elli: What do you need? How's your mom?

I can't answer.

I can't type the words.

I won't think them.

I won't believe them. The universe doesn't need that out there.

Mom swears by yoga and meditation. In Sanskrit, intention is called Samkalpa, which literally means what you create in your mind with will or imagination. Karma begins with intention.

I *intend* for Mom to be fine.

I *imagine* this is all a mistake.

I *will* the doctors to be wrong.

Mind Death

My mother is a deflated balloon, lying in the hospital bed. Small and diminishing. Floating away.

Not awake.

The doctors insist she won't wake up, can't wake up, and they tell me I have to be the one to choose. That's the downside of being eighteen. As if anyone is ever adult enough to deal with this.

I don't want to be adult. I only want my mother.

She doesn't look...she doesn't *need* this. Her face isn't damaged. Around the breathing tube, it's still lovely and almost peaceful.

I can't decide. I *can't*.

I place my phone beside her ear on the rough, sterile sheets and start the music playing. Sitting beside her with my knees drawn up on the chair, I rock myself back and forth.

The music knifes through the air in dazzling notes. I imagine her playing, her fingers skipping and sizzling and gliding and tip-toeing across the keyboard, the music pouring from her heart.

If I do what the doctors recommend, Mom will never finish her concerto. She'll never achieve what she's always worked for. Not the perfect piece. Not any future music. Not any future anything. But they tell me that's over no matter what I choose.

"Please come back," I whisper, picking up her hand. It's warm and limp, her and not her. I wait, and wait, and wait. It doesn't move. It doesn't change.

My beautiful, mercurial, passionate mother has played for royalty and performed in the greatest concert halls around the world. She brings audiences to their feet and conductors to their knees. She has never met a batch of cookies she can't burn or a bill she can't forget to pay.

Just last Tuesday, she emerged from her music and threw herself onto my bed, making me bounce where I was studying. "I need a sweet-tooth-ritual," she said. "Pack an overnight bag. Hurry up."

I gave the usual, token argument. "I can't go anywhere. I have school tomorrow..."

"I'll write the note," she said. "I'll fawn. I'll be *nice*. Please, *querida*. I need this."

In the pre-spring lull, Cape Cod was still bitterly cold and quiet. We walked on the empty beach and played Scrabble (which I always win) and chess (which she always wins), and we watched *Casablanca* for the thousandth time on the hotel cable while eating dessert for appetizers and dessert for dinner and dessert for dessert.

All that sugar made my stomach hurt, and I groaned and said, "We're getting too old for sweet-tooth-rituals."

Mom stole the last of my *crème brûlée*. "What do I always tell you? You only get one life. You may as well choose to live it brilliantly."

People who don't know my mother talk about the blinding speed of her hands, her dexterity, the absolute lack of a dominant side in her playing. She laughs at that. She says it isn't her hands she's training with all the practice.

Studies prove the mind of a pianist is wired differently, that it communicates in syntax instead of words. Pianists multitask. They make decisions at the speed of light. My mother's mind is what allows—*allowed*—her to make choices that communicate pure emotion. Choices that make people *feel*.

Brain dead. That's what the doctors call it.

Mind death.

The other driver was texting.

A scream builds in my chest, squeezing out the air. A scream that has no sound. A scream that has no relief.

This can't be real.

What kind of a text was worth my mother's life?

Letting Go

I sit on the floor with my hands wrapped around my knees and Elli's arm wrapped around my shoulders. I'm sobbing so hard I can't hear what Elli's parents are saying, shaking so hard my teeth chatter. I understand there are people Mom can help, that she wanted to be an organ donor. I understand I have to decide, even if the thought of life without my mother is impossible.

I'm supposed to trust what the machines and the doctors and Elli's parents tell me, that Mom will never breathe or move on her own again. Never think on her own again. I'm supposed to believe she will never be Mom again. She will never see me graduate from high school, or walk me down the aisle at my wedding like she promised.

Why did I run out this morning to meet Elli at Higher Grounds? That's an extra hour I could have had, listening to Mom, watching her. Being with her. It never occurred to me that the time I gave up might have been all the time I would ever have.

I don't want to let go. I don't want to, but I can't be selfish. Mom wouldn't want life without her mind, without her music. She'd want me to fight for what *she* wanted, the way she has always fought for me.

This isn't about what *I* want.

I have to choose for my mother because she can't choose for herself.

Malcolm
Paper Butterflies

The Duchess of Northumberland created an entire poison garden at Alnwick Castle, and the only ideas I've come up with for Halford Hall are a murder tour and paper butterflies. Butterflies. It's bloody emasculating, that's what it is. I try to tell myself I'm evolved enough not to mind that I'm spending Friday night hiding insects for the amusement of sugar-sozzled children. Still, I can't help a Neanderthal knee-jerk reaction that makes me long for a pint and a nice, bruising game of rugby. Not necessarily in that order.

Percy, my best mate, does little to hide his amusement as I get down on all fours to tack a Large Blue butterfly—only recently brought back from extinction locally—to a life-sized portrait of the eighth Countess of Mortimer. "I should snap a few photos of you doing that," he says, "and hold them in reserve for appropriate blackmail opportunities."

"Only if you have a death wish."

"You used to be more fun, you know, once upon a time. Right, so how many *Maculinea arion* are we up to now? Ninety-five?" He marks this latest butterfly on the tourist map of Halford's public rooms.

I knock the eighth countess's portrait as I scramble to my feet, and she chides me from her gilded frame. She's the one who introduced dark, arched eyebrows into the Halford gene pool sometime in the fifteenth century, and the way they draw together even when her lips are smiling makes her appear perpetually worried. But *she* lived here long before having a stately pile in the British countryside required tours, destination wedding weekends, community hearts and minds campaigns, and treasure hunts for children featuring paper insects, maps, and prizes. I doubt my own expression looks any happier.

"It's ninety-eight butterflies, not ninety-five," I say. "Don't tell me you've lost track?"

"Are you quite sure?" Percy's own blond eyebrows bristle like a pair of caterpillars.

"Of course I'm sure. But you're the one meant to be reading Maths at Oxford. I assumed you could count." With a sigh, I amble over, and we both frown at the map.

Percy's windblown complexion grows even redder as I take the pencil and mark the missing butterflies for him. His attention shifts strategically to the ceiling. "I'm thinking of changing over to Politics instead, actually," he says. "Which you'd know if you ever showed up for meals or anything remotely social."

That's about as close to admitting hurt as Percy'd ever get, and he covers it with a grin and a shake of his head. "The good news is," he continues, "starting out in Maths and Philosophy, I've done most of the core for Philosophy, Politics & Economics. I'll only need to make up a handful of courses."

I take in his pinched smile, his unaccustomedly rumpled shirt, the mop of hair that's untidier than usual, and the pallor beneath the ruddy cheeks he gets from rowing. Clearly, I've been a rubbish mate. I never twigged that offering to help me set up the butterfly hunt was a pretext for needing a sounding board. And when am I ever around for him to talk to? I'm down here every weekend now that Dad's seemingly chucked in half his responsibilities.

Which is no excuse. Friendship doesn't deserve excuses. I should have noticed Percy struggling.

"Look, I'm the last person to tell you to stick it out in Maths," I manage to say quite evenly, "but I wonder if it's escaped your notice that Economics isn't any better. And also, the PPE-ists are all first-rate dickheads. I can't see you swanning around college in a suit and planning clandestine *coup d'états* of the Doctor Who society en route to ultimately taking over Parliament. It's not your style."

Percy's shoulders curl, and his finger twitches on

the pencil. "I haven't got many other options, have I? I revise until my eyes bleed and my grades are still disastrous. Face it, I'm useless at anything to do with science or technology or management. History is soporific—no offense—and I've never had your dedication to keeping the family pile afloat. I can't see myself spending the next six decades of my life supervising meaningful community employment at Malming Abbey and researching the hidden history of long-dead blacksmiths. In which case, I might as well embrace the family tradition and wade into the swamps of government. Honestly, the thought of it wouldn't be half so bad if I didn't know it would put a smile on the old man's face."

The half-hearted grins we exchange at that are a show of solidarity. Our friendship, Percy's and mine, was forged in the crucible of admiration for the Leicester City Football Club and a mutual hatred of our paternal members. The reasons may be different—Percy blames his father for destroying the country and mine was only responsible for destroying my mother—but the intensity of feeling brought us together and bonds us still.

We duck into the state dining room, and I affix another paper butterfly to a sign about Grinling Gibbons, the man who carved the seventeenth-century wall paneling. The last of the hundred *Maculinea* goes in a corner of the corridor outside.

Then, thank God, we're done. Technically, I suppose, setting up the new endangered butterfly hunt is one of the things the tour staff could have handled. They're already overworked, though, since Dad's too depressed to care about what goes on these days. In the grand scheme of things, my butterflies may not do much to increase the number of mums and dads willing to plonk down hard-earned cash to force march their offspring through Halford's gardens and twenty-six public rooms. But it's almost free to implement, and it can't do any harm.

"That's it? Obligation discharged?" Percy marks the final butterfly on the map and checks his watch. "Because it occurs to me I could be convinced to forgo Mrs. Danvers' roast beef and Yorkshire pud in favor of LiveFriday at the Asmolean followed by an irresponsible night of drinking. We could still make it back to Oxford with time to spare. And in case you need more incentive, that red-haired Catherine was asking if you were coming."

I've no interest in any girl who's more enamored with an aristocratic title than the person it belongs to, but I refrain from mentioning that. "You swore you'd see me through the weekly dinner," I remind him instead, "and please don't call Anna 'Mrs. Danvers.' First, she's nothing like that, and second, her hearing is supernatural and her umbrages are legendary."

"All the more reason to get out whilst we can. You

may love her, but your housekeeper very nearly gives me fond feelings about my own family dinners. At least until I remember I'd rather have my teeth drilled out than attend another one. You've no idea how good you actually have it with your father."

"You only say that because you haven't had to live with him. And don't think I haven't noticed you're trying to change the subject."

"I changed that five minutes ago. Do keep up, Mal. The point is, I'm bound to be sucked into government sooner or later. I might as well embrace my fate as not."

"The whole purpose of fate is to give us something to rebel against."

"Nietzsche would argue that one."

"True, but embracing life isn't the same thing as embracing fate, is it?"

"All the more reason we should take time out to embrace LiveFriday and red-haired Catherine."

Though Percy's tone is light, his eyes tell a different story. I can't help giving in. Anna'll be disappointed, but I doubt Dad will even notice so long as I'm back in the morning before the tourists.

Percy and I cut through the book hall and the library, then stop in the office to drop off the annotated butterfly map. Tours are finished for the day and the guests for Sunday's wedding won't start trickling in until tomorrow. For the moment, the house is still:

ninety-eight cavernous rooms that have witnessed rebellions, treachery, treason, war, wealth, poverty, and everything in between. For me, it's a comfortable stillness, though, like the pensive quiet of an old married couple who know all each other's secrets.

The fight to save Halford is the one and only thing my father and I still have in common. He singlehandedly kept it from being turned into a hotel when he was little more than my age, and if he was able to do that, I can't see it gutted and sold off piece by piece on my watch.

Whatever daft schemes and ridiculous stunts I need to concoct, however many children's tours and community events I'll have to devise, I won't let Halford slip away.

Izzy
Claire de Lune

I'm packing.

Time is a tunnel and the world spins through it both too fast and too slow. Seven weeks have passed since the funeral. Seven weeks spent at Elli's house with everyone treating me as if I'm going to break. Even her brothers reduce their usual galloping up and down the stairs between classes at the local college. Their voices are perpetually at half-volume while they shout at each other. They even close their doors to drown out the clash of Ethan's rap music and Owen's techno-rock.

My suitcase is full, but there are leftover clothes still folded on the bed. Elli's mother keeps shopping for me as if dresses and blouses and jeans that I wear on the outside will fix the ugliness within. I've been wearing them because Dr. E went to a lot of trouble, because shopping is her way of trying to make me feel better, and because my old jeans are now too big. I'm down a size and a half. Food tastes like cardboard. But it's time Elli's family got back to their normal lives.

Not that Elli agrees with that.

"Come on. Just stay a while longer," she says. "I don't want you to be alone."

She flops onto the bed behind me, her legs stretched out and her back against the lavender wall in her room. The walls are actually white—her mother likes things uniform—but Elli has filled every inch of space with framed and matted photos, art, and posters of seascapes and marine animals. Each wall has a different predominant color. Lavender, mauve, azure, and lapis, going clockwise. Lavmaazlap, Elli calls it. Or palzaamval, counter-clockwise. Her speakers emit low ocean sounds, waves on the beach and whale songs, and together with the images of corals and bright schools of fish, it all creates a sense of being underwater.

It's impossible to breathe underwater. My lungs are starved of oxygen.

The problem is that now I'll always be alone. The space Mom used to fill is empty.

I need to get away.

Somewhere quieter.

I have a house to go back to. I'm eighteen, and I

can't keep hiding in Elli's room. I want to go home and scream into the silence where no one else will hear me.

Maybe I'll paint when I get home. Yellow walls would be cheerful. Or maybe I'll get a cat.

"At least let me come with you," Elli says. "I can help you sort. Hand you Kleenex."

"I'm thinking of getting a cat."

"Instead of Kleenex? I don't think cats like getting wet."

"The monsoons are over. It's time for the dry season."

"There's no time limit on how long it's okay to cry. You can use my shoulder."

"Maybe a gray cat. I could call her Rain. What do you think of Rain?"

"As a form of weather, I'm a fan. Not so much if you want to inflict it on a cat. Also, the Columbia dorms prohibit pets, which is possibly shortsighted of them given that high blood pressure results from every other kind of pressure and Mom says pets are calming—"

"Don't," I say, though I'm not sure what I'm *don't*ing. College. The logic of continuing to live a catless life. The fact that Elli still has a mother who can make pronouncements.

Is it possible to *rent* a cat? I imagine the internet listing:

<u>Cat Rental Store: Feline Emotional Support</u>
<u>https://www.CatRentals.com</u>
From dead-mother rage/loss/emptiness to college stress, Cat Rental Stores® offer cuddly kitties for all your temporary soul-recovery needs.
Over 1300 US locations.

Ghost Music

Even the house is mourning. Hushed. Whispering and heavy. Empty.

The tree Mom never got around to having trimmed out front drags its branches against the guest room window. In the silence, the wail is like a baby crying.

My mind plays tricks. The first night I'm there alone, I wake to Debussy's "Claire de Lune," the lyrical third movement of the *Bergamasker Suite*. The music is so clear that I follow it downstairs into the music room.

Mom is sitting there in the pool of moonlight that drifts in through the window, her corkscrew curls spilling over the ancient pale gray pashmina she wears thrown across the shoulders of black silk pajamas.

I stop beside her, and she looks up and smiles at me. "Tell me the story," she says, still playing.

I've always loved to tell the stories behind the music. Some exist, and some I make up myself, but

I've told this one a dozen times. It's so real, I can almost see the shape of it hovering in the air. There are dancers whose smiles are as much of a disguise as the masks they wear. Pretending happiness, they sweep and spin together across a checkered marble floor, their costumes jewel-colored or somber black and white, harlequins and swordsmen and ladies with wide silk skirts, painted lips, and tall, powdered, and stinking wigs.

They're all puppets in a courtly ballet, bottling secrets up inside them. There's the princess who would sell her soul for youth, who hopes for redemption while she continues to be the mistress of her sister's husband. A young duke plots to kill his brother for the sake of an empty title. A thief moves among them all, masquerading amid the masqueraders. Then there's fourteen-year-old Antonia. She's married to a man twice her age, a bald, fat, *smug* man she abhors because, in her heart, she's wed to Horatio, the third son of a second son. Antonia and Horatio dance to the edge of the dance floor, then slip away, out the high French windows into the still and silent moonlight, stealing illicit kisses in a topiary garden of fantastic beasts beyond the glittering fountains of the beautiful, lonely house.

The music fades as the story ends.

My mother fades.

I try to call her back.

I tell her how much I love her. I tell her how much I miss her. Tell her I will never wear my Oscar Wilde T-shirts again if only she will stay. Tell her I'll do anything if she'll fight a little harder.

She leaves me anyway.

When she's gone, I sit at the piano, but I never learned to play. She always said I was too stubborn to learn. I prefer to think I was too pragmatic. Mom's music already overflowed the house, overflowed our world, and there wasn't room for more.

My fingers sweep the keys.

Gently I close the lid.

Giving up the bench, I sit with my back to the wall in the still messy music room where photographs of me and Mom laugh down from the walls. I make a playlist of my favorites of her recordings: Debussy's "Claire de Lune," Beethoven's *Diabelli Variations*, Schumann's *Toccata*, Ravel's *Gaspard de La Nuit*. I play them over and over and over because they're all that remains.

Masqueraders

It's 3:04 a.m. I climb back into my bed.

The moon is low and round outside my window, the night's eye spilling across the carpet and my cabinet of museum curiosities, across the walls of bookshelves with books organized by topic and color into rainbow rows. I turn on the playlist, and Mom's "Claire de Lune" spills into the moonlit room.

As much as I love the composition, I've always loved the poem it's based on more, the image and quiet tragedy of Verlaine's masqueraders and bergamaskers dancing in their pretend happiness:

All sing in a minor key
Of victorious love and the opportune life,
They do not seem to believe in their happiness
And their song mingles with the moonlight,
With the still moonlight, sad and beautiful,
That sets the birds dreaming in the trees...

I've worn disguises every minute of every day since Mom died, pretending to the world that I'm all right. Inside, I'm a boat unmoored, in danger of drifting away from myself.

———◆�֎◆———

Washington Post, April 18, 2017

Marcella Cavalera, the world-renowned Argentinian-born American composer and pianist revered for her virtuoso work in the showpieces of the grand Romantic tradition, was killed in a vehicle accident in Arlington, Virginia, on April 17. She was 44. Electrifying to watch as a performer, she was lauded for her risk-taking and breathtaking technical agility and has been called the greatest pianist of the century.

Discovered as a piano prodigy at the early age of three, Cavalera made her performing debut at eight and was winning major competitions by the time she was sixteen. She achieved notoriety with brilliant performances of some of the most technically difficult solo pieces ever written. Her own compositions took futuristic approaches to the Romantic tradition, each at levels of difficulty that made them intimidating for even the world's greatest artists. Her solo recordings and performances with the National Symphony Orchestra turned potential rivals into fans.

Never married, Marcella Cavalera was rumored to have left a string of broken hearts behind her in her twenties. An enormous personality on stage, she was intensely private in her personal life, which only added to her enchanting air of mystery. She leaves behind few interviews or perspectives on her life, and she is survived only by her daughter, Isabelle Cavalera.

———◆❉◆———

Staring

Fifty-four days have passed. Most nights, Elli stays at the house with me until ten o'clock. We alternate between ordering pizza and reheating her mother's casseroles. Everything still tastes like cardboard, but I no longer have to restrain myself from screaming at every driver I notice texting.

So many drivers texting.

My homework is haphazard because even when I study with Elli, I end up doing a lot of staring into space. At school, I try to be polite when they voice concern or make concessions. Half the time I fail.

I'm called in weekly to check in with my counselor, Mr. Dewer, for "lack of coping." The sessions go like this:

I sit in the chair beside his desk. He steeples his fingers and leans back soberly. "How are you feeling, Izzy?"

"Fine," I lie.

"Are you eating? Sleeping?"

"Sure."

"Anger is a normal part of grieving. It's okay to be angry."

"I'm not angry," I say through gritted teeth.

He looks helpless. My lack of coping should result in a parent–teacher conference; I know this. But there's no one left with whom to conference.

Archaeology

I'm sitting at Mom's desk in her office, trying to sort the finances, surrounded by her awards and keepsakes and still more photos of the two of us. Her will took care of the money, the house, the big things. Still, there are a thousand details: stacks of insurance documents, sheaves of bank account statements, pyramids of credit card and electric bills mixed in with old airline boarding passes and coffee-stained scraps of notes and music.

There's no mortgage on the house, so it's mine outright. I can stay as long as I want. Do I *want* to? Should I sell it? Rent it while I'm in college?

I can't bear the thought of strangers inhabiting her space, touching Mom's piano, filling the house with someone else's music. My lungs squeeze so hard I have to put my head between my knees before I can continue working.

The piles in front of me loom larger: an unfilled prescription, the bill for putting new tires on her Lexus, the receipt for restringing the pearls she snagged on the corner of the knife drawer in the kitchen. There are hotel bills and travel receipts and notes for concerts she played around the world. Most of the dates are familiar and I can remember enough to fill in the details, but there are also hotel stays I didn't know about, trips to London and

Edinburgh and Oxford when I thought she was somewhere else.

It makes me realize there are things my mother didn't tell me. I feel like an archaeologist excavating her life, digging up clues and artifacts that make me re-examine the woman I thought she was. I only knew her the way a child knows her mother, as a teenager knows a parent. And I'll never know her in any other way.

One of the stacks in front of me contains letters and messages from people wanting interviews and a guy who wants to write her biography. I've had notes from musicians who want to annotate her music. Someone wants to make a film about her life. Fans are writing condolences, love letters.

They didn't know her, either.

She would have hated every bit of this.

Things Not to Think About

1. My mother's death
2. The twenty-six-year-old serial texter who killed her..
3. Who I am without my mother
4. Feelings of any kind
5. Final exams

6. Going to Columbia in the fall and having to function as semi-normal
7. Flunking my final exams and not being able to go to Columbia with Elli
8. Lawyers, houses, probate, bills
9. Films/television/books/interviews about my mother
10. People with questions
11. Answers I don't have

Sniffling

It's Thursday night. Elli glides out of the kitchen with a bowl of popcorn, settles on the sofa in Mom's office, and pats the cushion beside her. She kicks her feet up on the coffee table and pulls up *Frozen* on her laptop.

"Break time."

"I will kill you if you put that stupid snowman song into my head."

"Do you want to watch a snowman?" Elli sings. Her face turns serious, and she pats the sofa again and continues singing: "Come on it's time to play. You never see me anymore. Come across the floor. It's like you've gone away."

Guilt is bitter in my throat.

"Does it have to be a snowman?" I sing back.

She tilts her head with the beginning of a smile and

pats the sofa again. "What would you rather watch? Anything at all."

"*A Knight's Tale.*" I drift over to sit beside her.

"But it's Disney night."

"Fine. Pick a princess. Any princess."

Elli screws up her face, mentally shuffling through the options. "How about *Mulan*? You like the dragon."

"I like all the smart-mouth sidekicks. You're the one with the princess complex."

"No, I want to be both the princess *and* the smart-mouthed sidekick. There's a difference."

"Only because they haven't come up with a princess who does her own smart-mouthing yet."

"I *know*. The world makes no sense at all."

I swallow hard.

"You think?" I say with absolutely no inflection.

Elli turns and stares at me, then settles the bowl of popcorn on my lap. She curls her fingers around my hand where it's resting on the cushion. "The suckage will decrease eventually," she says. "It's bound to. And in the meantime, we'll always have each other."

We sit together through the entire movie, hands clasped and neither of us eating even a bite of popcorn. Tears dry on my cheeks and fresh ones fall. Elli pretends she doesn't hear me sniffing.

I decide that's the essence of friendship. Knowing when to ignore the popcorn and the sniffing.

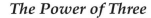

The Power of Three

Three's a powerful number. Fairy tales have three tasks, stories have three acts. It takes three points to define a plane, and any points after that reduce stability. That's why a three-legged stool is steadier than a four-legged one.

As far back as I remember, three has defined the boundaries of my family:

Mom + me + here = home

Mom + Elli + me = family

Since Mom died, though, I've been a stool trying to balance on two legs.

Now it's Friday afternoon, and Elli has one hand wedged under the padded strap of her overflowing backpack. Framed in the doorway with the sun-light behind her, her lavender hair is silver. She looks ephemeral as if she, too, could disappear on me in the blink of an eye. Logically, I know she's only going to her aunt's house in Richmond for the weekend, but until now, she's been five minutes away if I needed her.

She studies me as if she knows exactly what I'm thinking. "I wish I didn't have to go. I could still pitch a fit. Mom will cave. She'd come stay with us herself if it meant she could get out of two days of refilling glasses and washing dishes with Aunt Jude while everyone with any pretense of testosterone sits on their butts watching basketball."

"You should go, El. They're your people."

"They're my nightmare. And then they'll force me outside to play H-O-R-S-E to even up the numbers, as if I even care about basketball. The boys will spend ten minutes arguing about who got stuck with me on their team last time. Uncle Phillip will give them the good sportsmanship lecture and tell everyone that he's going to adjust the hoop so it's lower to make it easier for me. Then I'll end up spraining a wrist or an ankle or a knee trying to prove I don't need special treatment. See?" Elli slides me an exasperated look. "I don't even have to be there to experience the humiliation."

"Go. Experience. Live the dream."

"Come with me."

"I'll be there in spirit."

"You'll be thankful you've escaped."

"You aren't wrong," I say.

I'm getting better at faking normal. But probably normal after any death means dredging through the layers of denial and fury and failed negotiations with the universe. Probably *normal* is grief and loneliness no matter how many people are in the room.

Elli's the one who deserves to escape. She's earned

a break from me. She needs time with her family, a chance to appreciate that she *has* a family. She needs to take advantage of every minute she can have with them before the two of us go off to college.

I cross to the side table and pick up the gift bag with the manicure-in-a-jar I packed for her after she left last night. She extracts the mason jar filled with a nail file, cuticle cream, sugar scrub, and different colored polishes and plucks at the cascade of silver ribbons I tied around the top.

"What's this for?" she asks.

"An excuse for when basketball is imminent. You can't play H-O-R-S-E with a wet mani-pedi. Also it's a 'thank you' for always being here."

"Where else would I be, dummy?" she asks me softly.

She leaves. When she's gone, my ghosts and I are alone again in the empty house.

Izzy
Paper Remnants

The letters are in a shoebox in my mother's closet. Jimmy Choo. I find them on Saturday morning, and not knowing yet what they are, I wonder vaguely what happened to the shoes.

I'm so, so sick of paper.

Death is made of paper, piles and mounds and monuments of it. Mountains of manuscripts and compositions and condolences and fan mail.

What am I supposed to do with fan mail?

Finding still *more* paper makes me groan.

The envelopes in the box are all different kinds: fancy, plain, hotel stationery, and everything in between. And unlike the general chaos of Mom's office, they were placed in the box with care, neatly regimented against one side of the shoebox, newest to oldest. At least I suspect that's the case judging by the decreasing yellowness of the paper. I open the last one, and it's less than two months old.

---- ❄ ----

April 2, 2017

Dear Ian,

I'm finished with all but the opening of my C in E-flat Major. It ends with our beginning. Do you remember quoting William Blake to me that day?

"The spirits of the air live in the smells
Of fruit; and Joy, with pinions light, roves round
The gardens, or sits singing in the trees."

It wasn't the first time I heard music in words, but it was the first time I heard the music of you. The possibility of us. I find myself thinking more and more often about possibilities. One day, maybe I'll find enough courage to reach for joy again. To reach for you again.

Love as always,

Cella

---- ❄ ----

Questions

The handwriting on the letter is unmistakably my mother's scrawl, but as far as I know, she has never used an abbreviation of her name. Who is Cella?

More importantly, *who is Ian?*

And why is she Cella to him when she has never been Cella to anyone else?

My fingers stiff, I reach for the envelope on the opposite end of the box, the first envelope. The yellowest. The oldest.

The paper crackles as I unfold it, and my hand shakes when I read the date: April 22, 1996. My stomach clenches. I sink down cross-legged on the floor with the box in my lap because my knees give out.

April 22, 1996, is two years and eleven months before I was born.

Mom's been writing to some man I've never heard of for more than twenty years. She kept a secret my entire life. She kept *him* secret.

And she never sent the letters.

April 22, 1996

Dear Ian,

It's been two months and you haven't written back, so I'm accepting that you're done. I didn't realize I was hoping for anything else until after I started waiting for the postman every day.

I hope your ring arrived safely at Halford Hall. I know how much it means to you. Maybe that itself should have been the first clue that things could never work between us. I'm not naive to my own faults, and I understand I'm the sort of woman who will never be happy with someone else's ring, even if it's been passed down through seven generations of Halfords. I'm the kind who wants the ring to be a reflection of myself.

The ring is probably a metaphor for us. Your family is part of everything you are and do, and for me, my gift is always first. I'm too afraid I'll run out of time, of life, before I plumb the bottom of it. If that sounds selfish and pretentious, I'm only partly sorry. Gifts like this don't belong to just one person, or even to a single lifetime. If I'm to make music that will live on, I can't allow myself to be distracted. This is what I tell myself at night. The reminder drives me to work harder, and maybe it even makes the music inside me more powerful.

As painful as it's been for both of us, I'm glad I had the chance to love you. You taught me everything: passion, compassion, happiness, loneliness, heartbreak.

Be happy. You will, I know, and you deserve it. You're that sort of person.

Love,

Cella

Love and Longing

Goosebumps have crawled onto my skin in the cooling

air and set up permanent residence. My mouth is dry. I count the letters. Eighty-six. That's more than four letters every year.

Are they all like this?

I carry the shoebox out to the bedroom and flop onto my mother's bed, my back propped against pillows that still cling to the mandarin, myrrh, and amber notes of her Black Opium perfume. I hug a pillow as I read.

Eighty-six letters, one by one. Three times each. Some a lot more than that.

Some I nearly memorize.

They leave me numb. Confused.

Fascinated.

My muscles cramp from sitting still too long.

But the letters never say anything outright. They spell nothing out, make no promises, no arrangements for illicit sex in dark hotel rooms, nothing concrete.

No proof, just tantalizing questions.

My mother writes to Ian about *me*, about choices, about decisions, as if he's involved.

As if he has a stake.

Were there other letters once? Some she actually sent? Is that why there seem to be enormous gaps? Entire years left out, then years where the letters come more frequently?

As they stand, the letters give me nothing to grasp.

I feel like I've caught hold of the middle of a skein of yarn, and it's so long and tangled I can't find the ends.

Long Good Nights

My father isn't named on my birth certificate. All Mom would ever tell me about him was that he was a long good night in a string of long good nights, and that good nights of any kind don't make good parents.

I like to pretend I've gotten over being curious about him, but a lot of my stories have fathers in them. Good fathers. Bad fathers. I can't help studying the parental male of the species from the safe distance of my imagination, and sometimes, just sometimes, I feel my father's presence by his absence. The fact that I have to wonder about him. The fact that I don't know.

Not that my life was ever lacking. Mom always made sure of that. But every hero has an origin story, and we are all the heroes of our own lives. Until just now, just this moment, I've tried to convince myself knowing where I was going was enough. Only, can you know that, really know that, when you don't know where you came from? When you don't know who *both* your parents were?

As long as I remember, I've told myself I didn't need a father in the math of my life, that there wasn't even room because Mom + me + Elli was completeness. Without Mom, though, there's an empty space, a yawing, gaping black hole. And questions. Loads of questions.

About Mom. About Ian. About the other half of my DNA.

I assumed what my mother said about long good nights meant my father was one of a string of men. That he didn't matter. Instead, now here's a man Mom couldn't bear to part from. One man with whom the good nights never stopped.

Why did she write to him about me?

I can imagine the answer.

But then why didn't she ever send the letters?

Heart Worm

Three hours ago, I would have said I knew my mother. I knew her strengths, her faults, her demons. I would have sworn we had no secrets from each other, but I suppose it's inevitable that my view was clouded by familiarity and love and childhood. What do we really know through the filter of childish eyes? We see more than parents think we do, but I suppose we see without understanding what's really there.

Childhood is a cubist painting that's meant to be

realistic. Or maybe it's romanticism, emphasizing sense and emotions over reason and order. We give affection blindly as children. Our parents are our practice relationships. They shape our hearts, and that's how we learn to care for someone fully, unconditionally. We adore our parents before we see their flaws so that we come to understand that, when it comes to love, real love, flaws don't matter.

My mother's letters change nothing and they change everything. I don't love her any less, but I realize that I don't know her. I *never* knew her.

The paper of the oldest letter feels brittle as I fold it, as fragile as illusion. It makes me think of an E. E. Cummings poem about a tree called life that keeps the stars apart and about carrying a heart inside my heart.

My mother often told me to worry less about other people's words and find my own instead, but poetry is the barometer of emotion and the language that I speak. My mind drifts first to other people's words, and those are what help me gather my own nebulous thoughts into clouds of truth. Cummings was right. I'll carry my mother's heart with me inside my own forever, but I'm no longer certain what she carried in hers.

Who she carried there.

That's the bigger question. Who was Ian? *What* was he to her and me?

Ian, Halford Hall. Those three words and the internet, that's all it takes to look him up.

The search engine spits up a bunch of photos taken at society events. Below that, there's a website listing for Halford Hall. There are also several encyclopedia entries with biographies.

———◆❁◆———

Ian Halford, 17th Earl of Mortimer

Born 27 January, 1970, Ian William Edward Hector Halford, Lord Mortimer, is an English hereditary peer and practicing physician, the son of James Ian Malcolm Hector Halford and Lady Julia Anne Margaret Windsor, daughter of Prince Alfred, Duke of Essex. Educated at Eton College and Oxford, Lord Mortimer attended the Oxford University Medical School where he graduated with a Bachelor of Medicine, Bachelor of Surgery, and completed his medical training at John Radcliffe Hospital. He succeeded to his father's title in 2003. He was married to Lady Felicity Margaret Halford-Sloan, deceased, with whom he had twin children, Ian Malcolm Hector Roderick Halford, Viscount Halford, his son and heir, and a daughter, Lady Elizabeth Georgina Anne Halford, deceased. Lord Mortimer resides in Halford, Gloucestershire, where he is a consulting general physician at the Halford Surgery.

———◆❁◆———

Possibilities

I can't find anything more about the children, but there's a lot about Halford Hall, an entire website about tours and history and gardens and bringing back extinct butterflies. The pictures look like something out of *Pride and Prejudice*. Pemberley, I mean, not Netherfield.

Basically, Ian is Mr. Darcy. Without the happily ever after.

Except that even Mr. Darcy didn't have a title. I have to look that up. All of it. Basically, the aristocracy runs: Prince, Duke, Marquess, Earl, Viscount, Baron, Baronet, Knight. There are only twenty earls in England. And my mother was going to marry one whose mother also happened to be the Queen's first cousin. Which makes Ian second cousin to Prince Charles.

How did I not know this?

I can't stop thinking about him. About him and Mom. And me.

Leaving

Money is not a problem, and everything I need for the trip has a website: the airline, the hotel, the train, the cab company. Thanks to the internet, I can pretend to drive a car down the road past Halford Hall and past the office where Ian practices medicine and see exactly what he would see. I've already done it about a hundred times.

But that is not enough.

School is over. I walked across the stage for my graduation, and apart from my borrowed Elli-family, no one in the audience was there for me. Not a single person of my own.

After eighteen years of not having a father, I am now officially living a warped version of the P.D. Eastman early reader about a bird looking for its mother.

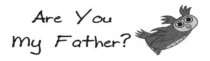

I pack a suitcase while Elli argues with me. She's read the letters almost as many times as I have, and it's not that she thinks I shouldn't go. She just thinks I can't—shouldn't—do this on my own.

I should. I can.

"Why don't you want me to come with you?" Elli's huddled on the floor, her hair almost the color of the dust on the foot of hardwood that extends beyond the boundaries of my blue Persian rug. "I can totally blow off working in the lab," she says. "Who wants to work when we could go be Jane and Eliza Bennett?"

"That's the point. I don't want to be Jane or Elizabeth Bennett. I want to be myself—whoever that turns out to be. And this isn't a Disney princess story. I'm Nancy Drew."

"You're crazy."

"That, too."

"Also you're going to need a bigger suitcase." She points at my carry-on roller with disdain.

I smirk at that. Elli requires pack mules when she travels. She throws everything she owns into a suitcase and gets her brothers to sit on it so she can force the zipper closed. I, on the other hand, am a champion traveler. Mom practically lived out of suitcases half the time, and I grew up going with her or at least visiting when she was playing somewhere. Rome. London. Madrid. Paris. Tokyo. Buenos Aires. Sydney. Oman. Beijing. Singapore. We have—we *had*—a game we played: five points for every continent, three points for every country, two points for every UNESCO World Heritage site, one point for every new concert venue.

I have 117 points.

If there was a world championship of packing, I'd be in the playoffs.

"At the very least," Elli says, "you should take a few nice dresses. What if Ian *is* your father, and he asks you to stay a while? What if there are royal balls or whatever? Teas? Or fox hunts?"

"Then I'll fall on my butt from a higher altitude. Remember summer camp?"

"That horse was meaner than the one in *Tangled*. You can't judge horses by one experience."

"I can judge fox hunting."

"Okay. Fair point." Elli's thin arms hug her knees as if she's afraid her legs are going to run away with her, as if she's going to dive into my suitcase so I can't tell her again that she can't come with me. The posture makes her look deceptively fragile.

Elli's the opposite of fragile, she's the iron to my carbon and together we are steel.

The first day of third grade, she gave Jason Evans a fat lip for pulling my hair at recess. In seventh grade, Shelly Hutchins tore Elli's favorite coat on purpose because they both got the same one as a Christmas present. I brought shrimp for lunch the next day and worked tiny chunks of them into Shelly's hem during gym. For a week after that, she was known as Smelly Shelly. I'd feel worse about that now if she hadn't continued on her *Mean Girls* poster-child trajectory undeterred.

I would love to take Elli to Halford Hall with me, but if I did, my impressions of Ian wouldn't be independent of her impressions. They would be *our* impressions, and I need to assess Ian with my own eyes. I can see how much that hurts El, though, and I don't know how to make it hurt any less.

"If he asks me to stay," I tell her, "I'll text you every hour. And if I go to a ball, you can be my fashion consultant."

"You better text me anyway."

"He may not ask. He may not even have a clue who I am. Or want to know."

"Your mom wrote about his opinion as if he had a claim."

"If she wanted his opinion she would have actually sent the letters. Just because she wrote *to* him doesn't mean the letters were written *for* him."

"He does kind of have your eyebrows, though, you have to admit. Looking objectively at the photos and the letters, it's a logical conclusion."

"That's why I need to go. I have to find out for sure—I can't stand not knowing." I tuck a plastic-wrapped sandal into the corner of the suitcase.

"On the other hand, I still think you could send an email. Or make a phone call. You don't have to go off without me."

She gives a drawn-out, dramatic sigh, but she looks worried enough that I want to hug her. She's right, but she's also wrong. I could call or send an email. People lie, though. Ian could lie. And I don't know what he knows. What I really want is a chance to find out if I *want* to tell him about the letters. To find out if I *want* to know him. For that, I need to see him face-to-face, to see the man who was this important to my mother, the man who quoted William Blake to her. If I see him first, then I can get an idea whether he might be willing to see me.

My head comes up and Elli and I stare at each other.

"What if?" I whisper to her.

"I know," she says. "It's crazy."

Enough

What if? has to be the saddest question in the universe.

Even if Ian isn't my father, Mom kept loving him for longer than I've been alive. She loved him so much that I wasn't enough for her, even though she always said I was.

There's a hole in the math of my life now, even bigger than the hole my mother left. Nothing is adding up anymore, and I need to meet Ian, talk to him.

I need to find out who he is to understand where he fits into my equation.

Tips for Packing

1. Temporarily suspend the paper-books-are-always-better-than-ebooks rule.

2. Roll clothes instead of folding and use compression bags.
3. Use packing cubes to group items for easier access.
4. Cover shoes with hotel shower caps.
5. Slip dryer sheets among packed items so clothes don't stink.
6. Store cords and gadgets neatly in plastic baggies.
7. Keep liquids from spilling by inserting squares of plastic wrap underneath the caps.
8. Pack layerable clothes and comfortable shoes to accommodate temperature changes.
9. Stick to dark, wrinkle-proof clothes that look clean longer.
10. Include scarves and small accessories to make the same outfits different.

Malcolm
Urgent Business

My mobile vibrates insistently in my back pocket as Mark Almsford and I emerge from our tutorial with Professor Kerr. The essay we've worked on all week is now dripping in red ink. Everything is dripping. Beyond the arched triple entrance porch to the History Faculty on George Street, it's raining cats. Mark turns up his collar, raises his hand in a cursory goodbye, and makes a dash down the steps and out the wrought iron gate. I stand in the gloom of the portico and return the fourth of my father's calls.

"Mal," he barks, "why didn't you ring me back?"

"This is me doing precisely that. My phone was off—I haven't even listened to my messages yet. What's the problem?"

"I'll need you to come home for a week or two. Something's come up, and I have to go to London."

He sounds a bit out of breath, as though he knows what he's asking, but it doesn't stop him from issuing an order instead of making a request. "This is the one weekend I told you I couldn't be there," I answer, working to keep the frustration from my voice. "I promised Percy I'd go home with him—"

"Surely you can do that another time?" There's a pause, and then he adds more quietly, "Please, Malcolm. I need you here."

Our relationship has been broken since I was twelve, so I don't know how to take that. The tour staff is more than capable of handling things, and Anna can make any decisions about the house. But I can't remember my father ever asking me for anything. Not quite this way.

I watch the rain come down beyond the Victorian arches, listen to it clatter on the rooftops and gurgle in the downspouts. On the street, a student unlocks a bicycle in the rack and pedals off in a spray of water, her satchel slung across her shoulders and her wet skirt clinging to her legs.

"Any particular reason," I ask my father, "you're going up to London?"

He clears his throat. "Some unexpected business I need to see to in person. But it can't wait, I'm afraid, and we have two wedding parties booked. Also, there's that Joran Masterson workshop on wood carving you've organized. I'm surprised you don't want to be here to see how it goes off."

"I would, if Percy hadn't asked me for a favor."

"Mal, look, I know you have a lot on, but now that it's summer, there's no real reason you can't come home and drive back when necessary to do your research. Is there? The point is, I'm not entirely certain when I'll be back."

PART TWO

Izzy
Eleven Centuries

The train ride from London wasn't quite two hours.
Counting back from there, I've also had a cab ride to
the station, a night in a nice hotel, another cab ride
from Heathrow Airport, and eight and a half hours
of flight time. Long enough to start reading three different novels on my tablet, only to give up because I
wasn't retaining a single word. I've resorted to *As You
Like It* now instead, which I almost know by heart.
Halford is only a few miles south of Stratford-on-Avon
where Shakespeare lived.

In spite of everything I said to Elli, I wish she was
with me, bouncing on the seat, cracking sidekick
sarcastic comments. I wish we were all here together,
her and me and Mom. Of course, if we were, then I
wouldn't need to have come in the first place.

> Text to Elli:
>
> Me: Shakespeare might have trudged down
> the road I'm on right now.

Elli: Thanks for that visual. Now I'm picturing naked Shakespeare trudging like
naked Chaucer in A Knight's Tale. Anyway,
I choose to believe Shakespeare was
Elizabeth I. She wouldn't ever trudge.

Me: You can't choose to believe something
that isn't true just because you want to
believe it.

Elli: Have you turned on the news lately?
Or met any actual people?

Me: That's beneath you. Truth is truth and
Shakespeare was Shakespeare, except
when he was Kit Marlowe.

Elli: I rest my case. Truth is whatever
serves us best. Also, do you think Elizabeth
could have gotten away with publishing plays under her own name? She had
enough trouble just being fat Henry's
daughter.

Me: She got away with chopping off her
own cousin's head.

Elli: Fine, it was a troubled family, but can't
you totally see her writing Rosalind?

Elli: Iz? Are you nervous?

Me: Way past nervous. But I'm trudging.

———◆❈◆———

Shakespeare's Country

It's not quite ten o'clock yet. The weather is cool, but even so, I'm sweating. I didn't use nearly enough deodorant, and my fingernails are shorter than they were when I left London. The closer we get to Halford, the more I wonder if this is a huge mistake.

Around me, the landscape looks like an idealized caricature of how an English countryside is supposed to look. I've been to London and Edinburgh several times with Mom, but we never went anywhere in between. And most of the time when I've been to England, there was at least intermittent rain. Now the sky is a clear, still blue the color of a swimming pool, and the sun rides high over meadows and rolling limestone hills. Mr. Corker from Cotswold Tours and Taxis assures me these are referred to as mountains by the locals. I guess everything is a matter of your frame of reference.

The ancient cab rattles over a wooden bridge, and then follows a road that looks like they forgot to add a second lane. I hold my breath every time there's a car or tractor coming from the opposite direction. But this is Shakespeare's landscape, or my imagination wants to make it that. It makes me think of a line from one of his sonnets, something about the sun *gilding pale streams with heavenly alchemy*. Except even that poem is less about landscape than it is about rejection.

Is it ominous that I'm remembering poetry about rejection? Probably. What if Ian is my father and he doesn't like me when we meet? What if I don't like *him*? How do I walk away?

The closer we get to Halford, the more I can't sit still. My thoughts shift from Shakespeare to Pablo Neruda, not just because he makes me think of Mom, but because he wrote poems about fear, about being afraid. Maybe I'm more afraid of being afraid. Is it too late to turn around and admit this was a huge mistake?

How do you get your bearings when everything in your world is shaking, sliding, disappearing?

"Are you sure you don't want me to wait for you and keep your suitcase?" Mr. Corker asks, watching me in the rear-view mirror. "I could sit down for a cuppa at The Green Man in the village while you take your tour at Halford Hall."

"That's really nice of you," I say, "but there's probably a cloakroom or something. And I may stay in the village tonight anyway."

"That'd be at The Green Man, too, then. It's the only place with rooms," Mr. Corker says.

"Yes, I called earlier and made a reservation just in case."

Mr. Corker has been very kind, trying to start up a conversation whenever I feel like I need to breathe into a bag or stop at the side of the road and puke up the sad pastry I had for breakfast. I'm trying to hide it, but I think I'm doing a rotten job. Either that or he is really good at reading teenage girls.

"Do you have a daughter, Mr. Corker?" I smile back at his reflection in the mirror.

He bobs his head then shakes it, as if he isn't sure. "Aye," he says, "not that she's speaking to me these days. She dyed her hair blue and pierced her eyebrow for her thirteenth birthday, and now we speak a different language. Not sure if that's my fault or hers, but I'd need a bleeding dictionary to translate half the things she says. On the other hand, I don't suppose she understands what I'm saying either. However hard I try."

I wonder if Mom ever tried to tell me things I didn't know how to hear.

How well did I really listen?

Expectations

There's a fork in the road and a sign for Halford Hall. Mr. Corker slows and glances back at me as he starts to make the turn.

I'm not ready. Now I really need to vomit.

"Wait," I say. "I mean, don't turn in. I think I want to go to the village first."

When I decided to take this trip, I thought about plane

tickets and train schedules, logistics. Transportation. I pictured myself going to Halford and finding out about Ian, something like that scene in *Pride and Prejudice* where Elizabeth takes the tour and hears the housekeeper talk about how wonderful Mr. Darcy is, how kind and handsome. But the way Mr. Corker talked about his daughter, now I'm not so sure.

I didn't want Elli coming with me because someone else's perspective will always paint their own version of the truth. But I've been picturing the BBC fairy tale: people saying glowing things, Ian arriving back, meeting me, and throwing his arms wide open. Now that I'm here, it seems more likely that if I show up at Halford Hall with a suitcase and start asking nosy questions, someone will have security throw me out.

I tap Mr. Corker on the shoulder. "Would you mind taking me to the village instead? You were right.

I think I'll go ahead and drop my bag at The Green Man, and maybe I'll stop by Dr. Halford's surgery instead of going on the tour."

He glances at me sharply. "Oh, do you know Lord Mortimer?"

"Not personally," I say. "My mother did."

Mr. Corker doesn't answer, and he's working to keep his face expressionless. Which tells me a lot right there.

Okay, maybe I didn't think all this through as carefully as I should have. Still, I might as well meet Ian head on, right? At least I know what to expect in a doctor's office. I can pretend to be a patient.

It's not that much of a stretch. My stomach already feels like I ate a bucket of week-old oysters.

———◆※◆———

Armor Optional

Downtown Halford is a toy village of ivy-covered cottages and pretty shops with high, stone roofs perched on top of walls of honeyed limestone that Mr. Corker tells me is called Cotswold stone. "You're fortunate," he says. "We're far enough out of the way to escape the madness here. Most villages in the Cotswolds are drowning in holiday homes and London commuters and shops no one local can afford to buy from." He slows to wait for an old woman walking her dog and then two people on horses come out of a side street and cross the road.

Text to Elli:

Me: I'm in an enchanted village. Want a souvenir?

Elli: A suit of armor might be good, or Prince Charming. Armor optional.

Me: I'd definitely need a bigger suitcase.

The horses clomp away. On the right side of the road, we arrive at The Green Man, an inn with a vacancy sign and empty picnic tables set out in the garden. Beside it, there's a grocer with crates of fruits and vegetables displayed out front. A few other assorted shops lie beyond that, and finally the road culminates in a small stone church surrounded by a cemetery. Off to the left, a side road is helpfully posted with an official-looking sign that points down to the "Doctor's Surgery."

I pay Mr. Corker, and he comes around to remove my suitcase from the trunk. I start to take it from him, but he walks off with it toward the inn. "Might as well have a cuppa myself so long as I'm here," he says. "Now don't worry if you don't need me again, but call in case you do."

I check in at the desk with a girl who can't be much older than I am. She's got burgundy hair cut in a trendy crop and there are miles of bare leg between her short, flowered skirt and her high-top canvas sneakers. It's not a look that goes with the village, but it works and I give her an oversized smile. "I'm checking in?"

She gives me a single nod. "Name?"

"Isabelle Cavalera."

"I'll need your passport, love. Just the one night, yeah?" She checks me in, makes a copy of my passport, snatches a key from the old-fashioned slot cabinet behind her, and hands it over. "Room's up those stairs and to the right. Third door on the left after that. Bathroom's down the hall."

I bump up the stairs with my suitcase and unlock the door to an aggressively charming room decorated with matching roses on the wallpaper and the bedspread. There's a standing mirror in the corner, a wingback chair upholstered in faded red velvet, and a pink enamel pitcher and washbasin with still more roses on a doily-covered dresser. It's an English country inn the way I picture it after watching television, which I'm betting is exactly the idea and a pretty good marketing gimmick. Not to mention that the owners don't have to waste money redecorating the rooms every decade.

I wander to the mirror and examine my reflection, trying to see myself the way Ian might see me, wondering if I should change into something nicer or at least pull my hair back into a bun. No. Wait. I deliberately wanted to see him in his element, yet here

I am wondering if I should change myself to make him like me better.

Bad plan, Izzy. Don't be stupid.

Ignoring the undeniable fact that my hair looks like something a rented cat threw up, I snatch my purse back off the bed, storm out of the inn, and march down the street.

The "Doctor's Surgery" sign ends up being a bit like the Cotswold "mountains." What it refers to is actually a smallish house built of the now familiar honeyed stone with an obligatory amount of climbing ivy and a mullioned bay window in the front.

Panic sets in the instant I pull the door open. A bell jingles, and the full complement of waiting patients turns to stare at me.

My hands begin to sweat. My mouth goes dry. But I remind myself of the Shakespeare T-shirt I'm wearing underneath my hoodie.

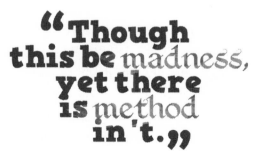

"Though this be madness, **yet there is** method **in't."**

There's a reason I am here. And I've come this far, so I can't give up.

———◆❊◆———

Stage Fright

Very few people know how nervous my mom always was when she performed. She hated the thought of failing her gift and letting down all the people who had paid to see her. She also hated the idea of being judged so much that she used to run to the bathroom and throw up before each performance. But she hid her nerves so well, I was fourteen before I knew anything about it. Even then, she only told me to make me feel better when Elli entered a story I had written into a writing contest.

Elli hadn't told me she was going to do it. She planned to confess when the results came in, but it turned out there were multiple rounds of judging and she hadn't read the fine print. She got the first email announcing I'd made it to the quarter finals and burst through the door of my room bouncing like a kangaroo. We'd been bouncing together on my bed, hugging each other and laughing madly for two whole minutes before she managed to say what we were celebrating.

"Here, read this!" She waved the printed email at me. "I sent your story to the Mid-Atlantic Fiction Competition."

"You did *what*?" I snatched the paper from her.

The thought of someone comparing me to other people, to expectations, made me puke into my trash can. People weighing my words, loving or hating my characters. Every night until the contest was over, I went to bed thinking about all the awful things the judges might be saying, and I'd wake up thinking about all the ways I should have made the story better. By the time I came in third, I was so sleep-deprived and depressed that I stayed in bed an entire day.

Mom brought me pancakes with *dulce de leche* and a cup of lumpy hot chocolate and sat cross-legged beside me on the bed while I ate. She'd been downstairs playing, still wearing her shawl and silk pajamas at 2:40 in the afternoon, her hair a tangle of dark curls around her head.

"Did I ever tell you about my first big competition?" she asked.

"The Chopin in Poland? You won."

"Yes, and I vomited on the edge of the velvet curtain before I went on stage and threw up all over again the moment I rushed off."

She picked up my hot chocolate and made a face as she took a sip. Then she frowned around at the neat orderliness of my room, which was so different from the disarray she left behind her everywhere she went.

"In between throwing up," she continued, "I concentrated on playing for just myself. One person. That was the only way I knew how to do it. After

MARTINA BOONE

the opening chords, the judges and the audience fell away, and it was only me offering up the music to the universe. That's all you can ever do. Offer yourself up, good and bad, and hope someone sees the beauty. If they don't, that doesn't mean you need to change. It means you need to work harder. If you've been true to yourself and your vision, if you've been honest, you have to keep going because you can't do anything else. You can lie about other things, but in art, you must be honest. That's the only way."

She kissed me on the forehead and hugged me so tight I couldn't breathe. When she pulled away, there were tears in her eyes. "You're going to write beautiful things someday, my Isabelle," she said. "Magical things. Trust me. You will make people laugh and cry and carry your stories in their hearts. All you have to do is find the courage to set the words inside you free."

———◆❃◆———

Excuses

The woman at the reception desk reminds me of a bird, fine-boned and quick, with improbably canary-colored hair swept thinly into a bun and a row of fat, red beads strung around her neck. I picture her in one of the pretty cottages we passed on the way, living there with a cat named Montmorency, a son who brings his family to her house for Sunday dinners each week, and a garden full of giant vegetables that she enters into village competitions.

I reach the window. She continues tapping at the keyboard for a very long minute before she looks up.

"Can I help you?" she asks in the sort of dubious tone that suggests she'd rather not do anything of the kind.

"Um." Suddenly, I have no idea what to say.

The phone rings, and she excuses herself to answer.

> Imagined/ Text to Elli:
>
> Me: Remember that scene in A Knight's Tale where William forgets his name?
>
> Elli: The "You've forgotten, or your name is Sir Um?" scene?
>
> Me: I'm here and I can't get out an intelligible sentence.
>
> Elli: You're trying too hard like usual. Just say what you need to say.

My fingers itch to text her.

But I have to be coherent instead.

"I was hoping maybe I could see Dr. Halford. Ian Halford?" I blurt when the receptionist finishes her call.

My face is so hot I think the blood is going to turn

to gas and expand and my head will explode and there will be a huge mess for this poor woman to clean up. And Elli will never hear about my utter and abject word-challenged mortification, unless she shows up for my funeral and demands that someone explains to her why my head exploded—which would totally be something that Elli would do. And then they would tell her and she'd be like, *Oh. Okay. Fine, then.* Because she would completely understand how I feel.

The reception lady is looking pained. "Do you have an appointment?"

"Not exactly."

Her eyebrows rise. Not one eyebrow in the cool way, but both in the go-away-you're-bothering-me-honey way. "Do you have one or don't you?"

"No, but—"

"Well, then. Dr. Halford's out of the office. I can give you an appointment tomorrow afternoon with Dr. Basrani who's filling in for him," she says efficiently. "That's the soonest I can squeeze you in."

"When is Dr. Halford coming back?"

She goes still, then peers at me over the top of her glasses. "What seems to be the problem? Are you ill or aren't you?"

"I'm not." My face gets even hotter. "I have something that might belong to him. To Dr. Halford. They— it—was my mother's, and my mother just died so I only now found them—um, *it*. I can wait for him."

"I'm afraid that won't be possible." For the first time, I see a flash of sympathy. "He's gone away. Perhaps you could leave whatever it is with me. I could see he gets it."

My stomach gives a high-speed elevator bounce, the kind that always made Mom take my hand when I was little. I can't help wondering if Mom would take my hand now, if she were here. Or would she drag me out the door and help me run away?

"Gone away where?" I ask, gathering up the fragments of my composure. "And when is he coming back? He is coming back, isn't he? I mean, you're being a little cryptic."

The moment I've said it, I hear how pushy it must have sounded. My cheeks burn like I'm standing beside a fire.

The receptionist blinks, probably wondering whether I'm certifiable or just American. Her expression freezes enough to drop the temperature ten degrees.

"I'm afraid I can't give out that information," she says. "If you have something to leave with me, please do so. Otherwise, I can't help you."

Well, all-righty, then. Strike number two.

———◆❈◆———

Roots

The cab turns off the village road, and Mr. Corker slows where the curved stone walls end in an open wrought iron gate and a pair of elaborate gateposts. A ticket-taker asks if I want admission to the gardens, the house tour, the children's tour, the upstairs/downstairs tour, the dungeon tour, the woodcarving workshop, or everything altogether. Since I haven't a clue, I shell out almost forty bucks for the works, and we drive on.

Beyond the gate, thick-boughed trees drape over a fenced expanse of lawn, and a small, gray lake reflects the honey-stone structure of Halford Hall where generations and generations of Halfords have lived and loved and died. People whose blood might run through my veins.

It's a shiver-inducing thought, and a cloud passes over the sun at that exact moment, turning the landscape into something ominous. I catch Mr. Corker looking at me in the rearview mirror again, assessing and sympathetic. He has to be thinking I'm behaving very oddly.

I am.

My mother's parents were teachers in Argentina. They died when she was five, and I know nothing at all about them. The aunt who brought Mom to America is long dead, too, and she never had kids of her own. Basically, my cultural exposure comes down to a love of *dulce de leche*—and really, who doesn't love *dulce de leche* once they taste it? Oh, and *Milanesa*, which is an Argentinian beef version of the Italian *Coteletta Milanese*—as in cutlet from Milan—which is the same as *Wienerschnitzel*, which is a cutlet from Vienna. Which is a little like me: something from nowhere in particular. Even the Spanish I know I mostly learned in school. Mom always said that was the great thing about America: it doesn't matter where people come from, they reinvent themselves when they arrive.

That sounds nice, but I wonder if she would have said that if her heritage had included a place like this. Probably she would have, though. She was always more interested in the future than the past.

Behind us, the Halford main entrance disappears. The long drive skirts the lake, and I can see a couple of tour vans parked off to the side of the house.

People are picnicking on the grounds and lined up

along the side of the building waiting to go inside. I didn't picture this many people, but on the plus side, it means I'll really be invisible.

This place could swallow a thousand people and no one would ever notice.

Up close, as we arrive, the house looks even more impressive. The website said it was built in 1588, which in *The Princess Bride* parenthesis terms—the book, not the movie—dates the structure before America and during Shakespeare. A few parts are even older because the foundations are set on top of a tenth-century building that was destroyed by Queen Elizabeth I to punish the Halfords for conspiring in the plot to put Mary Queen of Scots on the English throne.

Queen Elizabeth. And Mary Queen of Scots.

And the tenth century? I knew even less about that than I did about British aristocracy, so I had to look up what happened then. England was brand new, the French king gave Normandy to the Vikings, and the Norman invasion was still a century away. The Umayyad Caliphate controlled Spain, and Muslim Córdoba was the cultural center of the world. The wealthiest city in Europe was Christian Constantinople, women in a Chinese harem created playing cards, and the Toltecs took over Chichen Itza from the Mayans.

Seeing Halford, I can't help wondering if it changes you to have roots and foundations that go back further than most of the countries in the world. Roots that are deeply inseparable from the history of one place and steeped in ugliness disguised as glamour.

Does it give you a platform from which to explore the world? Or does it become a stone around your neck?

Malcolm
Wild Carvings

I can't help wondering how cultures around the world might be viewed differently today if sculptures survived as well in wood as they do in stone. How many civilizations have vanished without leaving any trace of their art behind? How many Grinling Gibbons or Balthasar Permosers, sculptors arguably on a par with Michelangelo and Bernini, have disappeared without a trace?

Even with the doors open, the tourists crowded into the workshop make the air feel close and hot, and the stench of sweat overshadows the delicate scent of limewood shavings. Joran Masterson speaks without looking up. His chisel digs into the light grain of the limewood cut from Halford's own grove of linden trees, sending shavings flying.

He's a small man, wide shouldered with powerful arms, a bare pink scalp gleaming with sweat surrounded by fringes of white, and thick white whiskers that obscure his chin. The three art students we signed up for the workshop in advance dwarf him physically as they stand in a half circle at his elbow, their eyes locked on his chisel as if watching for the single moment when the magic will happen and the wood will become as light as air. But the magic is in Joran himself, in the self-effacing confidence of his presence as much as the speed and genius of his chisels.

A girl with wild, dark curls and a T-shirt with a quote from Shakespeare's Hamlet threads her way through the crowd to stand at the front, and several other people press in beside her. Almost everyone is respectfully—surprisingly—quiet, so Joran doesn't need to raise his voice. Watching him and the way the crowd responds, I'm more convinced than ever he's precisely what we need at Halford—if I can manage to get him and Dad to agree.

"Grinling Gibbons," Joran says, "was probably the greatest of the Baroque woodcarvers. Possibly the best of all time. How many of you have seen the choir stalls and organ case at St. Paul's Cathedral?"

Fabric rustles as half the audience raises their hand. I'd be astonished if a quarter of them had noticed St. Paul's had any carvings at all, though.

Joran nods, still without looking up. "Gibbons was the go-to sculptor for Sir Christopher Wren, the famous architect. Wren became a fan after a friend happened to discover Gibbons carving a replica of

Tintoretto's 'Crucifixion' by candlelight in a rented cottage, and Wren, in turn, introduced Gibbons to King Charles II. There are Gibbons carvings at Windsor Castle, Hampton Court, Kensington Palace, Chatham House, and a handful of great estates like this one. But one of my personal favorite pieces is the Cosimo panel he did for King Charles to give to the Grand Duke of Tuscany. It's an allegory of art triumphing over hatred and turmoil—which I think is even more applicable today than it was in the seventeenth century. The whole panel was almost destroyed twice recently, first in a flood in 1966 and then in a fire in 1984. But those near-tragedies turned out to be blessings in disguise."

For the first time, Joran lifts his head and studies the crowd, which has grown even more attentive. "For centuries," he continues, "no one had ever been able to duplicate the lifelike effect Gibbons achieved in wood. But the Cosimo panel and another that was damaged at Hampton Court gave us the opportunity to study the techniques. It turned out that he'd laminated three or sometimes four different layers of limewood together, which ironically made the overall effect more delicate instead of heavier."

He holds up the rose that he's been carving while he spoke. The crowd murmurs and offers up applause, but Joran shakes his head. He whisks a white cloth off the piece he's had waiting on the table, and he holds the two side by side. The applause stops. There's absolute silence in the room.

Joran's rose is remarkable. But it's nothing to the other.

"Even I couldn't describe the difference between a skillful carving and one finished with Gibbons' method," Joran says. "It's something you have to see for yourself." He sets the two roses back on the table side by side and removes a cloth from a third object. But he doesn't hold that up just yet.

Scanning the crowd again, he asks, "How many of you are familiar with Horace Walpole?"

A few scattered hands go up. This time, Joran doesn't let it go at that.

"Good," he says. "So who was he?"

Most of the hands slip down again. Only the girl with the wild hair and two others keep theirs in the air. Joran nods at the girl. "Yes?"

"He invented the word 'serendipity' and wrote *The Castle of Otranto*, which was the first Gothic novel," the girl says in an American accent.

I find myself staring at her. Not because she's confident or young, or even because I'm surprised to discover she's American. Not even because her words are an intriguing description for a man who was more politician and art historian than writer. But something about her is familiar to me, as though I've seen her before. I'm quite certain I haven't. She isn't the sort of girl one forgets. The long, dark mass of curls tangling wildly around her shoulders and pale, triangular face reminds me of Joran's carving in a way that makes me want to touch it.

Joran, too, grins at her as though he's discovered some delightful new work of art. "I hadn't heard that about 'serendipity,'" he says, "but yes. That's the right Horace Walpole. In addition to everything else, he was a great patron of the arts. One night, he showed up at a dinner party wearing a point lace cravat. This wouldn't have been anything unusual at the time as they were quite fashionable, except that this particular piece of neckwear wasn't made of cloth. It was carved in wood by Grinling Gibbons—realistically enough to fool most of the dinner guests. I saw that same cravat myself at an exhibition in the Victoria and Albert Museum a few years ago, and I was so intrigued I spent twenty-eight months learning to make a decent replica of it."

He holds the carved result of his experiments in place beneath his chin to show it off. The wooden cravat is so delicate, I'd expect the fabric to stir in the lightest breath of air.

The crowd presses in for a better look, and Joran moves out from behind the table to let people closer.

I turn to search for the girl with the wild hair, wondering if she'll stay for the remainder of the workshop. Hoping for no sane reason I can think of that she will.

But it seems I've missed her already. She must have melted into one of the tour groups and walked past me out the door.

Izzy
Meeting

I dither in the driveway in front of the house, trying
to decide where to go. What to do. I've taken all the
tours and wandered through the sections of the gardens that are open to the public. I even took *the* first
part of the wood carving workshop.

The main thing I've learned is that Halford Hall
isn't a house as much it's an institution. There must
be forty or fifty people working here, and not one of
them is willing to talk about Ian. There's no charming
housekeeper eager to discuss her "kind master," no
helpful in-house phone that would let me casually ask
to speak to him, and the assorted Earls of Mortimer
in the portraits scattered around are long since dead.
Unless their ghosts are willing to point me to the
private quarters upstairs, dead earls are not the least
bit helpful.

So now what? Do I resort to hiding in a bathroom
or behind the shrubbery?

Not that *that's* likely to help me much. The guide made a point of using the two wedding parties that are staying overnight to illustrate how completely the thirty-two rooms in the private quarters are separated from the guest wings and the downstairs public portions of the house. Which is nice for Ian, not so good for me casually bumping into him.

"Can I help you with anything?" someone says beside me. "You look a little lost."

It takes a second to realize he's talking to me, and another second to realize it's the cute guy I saw in the woodworking workshop, the one who was leaning against the wall behind the velvet rope. Tall and lean-muscled, he's wearing a navy-blue zip-up sweater over a collared shirt and the sleeves are pushed up, leaving expanses of smooth skin and ropey muscle. His hair is dark with a hint of wave. It falls across his forehead, and his perfectly shaped eyebrows are faintly pinched together above light green eyes.

I'm not immune to boys. In principle, I admire a number of them from a distance, and I've dated a few that are eminently admire-able. Elli and I talk about band-boys and film-boys as much as anyone. But this is different.

This one is not strictly the best-looking guy I've ever seen. I'm not entirely sure that he's good-looking in the traditional sense. But every hormone in my suddenly wide-awake body stands to attention, and

I'm aware of exactly how close he is to me. Which isn't really that close, but it feels like he's right there, all up in my space, sucking away my oxygen so that it's harder to breathe.

Instant attraction. I've heard about that. Laughed about it in books and films. I mean, the whole idea is kind of ridiculous, isn't it? Not to mention dangerous and messy. Honestly, I've always assumed the concept began as part of a grand conspiracy designed to keep girls from giving up their virginity to the first guy who came along. *No wait, don't have fun with the guy you've been dating, honey. Not yet! However hot and bothered you think you are now, someday you'll meet someone who makes you feel much more.*

Well, hello, *more.* I'm Isabelle. It's awkward to meet you.

Okay, so maybe this isn't love at first sight. But lust? Oh, yeah. That's definitely a thing.

He grins crookedly, as if he's not sure whether smiling is appropriate, and we go back to the uncomfortable staring. Words swim around in my head like koi in a pond of hormones, and I vaguely remember playing some kind of a game once where you're supposed to feed specific fish while they mix themselves up so fast that you can't remember which ones you've fed already.

I stand there blinking at the guy like an idiot, not only because he's just that pretty, but also because I honestly don't know what to say except, "Um. You don't happen to know where I can find the Earl of Mortimer?"

The smile is gone like that. "Why?"

"Why what?"

"I mean," he says, "is there a particular reason you need to see him?"

What is it about an English accent that can make politeness drip with frost? Suddenly, I feel about three inches tall.

"Never mind. Stupid question." I shake my head and pull out my phone to call Mr. Corker to come and get me. What's the point of prolonging the agony any longer? Not to mention the humiliation. More and more, I realize this was a lame idea.

Imagined Text to Elli:

Me: You were right. This was an abject failure. I should have sent an email.

Elli: Normally I enjoy being right, but don't give up yet. Do something.

I start to walk away.

"Hang on." The cute guy gives me a worried look, his eyes softening and growing darker. "I apologize. I thought you were—well, never mind. Clearly something's wrong. Why don't you tell me about it? Perhaps I can help."

"I wouldn't know where to begin."

"'Begin at the beginning and go on till you come to the end; then stop.'" Cocking his head, he smiles again. Genuinely. Charmingly.

I find myself smiling back. "Did you just quote *Alice in Wonderland*?"

"That's the price of an Oxford admission, I'm afraid. It comes with an Alice quotation quota."

"Two quotations before breakfast?"

"Two quotations or two impossible things. Dealer's choice." He grins, full wattage this time, no holds barred, and he should register that as a weapon.

But I think of the reason I'm here, and how I've failed. "Some things," I say, "are more impossible than others."

"That's entirely possible. But I could use a bigger hint. Come on. I'm all ears, said the rabbit. Try me."

And there. He's got me doing it again. Smiling in spite of myself.

Okay. I'll bite. "Do you work here?"

He hesitates. The smile fades, and he's suddenly serious despite the fact that we're talking in absurdities. "I'm only here weekends, mostly, but I do know my way around. If you tell me what's wrong, I should at least be able to find someone for you to speak with."

He looks genuinely concerned, that wrinkle between his eyes has gotten deeper. He's got a dimple in his chin, a sturdy jaw that hasn't been shaved in a while, and those gorgeous green eyes that should be outlawed. Altogether, he's good-looking enough to be a heartbreaker, the kind of guy who's always on the make, but he doesn't have that vibe at all. He strikes me more as the trust-me-I'll-be-your-friend kind of a guy that girls can't help falling in love with. Not that there's much difference in the end, because a girl will get her heart shattered either way.

Some girls. Not me. I mean, the kind who are susceptible to that kind of thing. Which I'm definitely not.

Still, what do I have to lose?

"This is going to sound crazy," I say, "I fully realize that. But I'm looking for the earl because my mother was engaged to him a long time ago. Very long. And she died..."

The rest of whatever ridiculous-sounding explanation I was about to spew up dries in my throat, leaving me standing with my mouth half open. Because Prince Charming suddenly doesn't look cute anymore.

He looks mad. Like whoa *really* mad.

"You're her daughter," he spits out. "Marcella Cavalera."

It feels like a punch to the gut, the way he says the words as if they're four letters each.

"I'm Isabelle. Izzy." I nod vaguely, trying to think. Why does he know my mother?

He grabs me by the elbow and spins me toward the house, then drags me up the steps.

Halfway up, I manage to gather my lost wits

together again into some semblance of order, and I plant my feet and snatch my arm away. "Let go! What do you think you're doing?"

"Taking you somewhere private. I don't need you airing dirty laundry in front of every tourist with a bloody camera."

Wanting

Prince Cave Dweller drags me through the entrance toward a door marked "Private" behind the ticket booth. I find myself going along, pretending that my heart's not pounding like it wants to beat straight out of my chest.

Why?

Why shouldn't I go ahead and make a scene? I need to demand he tells me what's going on. I *don't* need to let myself get stuck behind closed doors with some deranged, pissed-off guy I do not know. Except that people are giving us *looks*. Watching. And the thought of arguing with someone about my mother in public makes me want to throw up all over again. Which I don't want to do on the pretty marble floor.

And now that I've thought all that, it's already too late. We're in an office and the door is closed.

I snatch my arm away again. "What do you know about my mother?"

"What are you doing here?" He counters, drawing himself up to his not inconsiderable height. "What do you *want*?"

What do I want?

So many things.

For my mother not to be dead.

For her to have had the life she wanted and the love that she deserved.

For her to have told me the truth so I didn't have to stand here humiliating myself in front of some jerkface Prince Not-Charming-At-All who's staring at me as if he's liable to grab the sword that goes with the suit of armor in the corner of the room at any second and use it to lop off my head.

This isn't how I pictured this visit going.

Malcolm
First Blood

I cram my hands into my pockets because they're shaking. No wonder I thought the girl seemed familiar. She looks uncannily like that obituary photo of her mother in *The Guardian*, the one where Marcella Cavalera won her first piano competition. That same hair. The same chin. Same lips. I can only be grateful Dad isn't here to see her.

She stares at me as though I've grown three heads. Not that I'm behaving well, of course. Clearly, I shouldn't have dragged her in here the way I did, but the thought of Dad passing a newsstand in London and spotting a photo of us rowing with each other on the cover of some sleezy tabloid.…Tourists with phones are as bad as the paparazzi.

I slump against the office door. "Do you intend to stand there gaping all day, or do you plan to tell me why you're here? What do you want?"

"Do you intend to tell me how you know about my mother? Who are you?"

Her inflection is a creditable imitation of my own, and my lips twitch. In anger, I think, not because she's funny. And I've every right to be angry. I cross to the bookshelf and pluck the stack of CDs from beside the disc player that Dad keeps there for when he's working. Marcella Cavalera's face is on them all, just as it's on the CDs in Dad's reading room that replaced the vinyl records I smashed to bits after my mother died.

The girl takes one of the CDs from me. Her fingers brush against mine, and the touch awakens my nerve endings. The ghosts of her fingers linger. I fist my hand, rubbing my fingertips against my palm as though they itch. It's a sensation I've never felt before, and I wonder if it's genetic. Is it me or is it her? Are we Halfords wired to something in the Cavalera women, or is there something about them that makes them particularly tempting?

Not that I *am* tempted. She's poison. Bound to be. And she absolutely needs to leave Halford immediately.

"I won't ask you again," I say. "Tell me why you're here, or I'll ring security and have you thrown off the estate. What do you want with Lord Mortimer?"

She wraps her arms around her waist, hugging herself for comfort. Her eyes are enormous and startled like a roe deer caught in the security lights. Her every muscle is tensed to run. Something twinges in my stomach but I shut it down. I won't feel sympathy for her. I refuse.

"After she died, I found some letters my mother wrote to him. *Ian*. That's what she called him."

"So?" The word comes out like a bullet.

She flinches and looks away. "She never sent the letters, but she kept writing. All this time, so I—" Shrugging, she looks away. "I thought he might want to see the letters."

I gape as though I've lost my wits when, actually, she's the one who's lost the plot. "You came here from America on the off-chance Lord Mortimer might want to see something your mother wrote and never sent? Are you mad? Why would you want to inflict that sort of pain?"

Izzy
Disappointment

When he puts it like that, he isn't wrong. God, I'm
an idiot. Why didn't I consider this from Ian's point
of view? I mean, I did wonder if he would want to
acknowledge me as a daughter—*if* that's what I am.
But I never stopped to imagine how he would feel
about my mother loving him all those years. I never
thought about him reading her words. All the *what if*s
and *could have been*s that would raise for him.

He's had a whole life in those twenty years. His
wife and daughter died. If my mother hadn't broken
off the engagement, that wife and daughter would
never have existed. Charm Boy here would never
have existed.

I dig my fingernails into my sides trying to keep
myself from crying. Because crying here would be
ridiculous.

I turn away with my chin wobbling and my shoulders shaking.

"Don't do that." Footsteps creak on the floorboards behind me. "Please don't cry. Are you crying?"

"I'm not crying."

"It looks as though you're crying."

"Then you must have X-ray vision." I sniff and shuffle around again as he tries to circle around in front of me.

He stops. "I'm sorry." His words are soft. "Do you want me to give you a moment? I could wait outside."

I need to call Mr. Corker and go back to The Green Man, that's what I need to do. But somehow the thought of that opens the floodgates. My throat clogs up and tears pour down my cheeks. I hear Prince Jerkface shift awkwardly behind me, retreat a few steps, then move back up, as if he's trying to decide what to do when he really just wants to run away. I don't blame him. If I could run away from me right now, I would.

Finally I take in a few solid gulps of air.

"Feeling better?" he asks. "Do you want to sit down?"

A chair scrapes, and I wipe my eyes and turn. The room is big enough for several offices, and there is one of those two-sided partners desks with a chair on either side. He's turned the nearest chair around and shoved it closer, so all I have to do is bend my knees and I'm sitting. I do that before it occurs to me that it will be harder to escape once I'm in that position.

I don't mean escape with my dignity intact—that ship has long since sailed—I mean escape, period. If I'd been thinking clearly, I would have covered my eyes, pretended I needed to go wash up, and never stopped running until I'd hit the main road into the village. This is why sneakers are an excellent choice of footwear. You never know when escape's required.

Also, now that I'm sitting here, I can't help looking up at him. And it's a long way up. Or a long way down. Depending on perspective.

"I truly am sorry." He shifts the few steps to the desk and props his hip against it, which doesn't do much for perspective, but he is, at least, farther away from me.

Farther is excellent.

We stare at each other without speaking.

I can't think of a thing to say.

Maybe he can't, either.

"So," we both begin at once. Then we stop.

"Sorry. Go ahead," he offers.

"That's all right. You go."

The corners of his lips tug a little, not a smile exactly, but not far off from one. "I was going to ask what we should do now. What do you want to do?"

"Apart from throw myself into the nearest sinkhole?"

He grins this time. "Yes, apart from that."

"I was thinking I'd slink back to the village. Feel

free to take all the cliché phrases about never darkening your doorstep again as written."

The grin widens charmingly. "It's rather a large
doorstep. Takes quite a bit to darken it."

"It sounds like my mother managed."

And once again the grin is gone. "I came on a bit
strong about that," he says. "It's only that her death
hit...Ian...hard. But he isn't here in any case. He's gone
to London, and I don't know when he'll be back."

"Oh. Okay." Why didn't it occur to me Ian might
have an actual life? Except, you know, for some obviously mistaken idea that country doctors hang out in
the country. But he's not your ordinary doctor, is he?
He's probably hanging out with Queen Elizabeth and
playing with the royal babies.

"Well, never mind, I guess," I say. "Thanks anyway,
and I hope I wasn't too much trouble."

I push myself out of the chair and cross toward
the door.

He gets there first and grabs for the knob as if he's
going to open it for me, only then he just stops and
stands there, holding it shut. "What are you going
to do now?"

That just makes it worse. Knowing I came this far
and I've completely failed.

"I don't know. Go home, I guess. Obviously, it was
a mistake to come."

Malcolm
Weapons

If tears could be weaponized, they'd be more powerful than swords. They certainly cut more deeply.

Watching Izzy trying to hold herself together, knowing I'm the one who's made her cry, makes me feel like the worst sort of heel. And the thought of letting her walk out the door and return to London, return to America, is even worse. She did, after all, travel 3,500-odd miles to get here. She was brave enough to travel all that way and risk humiliation.

I pause to consider the enormity of that. The amount of courage it must have taken. Whatever is in the letters must be important. Do I have any right to keep them from my father?

In any case, why should I care whether or not he reads them? Now I've had time to process, I'm not certain I mind if they bring him pain. He's earned every bit of that and more. It can't come close to the hurt he inflicted on my mother.

I keep my hand on the door handle to keep Izzy from bolting away. "Where are you staying tonight? In the village?"

"The Green Man, probably. Unless I go straight back to London."

"Oh. Yes, of course." I try to keep from scowling, but I picture Izzy trying to cope when the pub gets rowdy later, and I can't quite see it. Or I can, but I don't see it ending well. I'm torn about what I think she'd do—either bolt back upstairs and hide in her room all night alone or do something ridiculously ill-advised and put herself in danger.

We both look away.

Holding the door closed is getting awkward, but I don't want to let her go like this. It would be unpardonably rude, for one thing.

"You could always stay here," I find myself saying. "If you'd like. There's more than enough room, obviously, and I'm sure it's what... Ian...would want. I could try to ring through to him meanwhile. Find out when he's coming back."

I've no idea where all that came from, but none of this is Izzy's fault. As much as I've loathed Marcella Cavalera all these years, I've no reason to hate her daughter. And clearly, Izzy didn't know anything about Dad at all.

I remember how it felt losing Mum, and I try to imagine what it must be like for Izzy to find that her mother had an entire secret inner life. Twenty years of letters…It's been eight years since I found out about Dad and Marcella, and I still don't understand. I still can't manage to forgive them.

"Please," I say. "You should stay. Give me a chance to make up for being rude."

Izzy
Madness

The Jekyll and Hyde routine Prince Whosit has going on is giving me whiplash. Also, it's annoying to discover that I introduced myself but I still don't know *his* name. Anyway, he's too young to have the kind of authority it would take to give me permission to stay here, so what is up with that? Some weird attempt at a pick-up line? I'm not sure where he thinks that's going to get him, but I know what Elli would do. She'd totally call his bluff and enjoy watching him wriggle on her hook.

I, however, am not Elli.

"Much as I'd love to take you up on the invitation," I say, "you were right before. I'm not sure it would be fair to Ian to dump this on him out of the blue. I should have thought about that sooner."

"You must have believed the letters were important." He studies me, then slowly straightens and takes his hand off the door handle, either giving me the choice to leave or trusting I won't bolt out of the room. Where before there was only anger in his expression, now there's a measuring curiosity that intrigues me. Anyone else would have already asked me what was in the letters. I like the fact he hasn't.

"You never told me your name," I say. "Or what you do around here. At Halford, I mean."

His shoulders go stiff. An invisible wall builds itself around him, and he feels forbidding and remote as he steps past me. He stands a moment with his back turned, then he swings around and leans back against the desk, his arms crossed over his chest.

Alarm bells are going off in my brain again, but even so, I've never considered the erotic possibilities of forearms before. Or the base of a throat revealed between the open collar of a shirt.

And I'm definitely not considering them now. Nope. Not at all. It's just that his remoteness is so clearly self-protective I can't help seeing it as a challenge. An interesting package to be unwrapped.

His chin comes up slowly, and equally slowly, he smiles. It's hesitant and rueful and apologetic. "We haven't begun on the right foot at all, have we? At least I haven't. Do you suppose we could try and start over?" Peeling himself away from the desk, he comes toward me with his hand outstretched and that charming, disarming smile making him look like a mash-up of every dangerous weapon good-looking boys have in their arsenals.

"Hello, Izzy," he says. "I'm Malcolm Halford. It's very nice to meet you."

I'm already dizzy from the smile as his fingers wrap electricity around my own. Then the name processes and the boot drops with a great, fat, resounding thud.

Malcolm Halford.

Malcolm. Halford.

Oh. Dear. God. Prince Jekyll-and-Hyde could actually be my *brother*.

------◆❀◆------

October 26, 1998

Dear Ian,

There's life growing inside me—life other than my music. It's the strangest sensation, which is to say that physically I feel no change at all, and I can't help thinking that I should, that I must already be failing as a mother, as a parent. Shouldn't I have known sooner? Shouldn't I have suddenly felt more like a grown-up and less like an imposter dressed in grown-up skin?

The doctor tells me I still have options, but you'd hate that, wouldn't you? You'd be furious.

Of course, I can't even write the word, so maybe that's all the answer I need myself.

There's a part of me that's tempted to believe—to dream—this baby will have your intelligent eyes and cheerfully waving hair. Your eyebrows. Is it possible to love a man for his eyebrows? They were one of the things I first noticed about you. Now I notice them on every man I meet. I notice curling hair and green eyes and kindness.

In March, I will no longer be alone.

I hate you and I love you. Today, I also hate myself.

Cella

Escape

A surge of adrenaline carries me the first steps down the long drive toward Halford's main entrance. There's no way I'm going to stand around and wait for Mr. Corker to come and pick me up. I'm not even calm enough to call him yet without embarrassing myself. But on the bright side, it'll take me ages to walk to the gate, so there's plenty of time to call him.

Maybe by then, I'll have achieved some level of zen about the fact that I've used the word lust in thinking about a guy who could be my brother.

Holy crap.

I'm mean. Holy *crap*.

And poor Malcolm doesn't have a clue what's

going on. He followed me out to the steps when I bolted out of the room and out of the house. I screamed at him to leave me alone and took off, and for all I know he's still standing there looking bewildered and congratulating himself on having gotten rid of the lunatic relatively painlessly. *Relatively* being the operative word, even if he doesn't know it.

At least this makes my choices clear. I absolutely, positively cannot give Ian the letters. I don't want to see Ian. In fact, I don't even want to stay in the same village. London might not be big enough.

Because here's the problem. I knew Ian had a son. There was the biography, for one thing. And Mom's letters mentioned the children, but only as an extension of their effect on Ian, as if she didn't have any context for them other than knowing they existed. She didn't mention dates or ages, but I assumed they were younger than me. Because *if* Ian could possibly be my father, I figured it was because the breakup had taken a while to stick—Mom's string of long good nights.

All that changes if Malcolm's older. Ian and Mom would have had to cheat together. On Ian's *wife.* Which Mom wouldn't have done. She wouldn't have. Which means I can't be Ian's daughter.

Which means I've been an idiot.

A car pulls up beside me. I glance over, then quickly turn away.

"Get in," Malcolm says. "Please, Izzy. Allow me a chance to explain. You've every right to think I'm a sod for not having told you the truth. But at least let me give you a lift into the village. It's farther than you'd think, and it isn't safe walking like this."

I keep walking. After all the things I was thinking—feeling—how can I face talking to him?

On the other hand, hang on. If I can't be Ian's daughter, then Malcolm can't be my brother.

That's...totally not important.

Because I'm leaving.

Malcolm speeds up and then suddenly swerves over onto the grass in front of me, cutting off the line of cars behind him. Someone leans on a horn and shouts something obscene out the window.

I veer left to go around the front of the car, but Malcolm pulls further onto the grass until the hood of the dusty Land Rover presses right against the fence.

I whip around and snarl. "Are you completely nuts?"

"Given the situation, we're probably all entitled to straitjackets."

He's got the passenger window open, leaning across the center console to shout at me, and something about the tilt of his head and the mulish set to his jaw and the whole absurdity of the situation suddenly kicks in. I laugh, I can't help it, and my eyes fill with tears.

Malcolm blinks at me through the open window and shakes his head as though I've lost it. Which I kind of have. I admit it.

"Come on," he says to me. "Just get in."

I owe him an explanation. Frankly, that's the least I owe him.

"Fine," I say, and then because the steering wheel is on the wrong side in British cars, all I have to do is open the door that's right in front of me and climb into the passenger seat. But those few tiny steps are some of the hardest I've ever had to take.

Perspectives

Malcolm's down-at-the-heels Land Rover is badly in need of new shock absorbers. That makes it harder to talk as we bounce along the road toward the village, but given what I need to say, it would be next to impossible no matter what. The fact that his car is a mess, with ripped leather seats and the back littered with books and towels and soccer balls and running shoes in a way that reminds me of Elli's brothers, is actually weirdly comforting.

He listens while I explain about the letters and tell him what I've been thinking. His hand rests loosely across the top of the steering wheel as he weaves around deep ruts in the asphalt. That apparent relaxation is deceptive, though. There's tension roiling off him.

I finish, and he doesn't say anything. I wait another second to give him time to process.

Still nothing.

"I guess what I ought to say," I try again, "is that I'm sorry. For acting so weird. For showing up like this. For all of it. I shouldn't have jumped to conclusions. I know my mother, and she wouldn't have... you know. Not after your parents were married, but I assumed it was before."

"It couldn't have been before." Malcolm slows the car and downshifts as we come to the first stone structures at the village edge. He glances at me and then turns back to the road. "You're right, though," he says. "My father wouldn't have cheated, either. That isn't who he is."

"Then why do you hate my mother so much?" I fold my hands carefully in my lap.

"I don't hate her." His mouth twists on the lie, and he slams the brakes as a tabby cat runs across the road in front of us. "Well, all right. I suppose I do, but it's mostly the idea of her, obviously. The idea of her existence. The fact that she ruined my parents' marriage. My mother died because of her—"

"Died?" My lungs freeze in my chest at the word, and I can't breathe. I hope that's just hyperbole. Or some awful kind of a metaphor.

Except that his mother did die, and the bio I read didn't say how it happened.

Malcolm looks down at the fingers he has curled around the steering wheel. He says nothing as he pulls the Land Rover to a stop along the stone wall in front of The Green Man Inn.

I shiver, feeling very cold. Because suddenly it's all too easy to see how my mother must have seemed from his perspective. The other woman. The home wrecker. Camilla Parker Bowles to Malcolm's mother as Princess Diana. The woman who was always in the marriage even when she wasn't.

My mother was nothing like that—the letters were nothing like that—but how could Malcolm know?

"Do you want to read the letters for yourself?" I blurt out, and his face goes all hard and distant. "No, really. I think they—this whole thing—it's like those roses Joran Masterson held up in the workshop. You can't know what you aren't seeing until you see it, if that makes any sense. I don't know if it would change how you feel, but I think you should read the letters."

"I don't bloody want to read them." Malcolm rubs a hand across the back of his neck.

"What about your father?"

"I don't know." Malcolm snaps off the ignition and shifts around in his seat to face me. "Part of me thinks that after all the pain he inflicted on my mum, he deserves any amount of pain the letters would cause him. But he hasn't been the same since he read that your mother died. He still goes to the surgery every day, sees patients, runs the estate, but he's only going through the motions, as if nothing really matters. At night he shuts himself in the reading room and doesn't come back out. Then he rang out of the blue and asked me to come home this weekend because he needed to go to London. He refused to say how long for, and no one here knows anything except that he's arranged a *locum* doctor to stand in for him at the practice for as long as needed."

"And that isn't normal?"

"Far from it."

Malcolm's trying so hard to sound like he doesn't care that it makes my chest hurt to hear him. I hate that I came here and added to his worries. And I don't know how to get myself out of this.

"Well, I hope he—" What? What am I supposed to say? "Grief is hard," I manage, which is entirely feeble and obvious and lame. "Look, thanks for driving me back. And sorry I bothered you with all this. It was nice to meet you. So um. Yeah. Bye. Thanks again." I smile too brightly. I'm babbling, so I just have to stop. I need to go.

Snatching up my purse, I jump out of the car without looking at Malcolm, and I rush up the path. The entrance is set beyond a low wall bordered by the kind of perfect English perennial garden that looks as if it happened by accident but that—like everything else around here—probably took a hundred careful years of weeding and breeding to grow just right.

Malcolm jumps out of the car and comes after me. His legs are longer than mine, so he catches me in just a couple strides. "Don't do that. Don't get cold and polite on me. Don't leave."

He catches my hand and tugs me to a stop, and I feel every ounce of my body heat pooling in my fingers. I want to die of mortification so I don't turn around.

"All right, yes," he says. "Yes, I want to read the letters. Which is to say, I know I'll regret it if I don't read them. Also, I meant what I said earlier about you coming to stay at the Hall. Dad would have my head on a platter if he found out I'd left you here on your own."

I turn then, needing to see if he's serious. He gives me another one of those smiles, and it's the rose phenomenon all over again. Having seen the way his face can light up, I know this smile isn't completely real. I flail for a word to explain the absence of something special, but there isn't one. How can there not be one?

Well, heck, if Horace Walpole can invent "serendipity," I can come up with something.

A·splen·dor·i·a (Noun)
Perfectly executed but devoid of brilliance or genius. "The film's asplendoria made it enjoyable but unremarkable."

Malcolm's smile, this smile, is asplendorious compared to his usual one.

And I did that to him.

Anyway, none of it matters anymore, does it? Because I was wrong. And Ian was—is—still the man my mother loved, but that's all he is.

"Fine. I'll get the letters for you, but you'll have to read them here," I say.

"No. Check out. Come to Halford. Honestly." His head is tipped downward, but he slants a look at me that makes him look even cuter. Dangerous.

"Are you really sure?"

"Absolutely." The smile cranks up a lethal notch. "I'll be waiting in the car."

Text to Elli:

Me: I've met Prince Charming, and he's nice. For a minute I thought he might be my brother, but I was wrong about everything. Spending the night at Halford anyway.

Elli: What??? Ian's son? How old? What's he like? And where's Ian? Details, woman! And you call yourself a writer.

Me: London. Nice. 20. Ish. Yes. No, I don't.

Elli: Then send pics instead of words. NOW.
Do. Not. Keep. Me. Waiting.

Empty Halls

It's after four o'clock by the time we drive back through the Halford gate. A steady stream of cars plods down the lane in the opposite direction, and I feel like a salmon fighting its way upstream. Behind the house, the sun is lower in the sky, lighting up the rooftops and the lake, picking out flecks of mineral brilliance in the cobblestones in the forecourt.

Malcolm pulls around to a private entrance protected by a separate, smaller security gate. He opens and closes it by remote control and parks beneath a portico shaded by an enormous oak tree. Until now, I didn't even realize the house had a wing behind the main portion. You don't see it from around the front, and it's not included on the garden tour.

It's hard to fathom the scale of Halford. I wonder how long it would take to get from one end of the house to the other, how many manhours (or womanhours) it would take to mop the floors. How much money it would cost to paint the outside, never mind the inside where every surface is a separate work of art.

It's beautiful. Incredibly, opulently, royally beautiful. The acoustics are probably fantastic. But I can't imagine my mother ever living here.

"Do you like it?" Malcolm asks, watching me.

"I guess I'm trying to process picking a place, even this one, over the kind of love that was in my mother's letters."

"She's the one who broke things off." Malcolm slams the driver's door. Not hard, but a definite slam, and he circles back toward the trunk where he put my suitcase.

"I didn't mean that as criticism," I say. "I can see not wanting to give this up if you've grown up here. I guess I'm just trying to understand."

"What's to understand? Your mother shattered my father's heart. He never got over her."

He drags out the suitcase and shuts the trunk, and I snatch the suitcase from him and wheel it over the cobblestones myself. I don't know why I suddenly feel defensive, but there was something in his voice and in the way he's walking beside me that makes me feel I have to defend my mother again. Which pisses me off, because she doesn't need to be defended for choosing her career. It's a sad choice, but it was totally valid.

"She was the greatest living pianist," I say. "That's what people called her. If she'd stayed here, she was afraid her music would take a back seat to all this. Anyway, I guess if they had stayed together, neither of us would be here now. We don't have right to judge them."

I say that, and even while the words are coming out of my mouth, I feel like a hypocrite. Haven't I been judging Ian ever since I read the first of my mother's letters? I mean, you care about what you're raised to care about. I just naturally assumed it was sexist for Ian to expect Mom to be the one to compromise.

Maybe that's even part of the reason—a small part—of why I came. As much as I wanted to meet the man my mother loved, I also want to see the place that stole him from her.

Malcolm and I step inside the building, and I look around the enormous hall. The painted ceiling glows with color and the chandeliers catch rays of sunlight and transform them into bursts of fire along the parquet floor and walls covered in fading silk. I tried my best to take in details when I took the tour earlier, but there's too much all crammed together everywhere. Too many things collected over centuries and centuries. It's hard to know where to look.

I glance at Malcolm as he walks through it every day. Does he know the history of all these things? What they meant to whoever bought them? To whoever painted the portraits and landscapes, or carved and inlaid the furniture, or wove the carpets, or sewed the curtains. Or does he not even notice what's around him anymore?

As if he's asking himself similar questions, Malcolm pauses and looks around. His face has smoothed out into an expressionless mask, and I don't know him well enough to guess what lies beneath it. He turns back toward me as if he's going to say something, but a woman has materialized from somewhere in the dim recesses of the building, and she comes hurrying to meet us.

Disapproval

The woman is beak-nosed and hungry-looking, with stoop-shouldered posture and loose skin at her neck that looks pinched beneath the tight, white collar of a dark gray dress. She sees me standing there with Malcolm, and her face, too, pinches in. She looks me up and down. Her eyebrows rise.

Ignoring that, Malcolm stoops to kiss her cheek. "Forgive me. I should have checked in to say I'd be late for tea, but I've brought a guest. This is Izzy. Her mother was a friend of Dad's, so I've invited her to stay the night." He turns back to me again. "Izzy, this is Anna, who's been here since before I was born—which makes her family as well as the most long-suffering housekeeper in England."

Anna looks—what? Angry? Resentful? Malcolm's smile holds real affection and seems to let more light and warmth flood in through the windows. It makes my stomach wobble.

"It's nice to meet you," I say, holding out my hand to her.

In books, housekeepers mostly come in two varieties: the round, jolly, pleasant kind, and the other, the conniving, critical kind. I'm hoping looks are deceiving here. But I don't think so.

"Pleasure, miss." She gives a stiff, icy inclination of her head, and her skin is even colder than it looks. It's probably one of the briefest handshakes in history. Apparently, just because the house could hold the population of a small country doesn't mean she thinks there's room for another person.

At least not for *me*.

Does she know about my mother, too? Is that why she's looking at me like I'm something that Malcolm dragged in on the sole of his shoe?

No, now I'm just being paranoid.

She bobs her head at Malcolm. "I'll go see about finding something for a company dinner. Shall I take the suitcase up?"

"Don't bother; we've got it. And dinner in the kitchen's fine," Malcolm calls after her. "Only Anna? Would you mind bringing tea into the reading room for us? Izzy and I have some things to do."

Her shoes beat a disapproving rhythm as she walks away, and Malcolm stoops to speak into my ear. "Don't be offended—that wasn't about you. Anna stepped in to help after my mother died, but I'm not here as much since I went off to uni. She was probably looking forward to catching up a bit this weekend with my father gone, but she'll come around. And she'll consider it a point of pride to outdo herself with dinner."

His breath is warm as it fans across my cheek. When he pulls back away and straightens, I feel like he's taken my own breath with him. I stare at him as if I've never heard of food. As if I don't speak English. He stares back, our eyes locked together. Then he gives a tiny shake of his head. Steps back. We both stand there with silence unspooling like darkness between us, and I realize that he's taken the suitcase out of my hand while I wasn't paying attention.

"She cooks, too? I thought you said she was the housekeeper."

"She's both, really."

"What about all those cooks and people who were working in the kitchen when I took the 'upstairs/downstairs' tour?"

Malcolm's eyes crinkle at the corners, and he looks at me the way people look at a puppy who's done something cute but vaguely dumb. I should be offended by that, but somehow, I am not.

"What you saw was the staff that takes care of the cafés and tea rooms and preps for the wedding parties we have staying overnight. Dad and I and Anna use the separate kitchen in the family quarters. It's all much more modern here than it used to be. You didn't imagine we still lived like *Downton Abbey*, did you?"

"No, of course not," I say, although I totally kind of did. Does this mean they have a family kitchen at Windsor Castle? Kensington Palace? Actually, I'm incredibly relieved, because I think I would have to hate Ian if he thought it was okay to still live like *Downton Abbey*.

"Even Anna spends most of her time on the business of running the place," Malcolm says. "Coordinating between the private and public sides of the house. The rest of the staff—the butlers, cooks, cleaners, gardeners, event planners, and security people—all work for the tourism end of the estate, so Dad and I are fairly well self-sufficient in our own rooms. Now, come on. We're heading back this way."

I walk beside him, and suddenly I'm more aware of every decoration and piece of furniture, every vase and clock and cabinet and chair and piece of velvet drapery, that we pass. Where earlier today, I admired everything the same way I admire objects in the British Museum or the Smithsonian or the Met, now I'm also seeing all the work that must go into dusting, polishing, and repair. I can't help picturing the armies of people who have to do all that.

It's hard to know how to react, and the silence of the place feels oppressive now, as if it has acquired mass and heft. Like a heavy wool blanket that's smothering and itchy.

> Imagined Text to Elli:
>
> Me: I have lost the ability to speak.
>
> Elli: That is an impossibility. There must be nothing to say.
>
> Me: That is truer than you know.
>
> Elli: Then be wise and brilliant. You're good at that.
>
> Me: If I was wise, would I be here? No. I'd be there. With you.

Familiar Things

Malcolm leads me down several corridors until I'm thoroughly lost, then he stops at a closed door, pushes it open and steps aside to let me through. I'm careful not to brush up against him because I don't dare touch him. Does he know that? Does it show?

Did Anna notice? Is that why she resented me?

Oh, God. What if she knows about my mother

and she saw how I'm reacting to Malcolm? To all of this? Is that possible?

I'm mind babbling. Thought babbling.

Which doesn't keep me from being too aware that Malcolm and I are alone together in what's basically my wet dream of a room. He calls it the reading room. It's not as big as the library I saw earlier on the public tour, but that's both good and bad because this is cozier. There's a fireplace and a table and a comfortable Chintz-covered sofa and matching squishy chairs and ladders that slide back and forth on wooden railings over two whole walls of shelves filled with jewel-colored spines.

My mind stutters on the thought of what could be lurking on those shelves. First edition Shakespeares? Is there such a thing? Or at least a first edition Austen. Then there's another wall crammed with knickknacks and oddities, including a whole shelf of replicas of the Taj Mahal.

At one point, Mom used to keep a small ivory carving of the Taj on the bookshelf in her music room.

The real place is a tomb in India, an architectural wonder built by the Mughal emperor Shah Jahan to commemorate how much he loved his wife. Their romance puts Romeo and Juliet to shame.

I asked my mother about the carving after I started volunteering at the zoo with Elli. "How can you have ivory in the house?"

"I'm a pianist," Mom said. "I have an antique piano, so of course there's ivory."

"Do you know how many elephants have been killed so people can have *things*?" I asked. "Pianos and stupid bracelets and rosary beads and little carvings paid for with the blood of animals who feel joy, loss, and grief as much as humans do?"

My mother picked up the carving and held it a moment, wearing a strange, pained expression, then she brushed her finger along one of the minarets and set the Taj back on the shelf. "This 'stupid' carving was a gift. And it was an antique, so it wasn't illegal."

But we signed up to make a monthly donation to *Save the Elephants* that week, and Elli and I continued volunteering at the National Zoo. Mom quietly moved the carving into her bedroom, and I haven't thought about it since.

It's odd that things can become so familiar you don't see them anymore. Or you don't really notice what you're seeing.

I'm not sure what the Taj Mahal meant to Mom and Ian, but it obviously meant something. Which is weird, because Halford Hall is kind of like the *anti*-Taj Mahal. The monument that defeated love.

PART THREE

Malcolm
Possibilities

The filtered light in the reading room reveals a smattering of faint freckles across Izzy's nose, which is very straight beneath those sharp, dark eyebrows that could nearly be Halford brows. I *am* curious about what's in the letters that's made her think what she's been thinking. I've no desire to read the poxy things, but I don't see I have much choice. Dad's looked spent and old since the moment the news broke about Marcella Cavalera's death, and now I'm over the initial knee-jerk reaction to what Izzy's told me, I don't want him more upset than necessary.

Do I tell him Izzy's here? Not that I've any right to keep it from him.

I gesture her toward the sofa by the fireplace and park her suitcase in front of her. She unzips the bag and rummages around inside until she finds a yellowed parchment patterned shoe box in amongst the clothes. Her back is toward me, her rioting hair fallen on either side of her long, graceful neck and her elegant shoulders rounded and tight with tension. She straightens very slowly before she turns. The box is cradled in her arms as carefully as though it were a living thing. That in itself says a great deal about her relationship with her mother, and for an instant, I feel an irrational twinge of envy. Apart from running Halford, Dad and I've perfected the art of avoiding each other since Mum died. Once a week, we navigate dinner, most of our energy wasted circling around the shoals and rocks of the existence we have to share.

I take the box from Izzy. Briefly, we're both holding it, both looking at each other, neither of us ready to let go. It's ironic, I suppose, that we've both lost our mothers in car accidents. In senseless tragedies.

Izzy's the first to step away. She drops onto the dog hair-covered sofa and pulls her feet up after her as though she's building a moat around herself and hauling up the drawbridge. She looks back towards the bookshelf.

"Why the Taj Mahal?" she asks.

She has a habit of changing subjects in interesting ways when she gets uncomfortable. Interesting in a tip-of-the-iceberg sense that reveals hints of what she's thinking. I quite like the way she thinks.

I glance at the shelves that contain the various small sculptures Dad's amassed, and I wait for the usual wave of anger and resentment to fist themselves inside my chest. But for once, the carvings don't seem to matter.

"The Taj was where he and your mother were supposed to go on their honeymoon," I say without inflection. "He's collected these pieces ever since, even while he and my mum were married. He never told her what they meant, but she knew. She told him that just before she died, and it still didn't keep him from buying more."

The anger sweeps back in, a hard, cold bleakness so familiar I can't remember ever having been entirely without it.

"That's horrible," Izzy says, though I don't imagine she begins to understand. Her eyes are soft, the color of chocolate flecked with Cotswold summer honey.

I wonder what part of "that" she means, but honestly, Dad's obsession with Marcella Cavalera was awful from every perspective.

Now I just want to get this over.

Settling myself into a chair, I pull the shoebox on my lap and remove the lid. The envelopes are more yellowed on the far end, so I turn the box around and pull out the first of the letters. Izzy watches me a moment, then gets up and wanders toward the shelves as though to give me privacy.

Izzy
Mausoleums

I think of Ian collecting reminders of the honeymoon he and my mother never had, and my chest hurts as if every tear I've cried since Mom died has been pumped back into my lungs. At the same time, I want to run to her and bury my face in my mother's shoulder.

Sitting in his chair reading, Malcolm looks so much more together than I am. But living with this collection, all these Taj Mahals, knowing what they represented, had to have been hard for him. Especially knowing that his mother knew.

The black hole of missingness Mom left in my life hasn't gotten any smaller in the months since she died. Was it like that for Malcolm, too? It had to have been worse. He was so little. And all these years, he's been stuck here watching Ian grieve the loss of my mother instead of his own.

The truth is, he has every right to hate my mother. If I hadn't known the magical, flawed, struggling, human Marcella Cavalera, how would I be seeing her now? I suppose genius always requires selfishness, sacrifice, and collateral damage to the people around you, but that doesn't make it any easier to live with.

And Ian? Do I hate him?

I'm not sure I can hate someone who loved Mom that much.

To keep from staring at Malcolm while he reads, I wander over to a desk that's filled with photos in silver frames. The pictures are all of Malcolm at various ages. When he's very small, there's a little girl with him, and they look a lot alike. Sometimes, there's the two of them with their mother, who was very elegant. In other photos, Malcolm's older, wearing a school tie and blazer and looking rebellious and lost. There are shots of him with other boys playing soccer and graduating in a cap and gown. But there isn't a single photo of Malcolm with his father. No photos of Ian at all.

I turn to one of the bookshelves, running my fingers idly along the spines as I circumnavigate the room. Almost immediately, I find old friends: Shakespeare, Dickens, Homer, Goethe, Keats, Byron. Then I discover an ancient edition of *The Picture of Dorian Gray* and an even older copy of some of Oscar Wilde's correspondence. It's like finding a box of my favorite chocolates—I don't know which to sample first. I plop back down on the sofa, but instead of reading, I find myself watching Malcolm. Two envelopes lie on the table beside him and he holds a third in one hand while he reads the corresponding letter.

His eyes are the clearest I've ever seen, so clear it feels like I can see right into *him*. Reactions chase each other through them as he reads. Anger. Rejection. Surprise.

I wonder if reading the letters will change anything for him, alter the narrative of his childhood the way they've turned the wheel on the kaleidoscope of mine. Every new fact makes me see my mother and my life a little differently.

But the letters aren't proof in themselves. They're only twenty years of Mom thinking on paper. Talking to herself and pretending to talk to Ian.

Paper crinkles as Malcolm folds the third letter back into its envelope. His movements are stiff and careful.

"I can see why you wanted to come," he says. "Are they all like this?"

"More or less." My chest fills with spent air until it hurts. "She'd never told me anything about my father, but I knew she'd never fallen in love with anyone else. She never even dated, really, which she said was about her music. I suppose I knew there must have been more to it, but she always pretended it didn't matter."

"And of course it did."

I glance back at him, and suddenly my cheeks are so hot they're incandescent.

Darn it, I promised myself I wouldn't cry. Again.

Malcolm's chair creaks. A drawer in the desk opens and closes, and then he's standing at my shoulder. "Here."

He offers me a package of tissues. I take one, stealing a glance up at him. He looks less angry and more like the guy who wanted to believe as many impossible things as Alice.

Imagined Text to Elli:

Me: You know how Alice felt like she was shutting up like a telescope?

Elli: You mean after she drank from the "Drink Me" bottle?

Me: After she realized she'd forgotten the key so she couldn't get through the door. But by then she'd gotten into the habit of expecting out-of-the-way things to happen.

Elli: She kept going when the unexpected happened. That's the point. Otherwise, she'd never have found out what was on the other side.

———◆❊◆———

December 24, 1996

Dear Ian,

I have my first grown-up Christmas tree all decorated with my first grown-up ornaments and actual candles, and I thought I was getting over us until I realized my tree looked a little too much like the one at Halford. I thought putting up a tree would make me feel better. Instead, it makes me lonely. Candlelight fractures when I look at it too long, and my eyes blur.

I was invited out for the evening. I probably should have gone, but I didn't want to be the inevitable guest whose mood spoils everyone else's fun.

Tonight, I wondered again if you and I couldn't have made us work somehow. If we couldn't have compromised. After all these months, that question still hurts as much as if it's the first time I've asked it of myself. Then one by one, as if it's the first time I've ever considered those, too, I work through all the reasons I can't live at Halford and you won't live elsewhere. Can't and won't. So it isn't really me who left you, is it? I shouldn't feel guilty, but your silence reduces me to guilt.

If you'd write to me, I could say some of these things to you.

Your silence is too loud for me to hear myself.

Merry Christmas,

Cella

May 5, 1997

Dear Ian,

The music is like a wind, howling through my empty spaces. My heart feels hollow and light, and I don't think I would realize that if it hadn't briefly been filled by you. Maybe it would just feel normal.

I wonder if all great gifts demand a sacrifice in the way of ancient gods? If so, it's ironic. I would say such cruel gods weren't worth following, but I know my gift requires pain and a bloody worship.

Do you still think of me? Or have you moved on as if I never existed? I imagine you getting married one day, and I should hope she will be someone who understands you. Someone nice and kind. I can picture her, someone with enough money for Halford and the same kind of love for it that you have. I picture her filling the place with children for you so you can pass down the yoke of obligation to another generation. I think these things and I try to be happy for you, and if I were a better sort of person, imagining that you will have everything you need would make me happy, too.

Is it selfish to wish you happiness without wishing you were happy with someone else?

Love,

Cella

Infect the Messenger

I run my thumb along the edge of the book on my lap. "The saddest part is that your father must have already been married by the time my mother wrote that third letter. How old are you exactly?"

Malcolm unfolds another letter. "Twenty. My birthday's November 15th."

"1996?"

"Yes." He throws me a question with his eyebrows, but I ignore it.

I've been trying to remember what the letters say as he reads them. I know the important ones by heart since I re-read them so many times, and most of the early ones were etched in my mind by shock. And it's not just that Ian was already married. Malcolm and his twin sister were seven months old by the time Mom wrote that she was trying to wish he would be happy with someone else someday.

Every one of my mother's letters would have been too late, even if she had mailed them. The first was written only two months after she and Ian had broken things off, and she spent those months hoping he would reach back out to her. That they could repair things between them. But *he* didn't wait at all. Instead, he must have jumped straight into bed with Malcolm's mother. Which makes things worse. It makes Malcolm's mother a knee-jerk reaction. A rebound.

Not that I can say that to Malcolm.

Anyway, I don't have time to speak. Anna pushes the door open and sweeps in with a tray of tea and round scones with jam and whipped cream and little sandwiches cut into wedges on a serving plate. She's followed by dogs, insistent, jumping dogs: an Irish wolfhound about the size of a smallish horse and an aging cocker spaniel, two Jack Russells, and a pair of corgis that look like they fell off the ladders from way up high so that their legs compressed to half their intended size. All of them are wagging their tails, determined to be the first to inspect me and say hello.

"Dogs, sit. Stop fawning on the guest." Malcolm wades into the pack to haul them off me.

Either the dogs are boycotting the degrading command or they flunked their obedience training. If I didn't already look as though I shouldn't be allowed anywhere near this bastion of Anglo-Saxonness, the fact that I'm now covered with dog hair and saliva probably won't help my case.

"Sorry about this," Malcolm says. "My father's never had the heart to discipline them."

He removes the two bouncing Jack Russells into the corridor and shuts the door behind them. Once I've scratched the rest behind the ears and retreated protectively back to my seat, most of the others wander away as well, leaving only the Irish wolfhound staring at me with dark, intelligent eyes. I smile at him and he levitates onto the sofa beside me without any visible effort and plops his head into my lap. Tongue lolling, he wags his tail and turns to look at Malcolm, practically daring him to argue.

Anna sets the tray on the desk and starts to lay out the two cups to pour the tea, but Malcolm hurries over and picks up the teapot himself. "We can fend for ourselves, Anna. You already have a hundred things to worry about."

Her lips purse, and she wipes her palms on the skirt of her dress in a way that suggests she isn't happy. "I thought your father might have rung you. Have you heard from him?"

"Not a word," Malcolm says, glancing at me. "I might try to reach him in a little bit."

"Tell him one of the brides broke a window in the pavilion, apparently. A peacock had wandered in and she threw her shoe at it."

Malcolm's lips twitch. "I hope the bird wasn't hurt."

"It's fine, but the window can't be repaired in time for the reception, and the bride's mother is kicking up a fuss."

Malcolm raises his eyebrows without exactly raising them. It's a good trick and I'm kind of envious. Elli would love it. "I'm sure Pricilla will figure something out. Move a potted tree in front of it or something. The bride can't object if she's the one who broke it."

"Can't she just?" Anna sniffs as if she smells something unpleasant. "You'll see. Just remember you're meant to stop in and say hello to them before dinner. The Anderson–Shields people are in the east wing and Kendall–Grahams are in the Chiswick drawing room." She glares at me gratuitously and sweeps out again, but not before she manages to let the Jack Russells back into the room.

The two little dogs are both subdued now and on their best behavior, and they flop down in strategic positions under the tea tray to lie in wait for droppage.

"Do you take sugar?" Malcolm asks, pouring out a cup of tea for me.

I shift the wolfhound's head off my lap and get up to help myself, mainly because I don't want to end up with a whole plate of sandwiches that I'll have to sneak to the dogs. The housekeeper doesn't need more reasons to disapprove of me.

"I don't think Anna likes me much," I say.

"I wouldn't take that personally. She's worried about Dad, and she knows I don't like having to go and let people fawn over us as though we're part of the furniture."

"The tame earl?"

"Well, I'm only a viscount, technically, but yes. It's one of hundreds of things Dad and I row about. He sees the title as part of what he calls our 'unique selling proposition.' I'd rather focus on the history and what Halford means to the community."

I wonder if this is his way of answering my question about Anna. Does she see me as some kind of a royals groupie?

For the first time, I wonder if Malcolm has a girlfriend, some beautiful, Kate Middleton type who knows exactly how to drink tea in a room like this without worrying where to put the cup and where to put the plate without spilling food over the sofa and the dogs. Someone who wouldn't for a second worry about the housekeeper judging her and deciding she isn't good enough.

It was a mistake to say I'd stay here overnight. After Malcolm finishes reading the letters, there will still be dinner to get through and breakfast and everything in between.

Halford's long driveway and the distance to a village that doesn't even have a single Uber driver are a definite disadvantage. I mean, seriously. They filled in the moat and the protective ditch around the Hall centuries ago, but there's still no easy way to slink off without a fuss.

<hr>

Reading

There's something dangerously intimate about watching Malcolm read. Something sexy about a guy who knows how to be still and concentrate. I've never actually thought through the qualities I'd want in the perfect guy, but reading would be one of them.

He's settled in with most of the dogs at his feet, and there's a new aloneness written across his features as he moves from one letter to another.

I watch his brows draw together or rise faintly beneath his wayward hair, the way his lip softens or hardens, the way his jaw works, the way the muscles in his forearms tense as he folds each page back into its envelope and then extracts the next letter from the box.

Trust me to find a guy like Malcolm here, on the wrong side of an ocean. What I need is a Reader Boy on the first day of college, or in a chance encounter at a library, or when we bump into each other because we're both reading while we ride the subway and we each drop our books and realize we're reading the same one, or at least that we've read each other's books and loved them.

Malcolm absolutely, definitely, should not be inspiring me to start a mental list of things I like in boys.

———❖———

Characteristics of the Perfect Guy

1. He reads and thinks intelligently
2. He knows how to listen
3. He's open minded and wants to learn
4. He can change his mind graciously when he's wrong
5. He's comfortable in his own skin
6. He's kind, considerate, and respectful
7. He's honest
8. He has both passion and compassion
9. He knows how to have fun and has a sense of humor
10. He understands that A Knight's Tale is about more than a silly girl with a flower and a silly boy with a horse and stick.

Malcolm
Here Be Dragons

It's the eleventh letter, the one dated October of 1998, that must have made Izzy fly to England. If I didn't know my father, after reading the words Marcella wrote on discovering she was pregnant, I'd very likely have leapt to the same conclusion.

I reread the letter, and even knowing Dad, I can't help being taken aback by what Marcella wrote about him being furious. About dreaming. I try to imagine her sleeping with men who have eyebrows that remind her of my father's, and I'm not sure whether that's better or worse than Dad playing her music all the time and collecting monuments to longing.

Would it have been better for everyone if the two of them had simply given in and conducted an affair? Perhaps their feelings might have burned themselves out eventually. And if not, Dad might at least have done the decent thing and asked Mum to divorce.

Instead, there were all the arguments and accusations. I remember hiding from them in the priest hole and not being able to escape.

The priest hole—there's another thing I haven't thought about in years. I wonder if it's still there, whether all my old things are there. So many things I left behind. Suddenly, I'm twelve again, reliving all the fear. The hurt. The guilt.

I let the letter fall into my lap. Izzy's engrossed in a book, scanning the pages with a faint smile that makes the dimple in her cheek grow shallower or deeper as she reads. Gelert has settled beside her on the sofa again, his head on her lap. She scratches him absently behind the ears now and again and, though Gelert's notoriously reserved, he responds as though he's known her his entire life.

She raises her head. Her eyes narrow a fraction, and she studies me, then her focus drops to the letter and shifts up again. I don't know what I have written in my expression, but her chest rises and falls again in a heavy sigh.

"You're starting to see why I came," she says.

"If I didn't know my father, I might even be wondering a little. But I do know him. Duty and honor are everything. He'd slice his own arm off before he broke a vow."

"But you see how tempting it must have been."

"There's no proof. Nothing definitive. And her

obituary mentioned strings of men," I say, because that's what I'm thinking, strings of men with the Halford eyebrows, and never the right man. Because I'm not *actually* thinking.

I realize my mistake the moment I utter the words, but it's too late to bite them back. Izzy's expression freezes, and her fingers go still on Gelert's head.

"That was ugly." She drops her feet on the floor and stands up slowly. "Ugly and uncalled for and you can go to hell."

I jump to my feet. "No, wait. I didn't mean that the way it sounded."

"It's exactly what you meant."

"Maybe I was convincing myself—I *know* Dad wouldn't have broken his marriage vows, but I'll admit the letters are compelling. If I hadn't read that in the papers, I'd almost believe he—"

"So because you read it in the newspaper, it must be true?"

"But did she? She did, didn't she? Go out with a lot of men?"

"Not that I ever knew about."

"Izzy—"

"No, don't." She shakes her head as though she wishes she could shake my words from her ears. "If there were men before I was born, that was her trying to forget about your father after she was done waiting for him. Which is better than jumping in bed with another woman literally the second they had broken up. How long did he wait? A day? A week? At least Mom was honest with herself. She didn't go in for self-delusion. You'd know that if you'd ever heard her music."

"Heard it?" I throw the letter on the table. "Oh, I heard it. It was the bloody soundtrack to our lives until it drove my mother to suicide."

The letter shudders on the table, trembling against the wood, the bold, spiky handwriting blurring until the paper stops. I thought I'd finally gotten over the need to lob grenades. To wound people.

It isn't even as though I have any desire to be cruel to Izzy, but talking about all this shifts me straight back to old patterns and old resentments.

My head aches, and I rub my temples. Izzy steps closer and shakes her head. "Is that how she died?"

"I don't know. It was suspected, but no one could be sure," I say, fighting to pull myself together. "And I'm sorry, I can't seem to keep myself from making a proper bollocks of all this."

Her eyes are no longer subzero when she looks at me, but I think I'd prefer the arctic chill to pity. "I'm the one who sprang all this on you," she says. "It's still a lot for me to take in, and I've had months to get used to it."

I find myself wanting to wipe away the line that creases the skin between eyes that aren't what I think of as brown at all. They're dotted with honey gold flecks, and there's something clear and pure and honest about them that offers hints of tantalizing thoughts swimming beneath the surface. Potentially dangerous thoughts that leave me disoriented and a little short of breath.

Isabelle Cavalera's eyes should carry a warning marker akin to the dragons that medieval cartographers used to label unmapped territories. The mysterious unknown, something that intrigues and entices as much as it dissuades.

Here Be Dragons

Izzy
Beautiful Skin

The boys I know best are Elli's brothers. The older of them, Evan, is like I imagine Gelert the wolfhound would have been as a puppy, gangly and graceful and constantly in motion. Owen is a firecracker on a long, slow fuse. He simmers and then explodes in a single, massive burst.

Malcolm is something entirely different. An unknown. We walk side by side to the kitchen for dinner with the herd of sleepy dogs padding along behind us. I like the way Malcolm moves, loose-limbed but graceful, all contained kinetic energy and potential wrapped in beautiful skin.

He's only gotten through half the letters, but he's been quiet since he set the last one aside and slotted the envelope slowly back into the box. Now suddenly he stops and turns to me.

"I need to tell my father you're here," he says. "And he needs to read all this."

"You don't think that would be too painful for him?"

"It might help him to know your mother didn't forget him."

"It might make things worse."

"You do still want to meet him, don't you?" He scans my face. "Because if you don't, you could leave the letters with me. I swear I'd get them back to you."

I think about letting go of my mother's words. Her thoughts. Trusting them to strangers. And I can't.

"I'd like to meet him first," I say. "That's why I came in person. She must have had a reason for not mailing the letters, and you have every right to protect him—he's your father. But protecting her is my job."

Malcolm takes a beat to consider. "You want to know whether he deserves to read what she wrote?"

My nod is painfully slow. "More or less."

"He is a good man, you know." Malcolm's lips are stiff as he says this, as though it's hard to say. "Not always an easy one, but he tries to do what's right. Duty and honor, all of that. He's done his best to pass those ideals on to me, which I suppose I've always considered hypocritical of him, given that he destroyed our family by being in love with another woman. I never stopped to consider what that cost him. But it must have been unbearable giving up the sort of love I see in your mother's letters."

We've reached a long gallery that has no carpets

and not much furniture. Every sound echoes, and even the jingle of the dogs' collars and the click of their claws on the parquet floor is loud. The two long walls are lined with portraits, dozens of enormous paintings spaced a foot or so apart and hundreds of smaller ones in a collage of shapes and sizes mounted above those all the way up to the frescoed ceiling. Faces and faces and faces, all staring down at Malcolm through the history of his DNA. He glances up at them as he walks as though he's carrying their full weight on his shoulders. Tired. That's how he seems when he looks at them. And their eyes follow him expectantly.

He points them out: this ancestor died fighting Oliver Cromwell at Naseby, and that one was killed at Culloden. The one there with the smile that looks like Malcolm's was shot at Lexington fighting the wrong side of America's Revolutionary War. Others lost their lives at Salamanca, Waterloo, and Dunkirk. Halford Hall is a history of futile battles, a symphony built of blood and stone with variations on themes of honor, duty, and sacrifice. I wonder if Malcolm is seeing the connection the way I am.

> Imagined Text to Elli:
>
> Me: How do you live for yourself if you have to worry about everyone who died to put you where you are?

> Elli: What's the point? Better to live for the
> kids who'll hate you for doing that to them.

Doesn't someone eventually rebel? Say screw it, my shoulders aren't big enough to carry all this weight?

Maybe not. I think of all the commercials with lonely people dying to know they belong somewhere, rushing off to buy kilts or lederhosen or Native American crafts because of what they found out in a DNA analysis. Of course, you never hear much rejoicing when someone discovers a serial killer in the family tree. Except maybe the police when they're trolling through the databases and all those lonely people's DNA helps them figure out an unsolved rape or murder.

That's the thing. You can't escape your genes. Even now, walking past the rows of portraits, I can't help looking for myself in the faces, searching for something familiar. It's human nature, I guess. Even babies smile more at people who look like them. We all want to know where we belong.

Until Mom died, I never gave much thought to death. Then suddenly I was alone, the last person in my family, and I came running here, hoping for something to claim. Someone to claim me. These portraits are a record of Malcolm's genetic code, puzzle pieces of who he is: dark, thick eyebrows perfectly arched; eyes the color of sea ice—pale,

pale green—a straight, aristocratic nose; the dimple in his chin that looks like someone poked him with a pinky finger.

Beneath my feet, the gallery floor is ancient oak, like silk and honey and wax so thick I could skate on it. I picture myself taking off my shoes and getting a running start. How far would my socks let me slide?

I feel like I'm already sliding.

"There's only you and your father, right?" I ask. "No uncles? Cousins?"

"Cousins and an aunt—my mother's sister, who was Dad's second cousin. And no, that's not illegal. It's only marginally closer than our relationship to the Queen of England but we're something like forty-five steps from the throne, so no one's in any danger there."

His voice and posture remain casual as he says this. No inflection, no smugness to his grin, as if it's got nothing at all to do with him.

"There are also several great-uncles, two great-aunts, and slews of dusty, distant other relations."

"Including the queen, apparently."

"You know I made that up about forty-five steps, don't you? I haven't any idea, actually, how many people would need to die. My best mate Percy tried to count up his claim once, and we wasted the best part of an otherwise pleasantly beer-soaked night trying to devise a plot that could get him into Buckingham

Palace. But contrary to popular opinion, hereditary peers don't all congregate in one place the way they used to. Makes it difficult to plot a coup."

"It has to be hard, though, not having anyone close except your dad," I say, staring at the floor. "I mean, you must still miss your mom."

He gives me that startled look again, followed by that measuring I'm-trying-to-figure-you-out look. "It gets easier," he says. "I promise."

I don't say anything. I hate pity. But I guess I opened myself up to it. My own fault.

"I lost my sister, too," he says, "my twin, but you knew that. Her name was Ginny. She died of heart complications when we were eight. My father's only brother drowned in his last year at Oxford, and I was twelve when Mum died. I suppose I feel like I've had all the drawbacks of family, the drama and the obligations, without the best bits. The genuine closeness. Of course, we're British, so we show more affection to dogs and horses than to family anyway. You'll have gathered Dad and I have our share of problems."

His tone is dry, but he walks a little faster now, as if he's trying to outpace his feelings.

I've been really lucky—I know that—to have had my mother, even if I've lost her now. Malcolm's been alone most of his life. Too alone.

—◆❖◆—

Beautiful

Malcolm's phone beeps, and he mutters under his breath as he reads the text that just came in.

"I almost conveniently forgot about the wedding guests," he says. "Do you mind coming with me? We've only to pop in and shake hands, stay a few minutes. Maybe it won't be quite as painful if you're there, too."

I look down at my Shakespeare T-shirt, unzipped hoodie, and hot pink sneakers. I highly doubt this is the kind of attire people expect when the lord of the manor comes to thank them for shelling out silly amounts of money to help him keep a roof over his head. Not to mention my hair. My hair is *Princess Diaries* before the makeover.

"You look fine," Malcolm says. "You're beautiful."

"Liar." I turn away to hide my burning cheeks. "At least let me go change my shirt. Wait here, okay?" We left my suitcase in the reading room, so I run back in the direction we just came from with half the dogs giving chase.

Malcolm calls after me. "Izzy?"

I turn back. "Yes?"

"The letters—they're beautiful, too," he says. "I should have said that sooner. The way your mother loved my father was beautiful. My parents' marriage was nothing like that."

I nod, not trusting my voice. Sorry for him. Sorry for them.

It seems wrong for two people who loved each other the way Mom and Ian did not to have spent their lives together.

---◆�֎◆---

Punctuation

The first group of wedding guests mills around in a reception hall lined with dark paneling and tapestries that have faded out so that blues and greens are almost the only colors left. Tables draped with white linen make a U-shape on one end of the room, and forty or fifty people swirl around the other end sipping champagne or whiskey from cut crystal glasses. Chandeliers spill light across a black and white marble floor that makes me think of "Claire de Lune" and Verlaine's bergamaskers and charming masqueraders.

The whole scene feels familiarly dreamlike, as if I've pulled it straight from one of my stories. As if I'm looping back through time the way the portraits in the gallery telescoped through history. Even the French doors leading out to the garden with the fountain are there the way they're described in the poem, only in this case, it's a garden designed by Capability

Brown, who created poetry out of landscapes and wrote my favorite description of the proper use of punctuation:

> *"Here I put a comma,*
> *there, when it's necessary*
> *to cut the view,*
> *I put a parenthesis;*
> *there I end it*
> *with a period*
> *and start on another theme."*

Malcolm walks close beside me as we cross the room. Everyone is staring at us, and I feel ridiculously underdressed despite having changed into a blouse and the Gucci loafers Mom gave me last year for Christmas. Then the bride and groom and their parents come forward and Malcolm introduces us both, cloaking himself in a well-schooled easy charm.

They gush about Halford and ask a quick half-dozen questions about how many times he's met the queen and William and Harry—and has he met *her* yet. They don't specify which *her*, but from the mildly hostile way they glance at me I assume they mean Meghan Markle. Because we Americans are all the same and obviously all of us are out to steal members of the British aristocracy.

Malcolm handles it brilliantly. "My invitation to tea must have gotten lost in the mail," he says.

"I'd love to see a royal wedding. Mum went to Charles and Diana's, didn't you, Mum? She still has plates and biscuit tins as souvenirs."

Her mother is a pretty woman with improbably blond hair, a violently yellow dress, and one of those hats you only see at royal garden parties. She nods and smiles at Malcolm. "So sad what happened to Diana, isn't it? But that Kate is really lovely."

I can practically feel Malcolm wince, but he only shifts the conversation again and asks if they're all settled in and comfortable in their rooms. He's good at asking questions. Before they realize it, they're talking about their own lives instead of the royal family, about their work and the wine they like and visits to the John Rylands Library at the University of Manchester, which apparently is near where they live and well worth seeing.

The situation is familiar, as if I'm at one of the receptions to which Mom used to drag me. I'm no stranger to feeling like a shadow lost in the brilliance of someone else's light. Even the bride's mother struggles to find a label for me as other guests drift over to us and she tries to make introductions.

"And Izzy is Malcolm's...How do you know each other, dear?" She cocks her eyebrow at me as if I'm supposed to finish the sentence for her.

I flounder until Malcolm shifts closer and gives me that warm, comfortable smile of his.

"Izzy is a good friend," he says. "Practically family."

I don't think he meant it to sound the way it's taken, and he shoots me an apologetic glance in response to the sudden knowing smiles. He doesn't correct himself, though. Not that I can blame him. The people who have come over to us are mostly young women, and several of them have been looking at him as if they're hungry. But not for food.

We wander the room, handed off from group to group like gifts being passed around for admiration until we manage to extract ourselves. I think we've strategically shaken hands or kissed cheeks with every single wedding guest.

Peacocks

Malcolm catches my hand as we escape, as if holding my hand is completely normal. As if it isn't kind of mind-blowing.

> Imagined Text to Elli:
>
> Me: I am holding hands with Prince Charming at a receptionish-type thingy where he had to go be princely and charming. Um, what does a future earl do when he behaves like an earl?"

Elli: How much have you had to drink?

Me: Not enough. I am drunk on the absurdities of life.

The two of us hurry off to the next reception, where most of the conversation revolves around the Great Try-to-kill-the-peacock-with-a-shoe incident that took place in the Pavilion earlier. The Pavilion is apparently a former greenhouse that Ian and Malcolm have converted into an additional wedding reception space. The actual vows are taken beside a pond with a Gothic folly and a fountain in the center.

I'm not sure a fountain is a good idea. The groom is swilling back whiskey as if he'd like to drown himself, and the bridesmaids aren't far behind him. The bride and her mother, meanwhile, keep insisting that they didn't *deliberately* bean the peacock. The bride only meant to shoo it out of the building so it wouldn't poop on the reception tables.

"They're such large birds, aren't they?" the mother says. "And the droppings are rather enormous. Not to mention they carry all sorts of diseases. I looked it up. Not only salmonella and E. coli and the like, but chlamydiosis, cryptosporidiosis, and histoplasmosis. It's all there on the internet. That bird shouldn't have been allowed into the building in the first place while we were setting up for tomorrow. The health inspector would have something to say about that, I imagine.

And Olivia only waved her arms to herd the creature back outside. It turned on her with those cold yellow eyes and rushed straight over to peck at her."

"Did it?" Malcolm asks. "Peck at her?"

"It would have. If I'd let it." Olivia Kendall, the bride, is about five feet tall and not what I'd call athletic. She also has a nasal voice that sounds screechy when she's defensive. "Mummy's not exaggerating. It was a *dangerous* bird."

I can picture the scene in my head like a silent movie. Cue screaming women. Rabid peacock. Twenty people chasing each other. Chairs toppling and flying shoes.

Malcolm's trying not to laugh, and we both need to turn away fast as we catch each other's eyes. I suspect he has the same video playing in his head. We make a point of not looking at each after that until it's safe to make our exit.

"And the good times continue." He shoves his hands into his pockets as we leave the reception.

I'm not disappointed that he didn't take my hand again. Not at all. Nope.

"I'm going to have to put that into a story someday," I tell him. *"The Curse of the Vampire Peacock."*

"I wouldn't have had you down for that sort of story." He sends me a sexy, crinkle-eyed sideways glance.

"I'm not proud. Whatever will pay the bills and let

me keep writing. I'm perfectly willing to be a story whore."

The smile widens. "You're not holding out for the Great American Novel, then?"

"How many of those can anyone really write in a lifetime? Anyway, I'd rather be Ursula K. LeGuin, I think. Or J.K. Rowling. Or Stephen King."

"I'll expect a credit if you ever sell the peacock story. And it was good to have a witness. Who'd have believed it otherwise?"

"Are all your guests like that?"

"Not all of them. Most are grand, actually, but I feel a bit like a trained seal at these parties. Then I feel guilty because they're usually very nice people and they're paying us to give them a memorable wedding."

He holds the door open into the formal garden that sits between the three wings of the house. It's almost eight o'clock, but the sun has yet to go down. A cool wind rustles the leaves on the hedges and the three large fountains create a fine mist that hits my skin and leaves goose bumps behind. But it's far shorter to cut through the garden from where we are than it is to go through the house.

"Too cold?" Malcolm asks. "Here." He peels off his V-neck sweater. I start to drape it around my shoulders. He laughs and shakes his head. "That won't accomplish much."

He helps me slip the sweater over my head. The yarn is soft as a kiss and smells of him, some kind of delicious aftershave that's spicy like cardamom and sweet like the bergamot orange that isn't orange at all but either green or yellow and entirely surprising. Malcolm is surprising.

It's hard to breathe normally as he rolls up the sleeves so that my hands are visible again. The sweater comes nearly to my knees, so I could easily wear it as a dress, but I don't mind. I've gone from cold to overheated in the span of twenty seconds.

"There," he says. "Better?"

I nod and he steps back, and we start walking again. Did he feel that, too? Was he holding his breath the whole time we were close, waiting for something more to happen? Wanting it to happen? I look around at the garden, at the house, at Malcolm's profile, and I can't help thinking Halford is just as magical and unreal as Alice's Wonderland—and every bit as dangerous.

Malcolm
Pretending

For years, I've done my best *not* to think too much about my childhood. That's infinitely healthier than dwelling on it. Dad and I have mostly achieved an awkward truce that allows us to coexist in the interest of running Halford. Now Izzy and her letters, her questions and even her very presence, are dredging up the sediment of things better left undisturbed.

We've taken the shortcut across the garden, and I'm about to open the door to head up to the kitchen, but it feels as though my father's shadow looms over us. I don't want any shadows.

"I never did ring Dad," I say.

Izzy's quiet, then she looks up at me. In the twilight, her face is full of angles and curves I ache to explore with my fingers.

"No," she says. "You didn't."

I dig the phone from my pocket and step away to make the call. I half expect to reach his voicemail, but he answers and there are voices in the background. He sounds faintly out of breath as though he's had to run to reach the phone.

"Everything all right, Mal?" he asks.

"Fine, but..." I'm still not sure how much to say. "Marcella Cavalera's daughter is here. She flew over from the States."

He's silent so long, if not for the background noise, I'd be worried I had lost him. "She's there?" he asks finally. "At Halford? Hold on." There's a thud as though he's shut a door, and the line gets quieter. "Did she say what she wants?"

I give him only the barest minimum. The letters are Izzy's to share. "She found out about you and Mum, so she'd like to meet you."

He's silent again. Then: "Don't upset her, will you, Malcolm? Please. I know this is difficult, but do try to be kind to her. I shan't be able to get back until tomorrow."

His voice is even more breathless now. He's hurrying somewhere, and I try not to resent the excitement I hear. Excitement I haven't heard in ages.

But then he adds something. "You must be angry. Upset."

"No," I say. "I'm not."

"I'll do my best to explain if you'll give me the opportunity."

I push down the need to tell him I am not a child,

that I don't require his explanation. But perhaps it's up to me to help break old patterns as much as it's up to him.

"Izzy and I will be fine until you get here," I tell him, and despite my best intentions, my voice still sounds stiff and cold, unfamiliar. I'm too often someone with him that I'm not with anyone else.

We ring off, and I go back to rejoin Izzy. She looks up at me, questioning. "Is he coming?"

"Tomorrow." I open the door for her and follow her into the corridor, and suddenly I want to forget it all. All the history that isn't ours. All the awkwardness.

"Let's pretend," I say. "Pretend we're meeting somewhere else, under entirely different circumstances. No letters and no obituaries between us. Pretend this is the British Museum. Have you ever been there?"

Her smile is beautiful, the way it grows slowly and spreads to warm her entire face. "Several times," she says. "Mom used to drop me off while she rehearsed in London a couple of summers ago. Museums are some of my favorite places. I like to make up stories about the artifacts, about the individual people who owned them. That probably sounds weird, though."

"No, it's nice. History happens one person at a time."

I can picture her so clearly, standing like a rock amid the stream of people that always move through museum exhibits too fast to take them in. She'd have the same expression that she was wearing when I first saw her this afternoon, curious and intelligent and intensely alive.

"I don't choose the important people. My stories are never big. They're about the priestess who fed the cats at the temple of Bastet, or the mother who left the Gayer Anderson cat statue as an offering, begging Bastet to protect her son. Or the little girl who played with the Greek horse sculpture in Corinth while her father was away. Mom used to bribe me with museum stories. If I told them well enough, she'd buy a copy of the object in the museum shop. Or something else if there was no copy. She'd have made a terrible critic, though."

"Not very critical?"

"My biggest fan." Izzy laughs, and once again, I'm jealous of her relationship with her mother. Of anyone who can make her laugh like this.

It's getting harder to keep hating Marcella Cavalera. But I've spent a lifetime hating her. It's not easy to give up.

I lead Izzy through into Countess Eugenie's morning room and lock the door behind us.

"So imagine," I say. "Pretend this is the Egyptian gallery of the British Museum, and you and I are walking in opposite directions around the statue of Ramses II. You're concentrating, looking up, imagining what he had for breakfast and whether there are crumbs caught in his beard. We collide. Two strangers. No preconceptions. I apologize, because I'm polite that way—"

"We both apologize, and I smile because you're cute," she says, playing along.

She's completely caught in the moment, and I find myself leaning toward her. "You think I'm cute?"

She blushes, and the shoes she's wearing must have suddenly become fascinating. She stares down at them, long lashes hiding her beautiful eyes.

"I don't believe in leaving out facts," she says, "merely because they're inconvenient. There are probably a hundred girls who've told you they think you are."

I can't remember any other girls at the moment. All I can see is Izzy.

Izzy
Blame

Text to Elli:

Me: Hormones have a lot to answer for.

Elli: Mighty morphing tree lizards. Just saying.

Me: Is it me or was that weirder than usual, even for you?

Elli: Tree lizards. Hormones completely change them. Seriously, look it up.

Me: Focus, El. I told Malcolm he was cute. Is a hormonectomy a thing? Because I should probably have one.

Elli: There are worse things than telling a boy he's cute. But this is not a thing you usually do.

Me: This is not a usual boy.

Elli: There's your problem. Unusual boys are usually the ones to worry about.

Roast Gammon

The Halford family kitchen isn't cozy and old-fashioned the way I pictured it when Malcolm explained
the Halford setup. It gleams with modern stainless
steel appliances and efficient white-painted cabinets
that his mother had put in, but these definitely did
not come from Ikea. Neither did the ornate tile and
woodwork that make the room feel as if everything
in it could plausibly have been here centuries ago.
It shows that Malcolm's mom understood Halford
and loved it, and somehow that changes how I think
of her.

Anna looks a little like she's been here for centuries, too. She's put a gray cardigan over her dark
dress, which only emphasizes the grimness of her
gaunt, sharp angles. She glares at me again as she
hauls the dogs off to a separate room somewhere, as
if *I'm* the reason the dogs dared enter her domain.
Or maybe she just blames me for keeping dinner
waiting. Which wasn't my fault. Not completely.
Unless she saw us outside, in which case, I'm totally
busted. On the bright side, I remembered to give
Malcolm back his sweater before we stepped into
the kitchen. So what can she have actually seen?
Nothing happened.

Practically nothing.

Nothing to make her bang pots and pans around on the stove and shoot laser beams out of her eyes.

"Can I help you with anything?" I ask her.

"I've kept everything warm." She graduates from lasers to photon torpedoes. "It's nothing special. Only a gammon roast."

"Which happens to be my favorite," Malcolm faux-whispers to me, "so don't let her fool you."

Anna sets a porcelain tureen of soup and a basket of crusty, homemade bread slices on the table, and I take the crisply ironed linen napkin off my plate and spread it across my lap.

Who actually has linen napkins in the kitchen? Is this how it was for Malcolm growing up? Floating around in this huge empty house that has to be kept neat and perfect. Except for the dog hair. With only his dad and Anna for company.

I wonder how different he would be if he'd grown up in Elli's house instead, with its overflow of shouting and laughter and running feet. With the messy rooms and rock music blaring in competing bursts as her brothers opened and slammed their doors. Then I remember the soccer balls in the back seat of Malcolm's Land Rover. Maybe he wouldn't have been so different. I can picture him pounding up the stairs in his cleats with Owen and Ethan, kicking the ball through the house the way I've seen them do a thousand times.

Elli's brothers would love this place. All this room. They'd break every window in the portrait gallery inside a week playing one-on-one, and Anna would kill them.

What kind of a dad is Ian? Would he yell if Malcolm broke a window? Ground him? Hit him? Somehow, I don't think so, but the thought makes me miss my mother with a hard, hollow ache. She never yelled or looked at me with disapproval.

I decide to make a bigger effort to win Anna over. "Couldn't you sit down with us, Anna? I feel bad disrupting your night with Malcolm."

"That wouldn't be my place. Not with company."

"Don't be snobbish." Malcolm shakes his head at her. "You've eaten dinner with my mates many times."

"You're older now. It's different. Anyway, I've far too much to do to waste time amusing you. Get on with you now. Eat your dinner." She turns away to check something in the oven, and Malcolm nudges the soup tureen toward me.

"We'll need to have Pricilla add the cost of a replacement window directly to the Kendall—Grahams' final wedding bill," he says to Anna's back. "They're likely to kick up a fuss if we try to bill them for it later."

"They're like that, are they?" Anna asks.

"They seem nice enough, but the mother did mention the health inspector."

Anna turns sharply around. "Did she? After they're

the ones who left the Pavilion door open? Not that being wrong ever carries any weight with that sort."

She sniffs loudly and bangs the oven closed. The smell of ham escapes into the room. Which explains what gammon is, I guess—I wasn't going to ask in case it was some cuddly rabbitty creature I'd rather not know I was eating.

Straight up, Anna scares me, especially with all the pot and cupboard banging that seems to be a language of her own. She's somewhere between the housekeeper in *Rebecca* and the witch in *Hansel and Gretel*. The original Brothers Grimm version where the parents abandon the kids in the wood. (Which is not a fairy tale that should ever be read to children.)

My brain has wandered, so I curb my thoughts and concentrate on ladling out soup that smells of onion and tarragon and a rich, beef broth together with caramelized chunks of roasted carrot, leek, and cauliflower. Malcolm and Anna have drifted into a conversation about his research project concerning the family's involvement in the plot to make Mary Queen of Scots the Queen of England. He wants turn that into a "Two Queens" exhibit on the Halford tour.

I can't help wondering how many great stories like that are lurking in this building. Living here must be like getting to play in your own private museum. Malcolm and Ian could probably sleep in a different bedroom every night of the month, if they wanted to, and I can only imagine all the important people who must have slept in all these beds. Plus there's no one to stop them touching the treasures, the chess set that some long-ago Earl of Mortimer got from Charles I before he was beheaded—Charles, not the earl—or the chair that still has faint scratch marks from when Lord Byron brought his tame bear with him on a visit down from Cambridge.

The fact that Lord Byron was *here* almost trumps the fact that Byron took an actual bear to college. Cambridge didn't allow dogs, according to this afternoon's tour guide, but there was no definitive rule against pet bears. Which tells me everything I need to know about Lord Byron. And the fact that no one at Halford kept him from bringing the bear into the house when he visited makes me think the people who worked here then weren't anything like Anna.

"So how often do you change the tours and exhibits?" I ask when Anna hurries out of the room for something.

"It varies," Malcolm says. "We add on seasonal tours here and there, but we also try to switch out what we spotlight on the main tours. We've found that creating an overall theme helps give visitors a feel for the place and keeps them coming back."

"That was Malcolm's idea," Anna says, coming back in carrying a bowl of fruit. Her fish eyes light up when she looks at him.

We've finished the soup, so she brings over the ham and a serving bowl of potatoes. She's baked the meat with a honey-orange crust, and it's sweet, tangy, and delicious, and Malcolm and I both eat too much of it while she still bustles around, first making dessert and then starting on washing up the dishes.

"I can do that for you later," Malcolm says. "Why don't you come sit down?"

"I won't have you washing up on one of your few nights home. We don't get you often enough as it is."

"And you think a few dishes will frighten me away?" He gets up and turns off the faucet, then steers her toward the table.

She ducks around him and turns the water back on with a giggle that makes her sound two decades younger. "Oh, get on with you. Let me do my work."

He captures both her hands in his, dances her around the kitchen, then spins and sweeps her into a dip. Behind them, the water is still running, tiny soap bubbles drifting up to catch the light. Both of them are laughing. I can see what Anna must have been like years ago, and I wonder if it's the work or the house that etched the hard lines into her face, or whether there's something else. Has she always lived at Halford? Has she ever married? She doesn't wear a wedding ring.

"Very well. If you're so eager to do the washing up, I'll leave you to it. I've paperwork to finish anyway." She reaches up to pat him on the cheek. "Only mind you don't leave food drying on my good pots or I'll have something to say about it in the morning."

"Dad's coming back tomorrow, by the way," Malcolm says.

Anna freezes, and for a moment there's a look on her face that makes my heart thud. I don't know her well enough to be sure, but I think it's fear.

"Is he?" She picks up the red and white patterned dishcloth hanging on a hook, and she very deliberately dries her hands. "I thought he had business he needed to attend to in London."

"What sort of business?" Malcolm asks.

She hangs the dishcloth up again. "Now, how should I know that?"

"You're not answering the question."

"I told you before—he didn't confide in me. Now, if you're quite done with the inquisition, I'll go and leave Pricilla a message about billing for that broken window," she says, and she sweeps out of the kitchen.

Dirty Dishes

Malcolm watches Anna go. I watch him.

He turns and catches me.

"What are you thinking?" he asks.

I jump to my feet and start stacking plates to take to the sink. "I'm thinking that love is complicated."

He arches an eyebrow at me. "I'm afraid that you'll need to explain that one."

"Anna's obviously in love with your father. Probably has been for years. I don't suppose they could have been..."

"Having an affair?" Malcolm laughs. "Anna would rather die. She's much too old-fashioned."

"But your mom's been gone so long."

"But unlike Mum, Anna wouldn't take anybody's cast-offs." He takes the stack of dishes from me and lowers them down into the soapy water. "You really think she loves him?"

"She might." I walk over to stand beside him.

He turns with his hands dripping bubbles onto the floor. "Do you blame my father? For hurting your mum, I mean. Only it seems from the first letters that she may never have meant to break it off with him. That it was more of a shot across the bow, looking for reassurance or compromise. And he married my mum instead."

"I'm not sure either of them deserve to be blamed."

"Someone does. At least for what it did to my mother." He picks up a plate and starts to scrub it. "She might have hit that tree by accident, no one could say for certain, but she drank too much after my sister died. And Dad was too caught up in himself to help her."

"You can't always help people. Sometimes they won't let you," I say with my heart aching for the little boy he must have been.

"I know that." He glances over. "I remember them fighting. About the drinking, about your mother. Everything. Only a few weeks before Mum died, she accused him of never trying to make a go of their marriage. Told him he didn't know how hard it was to be silently compared to Marcella all the time."

I brace my hip against the counter. My body feels too heavy. "She let you hear her say that?"

"I was in my secret place, but she was drunk and loud and they were walking up the stairs. They didn't know I was there." Malcolm gives a shrug like it doesn't matter. "Don't feel sorry for me. That isn't why I'm telling you."

"Why are you, then?" I want to reach across and take his hand, let him know that I understand, that he's not alone. But I remember what happened in the garden when he gave me his sweater.

Touching him isn't a great idea.

"I was wondering how long it would have taken me to get over casting blame if you hadn't come here," he says. "How long would I have spent seeing my father as though I was perpetually twelve years old?"

"That's how I felt when I found the letters. As if I was seeing my mother for the first time as a person instead of as a parent. Maybe that was part of the reason I came here, to try to find out more about who she was. But you're lucky. You still have a chance to know your father in a different way."

"Possibly."

"Definitely."

We load what we can into the dishwasher, but the plates are probably the Halford umpteenth-best china or something with silver around the rim, which is why Malcolm gets down to the business of washing them by hand. I dry them as he hands them to me, and I don't know what's changed between us, but there's something both comfortable and electric.

Something expectant.

Malcolm pulls the plug and rinses out the sink, and I'm hanging up the dishcloth when he starts to laugh. "You're humming classical music. You really are your mother's daughter."

"It's 'Claire de Lune,' and what's wrong with classical music?"

"I imagined you as more of a rebel." He smiles in that way that makes the room light up, and the stark plains of his face no longer look as sharp and lost. If music did that for him, then we need more music.

I take a mental stroll through my Beatles repertoire, searching out something we can sing together.

A second later, I belt out the opening to "Here Comes the Sun." He doesn't join in.

"Come on," I say. "I know you know this one."

"I don't sing."

"Friends don't let friends sing alone."

"You'll only regret you asked."

He comes in at the top of the second verse in a rich tenor, but he's right. I do regret it, because he cannot sing. I mean, he cannot stay on key. Soon, we are both laughing so hard we're doubled over.

Amusia, the inability to process pitch, occurs in only about four percent of the population. Charles Darwin was tone deaf, and so was William Butler Yeats. Malcolm is in outstanding company.

I love the way he laughs. I love that he's laughing when he's been so full of tension. I want to keep him laughing, so I tap the "Elli's Dance-off" playlist on my phone.

"Let's dance," I say. "I dare you."

Elli's Dance-off Playlist

1. The Troggs: Wild Thing
2. The Clash: Rock the Casbah
3. Isley Brothers: Shout
4. MC Hammer: Can't Touch This

5. Beyoncé: Single Ladies
6. Aretha Franklin: Respect
7. Carly Rae Jepson: Call Me Maybe
8. One Direction: What Makes You Beautiful
9. Montell Jordan: This Is How We Do It
10. Kool and the Gang: Jungle Boogie
11. Little Eva: Locomotion
12. Black-Eyed Peas: I Gotta Feeling
13. Whitney Houston: I Want to Dance with Somebody
14. Bruce Springsteen: Dancing in the Dark
15. Village People: YMCA
16. No Doubt: Hella Good
17. Daft Punk: Get Lucky
18. Rihanna: Don't Stop the Music
19. Prince and the Revolution: Kiss
20. Lady Gaga: Just Dance

Witness

The first beats of "Wild Thing" come on, and I hop into the space between the table and the ovens and start jumping and pumping my arms like a fiend.

"I can't dance to this," Malcolm says.

"No one can without looking like a moron. That's why it's the best dance music ever. You have no choice but to lose all your inhibitions when you try. Come on. Hurry up."

We dance until we're breathless. My feet hurt and so do my lungs, but neither of us wants to stop.

I don't notice the man who's arrived and paused on the threshold until Malcolm freezes as if someone's flipped a switch in his back and turned him off. As if someone turned off all his joy.

"Dad," he says flatly. "What are you doing here? You said you couldn't make it until tomorrow."

PART FOUR

Malcolm
Tea and Whiskey

My father has been fragile since he heard about Marcella's death. Now his hand has become a claw, clutching the door frame as though Izzy is a ghost, his skin leached to the color of parchment paper. His eyes, though, have sprung to life. They burn with emotion, and I can't tell whether that's from happiness or fear or anger.

Not for the first time today, I wish I knew him better. And precisely because I don't know him well enough, I don't have any words for this situation.

Apparently, Izzy doesn't, either. She rocks on the balls of her feet, back and forth as if she's trying to comfort herself. I shift over and slip my hand in hers.

"Dad," I say, "this is Izzy. Isabelle."

He's trembling as he comes forward. His hand rises as though to cup her cheek, but she flinches almost imperceptibly. Catching himself, he drops his arm and offers her a handshake instead.

"Hallo, Izzy. I'm Ian." His voice trembles, too. "You look very much like your mother."

"Do I?" She forces a smile as her fingers escape my grasp.

"You do indeed." He clasps her hand between his own, his eyes fever bright as he drinks her features in.

This is nothing like my father. But then, maybe this is simply a version of Ian Halford I've never met. A version that needed to be himself first and a Halford second. I've certainly felt that, too.

Izzy pulls away wearing a determined smile, as though she doesn't want to hurt his feelings. I don't reach for her hand again. This shouldn't be us against my father. He and Izzy both deserve better than that.

It's hard to watch them, him and her.

Tea. That's what we all need. Without tea, the whole quiet, soothing ritual of tea, I suspect the British stiff upper lip would fall to pieces. I shift to the stove to put the kettle on.

Dad clears his throat. "This calls for something a bit stronger than tea," he says. "Whiskey for me, I think. Izzy? Are you old enough to drink?"

Ian
Dark and Bright

I never told Cella how much she reminded me of that line of Byron's poetry for fear she would think it too cliché. It runs through my mind now, as though I'm seeing her for the first time all over again, as though she's here in the kitchen with me where she should have been instead of buried cold beneath the ground. As though I've been given a second chance.

> *"And all that's best of dark and bright*
> *Meet in her aspect and her eyes..."*

What I wouldn't give for a chance to repair the mistakes I've made.

Hand trembling, I pour two fingers of whiskey into a glass. The decanter knocks the rim in a telltale clink, and my heart stutters but I ignore it. Marcella's daughter is here, and I don't know why she's come. That's what matters most. Malcolm's been through quite enough already in his life, so I had damned well better pull myself together.

The whiskey sets fire to my throat and braces my legs, and I manage to walk back to the table almost steadily and lower myself into a chair. It's odd, seeing Mal with her. Izzy. My son and Marcella's daughter. They seem comfortable, as though they've known each other quite some time. Have they? Did they find each other somehow and start a correspondence? I'd like to think Malcolm wouldn't have kept something like that from me. But the wall he's constructed to keep me out has been effective all these years. I can't say what he would or wouldn't do.

Izzy hovers between the sink and the table as though she's not sure what to do with herself. Light from overhead catches in the dark curls that are so much like Cella's, in the round cheeks and familiar vulnerable generosity of Cella's brown-gold eyes. The hesitant smile she gives Malcolm when he hands her a mug of tea slices my heart wide open. I remember the last time I saw that smile, and the heartbreak that came after.

No, enough of that.

I'm meant to be the adult in the room. I need pull myself together.

"I hope you'll feel free to stay with us as long as you like, Izzy. You'll certainly be most welcome, though I admit I'm surprised your mother mentioned me. She was determined to cut me out of her life the last time we spoke."

Izzy
Colors

Lying would not be the way to start a relationship with Ian, so I don't. I only shade the truth a little.

"She wrote about you," I say.

His eyes stop blinking and turn distant, as if his mind has darted away. He looks older than I imagined but still handsome in that way that turning gray makes some men look distinguished. His hair is thick, and he has a close-cropped beard around which his skin looks like he spends time outside. But there's also an air of vulnerability about him, as if the wrong words could blow him over. That's the opposite of his son. Malcolm's like an oak tree, strong all the way to the core so he can withstand wind, hail, and lightning. He's had to grow up like that.

Ian takes a sip of amber whiskey and lowers the glass back to the table with a hand that quivers. "I loved your mother very much. I hope she understood that."

"What she wrote about your relationship, her feelings about you, the memories she had—it was beautiful. I wanted to meet the man who had made her feel like that."

"She was the love of my life. But being with her was like holding a flame. You can't hold fire without it scorching through you. Still, even if you only spend a moment with someone who burns that bright, you never get over it."

He's crying now, silently but without bowing his head, as though, if he doesn't turn away, maybe we won't notice the tears slipping down his cheeks. That much naked emotion makes me ashamed to look at him, and I don't understand why we are taught we shouldn't cry, that we're weak if we do and stronger if we don't. I think part of the reason I like Malcolm so much is because he has the courage to be honest about his feelings.

I ease myself into the chair beside Ian, and the floor groans behind me as Malcolm crosses the room and pauses with his back to us. He stands with a mug of tea cradled in his hand, a big swath of distance between himself and the table where his father and I are sitting. If it's hard for me to hear Ian's words, to see Ian's tears, it must be far more painful for Malcolm. And it's unfair. Unfair that he has to hear this.

As though he realizes that, too, or belatedly thought about how his words must sound, Ian glances back at him. "It's painful, a love like that. Painful for everyone, including people you never meant to hurt. Your mother and I knew we were making sacrifices, but it took us too long to understand that other people would be paying the price of those along with us. You, Malcolm, my wife, your father. We weren't fair to any of you."

He's still speaking to me, but his attention has shifted and he's watching Malcolm's reaction. Of course, he doesn't realize what he's said. I wrap my feet around the legs of the chair and hold tight to the wood even as I let go of the last bit of tenacious hope I hadn't even realized was still alive. I'm glad I was prepared, thanks to Malcolm. I'm not disappointed. Not too disappointed.

"I never knew my father," I say, sounding perfectly normal. "Mom wouldn't say who he was. I hoped you might know."

He peels his eyes away from Malcolm. "She never told you?"

"He's not even on my birth certificate. To be honest, for a while I thought...I mean, obviously I was wrong. Malcolm and I figured that out, but it did seem possible."

I'm babbling because it all feels so stupid now, so much a product of irrationally wanting something I've never had.

"No." Ian smiles at me, a sad smile. "I'm sorry. Can

you please excuse me?" He stands up, and his skin is pale with strain. Sweat has broken out in a sheen across his upper lip. "I'm still a bit tired after the drive from London, and this has all been a shock. Would you mind very much if we continue in the morning? I'm sure Malcolm can see you settled in."

Personal History

If silence were a color, the shade in the kitchen would be achromatic gray, the kind that hangs in perfect balance between red and blue and green, anger and sadness and healing. Or at least I'm telling myself there's healing coming at the end of all this, that the three of us each have had these deep wounds we've been carrying around. Maybe ripping the scabs away will let new skin begin to grow. That could just be me kidding myself, though. Probably all I've done is expose deep pools of sucking infection.

Did I mention I'm waaaaay out of my depth?

I sigh. Malcolm glances over at me, then stares after his father as if he's trying to decide if he needs to follow.

"Go on," I say. "He didn't look good."

"But if I question why he left like that, he'll take it as criticism and only get more upset. That's what we do to each other." Malcolm's lips twitch into a frown.

"You should try, at least. Patterns can change."

"I'll give him a minute." He sits down in the chair beside me. "I'll admit, that was odd even for Dad. I suppose it must be hard, though. I didn't warn him about how much you look like your mother. Maybe I should have done."

We sit, neither of us saying anything at all, and then Malcolm eventually says, "Are you tired?" at the same time I say, "I should be tired but I'm not."

We both laugh awkwardly. Instead of talking at once a second time, the way people so often do, we both wait, so neither of us speaks. After a few seconds, we both smile again, politely, like we're back to being strangers. I hate the distance that's sprung between us.

"I could show you where your room is," Malcolm says, speaking too quickly. "Or you could watch some telly or read while I finish the letters. What do you normally like?"

"Like to do?"

"Or anything. Tell me seven things. I'm curious."

"Why seven?"

"It's the searcher number, the seeker of truth. If you believe in numerology. That and I can usually manage to remember seven things."

Even when I don't feel like smiling, he can make me smile.

"Seven things I like? All right," I say. "I like reading. And Mom and I liked watching old movies—really old, not seventies and eighties and nineties old. I like sweet desserts, and Scrabble. I also play a mean game of chess—by which I mean that I like it but I'm nasty when I lose, not that I'm any good. Mom got me into yoga. And I love elephants."

He grins, though I don't know why. "Elephants?"

"Never underestimate an elephant. They're smart. They're also compassionate, cooperative, self-aware, and playful. They have a sense of humor, and they're musical. Did you know they keep better time than human drummers can? They've even learned to speak human words in context."

"I didn't know any of that."

"The world would be better if more people were like elephants. I only hope my grandchildren and great-grandchildren will still be able to see them. In the wild—not just in zoos. I want there to be elephants and rhinos and tigers and leopards and whales—all the animals we're too selfish to consider as important as humans."

Malcolm grins again, and I'm like Pavlov's dog: I want to smile every time he smiles.

"What about you?" I ask. "You're studying history. Is that all because of Halford, or do you want to do something else with it?"

"It started with Halford. Thousands of different

people created this estate. The masons who put up the stonework and the workers who cleared the land and tilled the soil and tended the farms. The woodcarvers, painters, and servants who kept it running day to day down the centuries. We Halfords probably caused a lot of misery, but the Hall also supported the entire village and surrounding area. The descendants of all those people have a connection to it. And I don't think it's finished being relevant yet. It should have a role in the community now that gives back, provides security and jobs and opportunities and context for the past. A living history for the masses, if that makes sense. Sorry, you touched a pet subject with that question."

He's cute when he's embarrassed. "Living history like your 'Two Queens' exhibit?" I ask. "Because I think that's a great idea."

"I'd like to write a book about them as well. Mary as figurehead and the role of spies in the plot to assassinate Queen Elizabeth. Popular nonfiction. Or hopefully popular, at least—that being the only sort that might make money."

"Spies are always good. And I'm all about strong women."

"I suspected you might be." Now there's only the ghost of a smile lingering in his eyes.

I busy myself looking elsewhere. "I wish there had been more stories about individual people on the tour," I say. "You couldn't include too many at once, but maybe you could rotate them like you do exhibits. Showcase a few who all lived at the same time and spotlight some of the objects that were purchased then and the things that happened while those people lived. Not just the Halfords, though. A particular stonemason or painter, a maid and a butler and a cook as well as the earl and countess and their children. Like *Downton Abbey,* only in objects they owned or used. Or is that stupid?"

"It's rather brilliant, actually." Malcolm leans forward, his elbows on the table. "All we'd have to do is include a program that picks out a new story as people move from room to room. We could even let them choose the year they wanted as they bought their tickets—then they'd know there was a reason to come back to find out more. That really is brilliant, Izzy. You're a natural."

"I like personal stories." I shrug, feeling too warm all over. "That's what most people relate to, anyway."

Malcolm's chair scrapes as he gets up to dump the remnants of his tea into the sink. He leans back against the counter, watching me. But I get the feeling he's lost in shadows that have suddenly swept back in.

"Dad was the one who taught me that we need to keep bringing people back. I suppose that's something else I don't remember often enough. He was only sixteen when my grandfather decided to sell Halford to a hotel developer. The upkeep was too expensive. The roof needed redoing, and the money wasn't there—you can't imagine what a roof costs for a place like this. My father's the one who managed to raise the funds. By the time he met your mother, he'd spent years fighting tooth and claw to save the place. I can't imagine him having to choose between being here and living elsewhere with your mother—even part of the time. Halford couldn't have survived."

"Maybe there was no good answer."

"Yes, well." Malcolm's face is solemn, there's something new in his voice. Something softer. "I'd better go see if he's all right."

It's funny that the things our parents love so passionately can almost make us hate them, I think as Malcolm leaves. That's how I felt about my mother's music.

Love and hate are two paths to the same destination, the way that some philosophies look at hell and heaven. The more you love something, the more it has the power to destroy you.

Malcolm
M i s c o n c e p t i o n s

Anna answers my father's door, and she's wearing a blue quilt robe over a long white nightgown. My mind flies back to what Izzy said, and I wonder if they've been...But no, of course not. They wouldn't. Neither of them.

"Your father's tired," Anna says, giving me her fiercest gimlet eye. "You should let him rest." She steps out into the corridor and tries to close the door behind her.

I catch it and slip through despite her efforts. "Don't worry. I won't stay long."

Dad swings his feet over the edge of the bed and fumbles them into his slippers, but the pillow is dented where he was already lying down. "Something wrong, Mal?"

"No, I was only coming to check on you," I begin, searching for words. "To apologize for springing Izzy on you like that. I should have prepared you better."

He reaches for the brown paisley robe at the foot of the bed and starts to put it on. "I'm the one who owes you an explanation."

"You don't, actually." I'm uncertain how to approach what I need to tell him. It's as though speaking with Izzy has knocked a hole in a wall inside my head, revealing an entire boxroom of cobwebbed and dangerous things I need to sort.

I've been angry so long I don't know if I know how not to be angry anymore.

"I never stopped to consider you in all of this. Not really. I was too busy blaming you," I say, "when you were trying to do what was best for Halford all along."

Dad moves toward me, his steps tentative as though he's afraid to spook me. "Malcolm—" He stops and shakes his head, then catches the bedpost and leans back against it to compose himself. "You were too young when it all happened with Mum for me to explain things properly. And then—"

"Then I didn't give you an opportunity," I admit.

In the dim light of the reading lamp on the nightstand, his eyes shine. "You can't blame me for your mother's death any more than I already blame myself, believe me. But I should have told you more. I should have tried harder."

"More about what?" I sit on the edge of the bed, and he stands a moment looking down at me before lowering himself slowly beside me.

As though it's simpler to think when we aren't looking at each other, he seems to be studying a water-color painting of the Halford lake that hangs on the wall across the room. It was painted by Margaret, the eleventh countess, and it isn't bad—but it doesn't deserve this much attention.

"Your mother knew about Marcella from the beginning. I never promised to love her. I couldn't, but I needed an heir for Halford, and she already loved the place. It was her own history, too, so she understood how much it demanded of us. And her branch of the Halfords still had money."

"Probably because they hadn't had the Hall to spend it on," I can't keep from offering.

"True enough." There's not much humor in my father's small bark of laughter. "She'd also inherited from an aunt who'd married a shipping fortune, though, so she brought a much-needed infusion of cash. Our marriage was a partnership."

"You married her for her money."

"That wasn't so unusual then. But we were friends and she...well, she got something out of it, too. She thought Halford and friendship and children would be enough for her until we lost G-Ginny. Then she needed more."

The way he stutters on my sister's name, it sounds exotic and reverent, like a beloved word in a foreign language. I think back, trying to remember the last time he said it, but we don't speak about her. We don't speak about much at all apart from school and Halford.

His robe rustles as he turns toward me. It looks too big for him, as though the strain of Marcella's death has carried a physical part of him away.

"I was weak," he says. "Your mum needed me, but I couldn't forget Marcella. I told myself I'd never promised her I would. Which was true, but it still wasn't fair. When I saw that your mother had fallen in love with me, I should have done the right thing and made her see it would be too painful to stay married. In her mind, I was unfaithful by loving Cella, and after Ginny died, she retreated into her gin and tonics. I should have found a way to help her, but I was too trapped in my own pain."

"It wasn't entirely fair to blame you. Not if you weren't unfaithful in the physical sense."

Dad's breath comes hard and fast, squeezing his voice. "I was once. Cella and I both realized it was a mistake immediately. We never repeated it."

A hard knot forms in my chest, and I can't breathe. "You slept with Izzy's mother after you and Mum were married?"

His fingers burrow into the bedclothes, the knuckles white. "It shames me to admit it, but yes."

I stand up slowly, and I can't look at him. The one thing I knew about him, the one thing that has always been a constant, was his sense of honor. His basic decency.

"When?" I demand. "Does that mean Izzy *could* be yours?"

"Of course not!" He shakes his head. "Her father was a conductor Cella met on a European tour. She told me that specifically, but that doesn't matter—"

"Of course it matters! You had a duty to Mum! To me and Ginny. And you betrayed it. You betrayed us."

He's gone pale again, even paler. "I'm human, Mal. God knows I live with my regrets and failures every hour of every day since. What I meant to say was that it doesn't matter that Izzy isn't mine. She's still Cella's daughter. I can't expect you to understand what that means to me, but I'd like to get to know her—so long as that doesn't create a problem for you. You're my first priority. You and your sister always were."

It clicks then. The way he looked at Izzy. "Is that why you want Izzy to stay," I say very quietly, "because she could replace Ginny for you?"

"How can you even ask that?" My father colors furiously.

I stare at him, but I wonder if he realizes what he's done. Has he really seen Izzy at all? Or was it only Marcella and Ginny he saw when he looked at her, his own needs? He didn't see her any more than he's ever seen me without seeing Ginny's ghost beside me. I cross to the door, each thud of my footsteps echoing the hollowness inside me.

"Malcolm, come back here!" Dad calls after me. "I swear Izzy has nothing to do with you or Ginny. Nothing at all."

"I don't believe you." I turn back to him, and there's a stranger standing in front of me, one refashioned without my lifelong misconceptions.

I've believed many things about him throughout the years. I believed he mistreated Mum by loving Marcella. I believed he was selfish. I believed he helped push Mum into drinking herself to death. But the one thing I've *known*, the one thing I was certain I knew, was that he would never have betrayed his marriage vows.

"How can I believe anything you tell me?" I ask, but I don't wait for him to answer. I push the door open and let it slam behind me.

Izzy
Ghosts

It's eleven o'clock, and I'm shivering beneath the comforter of a four-poster bed hung with thick, green floral fabric in the same pattern as the bedroom wallpaper. The heating thumps and the floorboards groan, and I'm reading because it's only six o'clock at home, and who goes to bed at six o'clock?

I keep thinking of Malcolm. About his life and how he turned out. It's impossible not to think about him.

Then suddenly there's a bang somewhere and feet move down the hallway. Angry feet. I throw on a sweater and open my door a crack.

Malcolm stalks to the threshold of his room, and if he had a tail it would be lashing back and forth. Then he stops and his head snaps up. Instead of going into his room, he continues down the corridor.

I'm not sure what makes me duck back against the wall, but he passes my door without even glancing at it. His footsteps are a metronome of anger.

I follow him.

The family section of the house runs above the public rooms and part of the guest wings on either side. Malcolm turns onto a staircase and takes the steps up two at a time.

I follow more slowly, still uncertain what I'm doing. It's dark, and the hallway here is narrower, the ceiling lower. After only a day at Halford, I'm surprised to find only stark white walls bare of the decorative moldings and elaborate woodwork downstairs. A yellow pool of light on the dusty floor reveals an open door, and I only hesitate a second before I walk toward it.

> Text to Elli:
>
> Me: I think I'm turning into you.
>
> Elli: At last my work is done. In what way exactly?
>
> Me: I can't seem to mind my own business.
>
> Elli: Welcome to the human race, honey.

Rocking Horse

The room Malcolm enters is a nursery, dusty but not

choked with dust, as if the downstairs rooms get a regular cleaning, but up here it's on a less frequent schedule. Most of the furniture is covered in sheets. A dappled gray rocking horse with a mane and tail of what looks like actual hair and a genuine leather bridle and matching saddle is uncovered, though. Malcolm sits on the floor beside it with his back to the door and a dust cloth puddled at his feet.

"Do you believe in ghosts?" he says without turning toward me as I stop on the threshold.

"Actual ghosts?" I ask.

"We put on a special 'haunted weekend' at Halloween with rooms going for a bloody fortune so people can have a peek at the Halford ghosts. We even rented the place out to one of those paranormal investigation reality shows last year. They spent a week measuring everything they could possibly measure and came up with nothing except some cold spots and bits of mist. But people claim to have seen all sorts of ghostly things."

I'm sure there's a reason he's telling me this, and obviously there's a reason he's sitting up here by himself. Emotion rolls off him, filling up the room.

I take a few steps toward him then stop again. "Have you seen something ghostly?"

"Once. My sister." He glances over his shoulder, and the dim light paints dark shadows into the sockets of his eyes and etches marionette lines around his mouth. "I swear it was real. Sounds mad to admit it aloud, though, doesn't it?"

"Not if that's what you saw," I say.

"This used to be our playroom. Ginny's and mine. That's what Mum used to call it, but it was the nursery when Dad was a boy." He hangs his head, not looking at me, and I go over and drop down cross-legged beside him. "Ginny and I had our books and toys and paints and papers up here. I'd stopped coming after she died, but I finally came up with a packing box to get a few more thing I wanted. She'd been dead about ten months or so by then."

He looks up briefly, and I swallow hard at the rawness of his expression. "The door was closed," he continues, "and when I opened it, Rosy— Rocinante—the old rocking horse was rocking. Not swaying due to currents in the air. I mean rocking, the way he'd used to when Ginny would ride him full tilt, pretending she was racing. Then he bobbled suddenly, and I heard Ginny's feet hit the floor and run toward me, and I felt her hand take mine. I felt the slide of her palm and the small webs of skin at the bases of her fingers and all the fragile bones in the back of her hand. She led me to that window there and showed me where she'd slipped two of my best game cards behind the window seat. They would probably have stayed down there until the house was demolished if she hadn't shown me."

He stands up abruptly and pulls me to my feet. Still holding my hand, he draws me to the window and shows me a narrow crack between the seat and the wall where the molding has warped. The wood is splintered a little on one end as if someone tried to work it loose—or pry something out—but it's been a long time since then. The wood is yellowed and dried out.

"She pushed my hand right up to that crack, and I couldn't see anything. And she didn't talk—I didn't know what she wanted until I pried it open a bit more and saw the edges of the cards. I had to use tweezers to pull them out."

Goose pimples have broken out all along my arms and the back of my neck, and I can't help shivering. "That's a gift."

"Sounds ridiculous to say something like that aloud." He smiles weakly. "But I've always thought it was Ginny's way of settling unfinished business. Saying goodbye."

He looks down at our hands. He's still holding mine, and I wonder if I should pull away. I definitely should.

I don't, though, and he doesn't, either.

"Coming here to Halford, that was your unfinished business, wasn't it?" he asks me.

"I suppose. Not that it's finished anything so far. Did I upset your father? Is that what's wrong?"

"If you did upset him, it's far less than I have. Not that he didn't deserve it, but I did the same thing I always have—shut him out without giving him a fair hearing."

"I'm sure it's not too late."

He turns to me, looking broken. "You don't need to listen to all this. It's the middle of the night."

"Not where I'm from. But maybe we should both go."

"Don't."

"Why?" The word comes out hoarse, and I start to pull my hand away.

His fingers tighten on mine, certain and electric. "I've no idea," he says quietly, and I say, "Then we shouldn't stay," and the distance between us gets smaller all by itself, or maybe I'm just leaning in and Malcolm's leaning down and it's inevitable.

He's going to kiss me. We're going to kiss each other. There's only an instant for the thought to register, for me to notice the little concentration line between his eyebrows and a tiny scar above the corner of his mouth. It's an instant that fills every cell in my body with awareness, and our lips meet halfway, as if they have no other choice, as if a kiss was always going to define the space between us.

I've been kissed before.

It didn't feel like this.

Boy Math

Through the last year of high school, Elli and I had a no-dating pact. Not that we couldn't date, just that we wouldn't unless the boy was disruption-worthy. It was bad enough trying to coordinate going to college together. Introducing another factor was a complication we didn't need. And what was the point anyway, unless there was a chance of forever? Too many girls arrange their whole futures over boys they meet in high school, and how many of those turn into happily-ever-after? Most of them are barely happily-after-first-semester.

Plus, our love lives to that point hadn't exactly been the stuff of poetry. Our first real experiment was me dating Liam Hoult in junior year. Liam was cute, and he wrote lyrics and sang in a ska punk band, and everyone in the whole school knew him. I'd noticed him, but not really *noticed* until we ended up lab partners in AP Chem. Then suddenly I noticed. A lot. And I thought about him. A lot. Elli and I talked about him. Also a lot. Long before he asked me out, she and I had already dissected what I would say and agreed that I would wear my plaid skirt and favorite lavender sweater and disagreed in our opinions of how long I should wait to let him kiss me. Elli doesn't believe in wasting time. I believe in buildup and being sure.

Or at least I did until this moment.

In Liam's case, the buildup was longer. And kissing him was good. Worth thinking about. But his lyrics were bad, and his favorite book was *Foundation* by Isaac Asimov, the first in the series, which is basically the Soylent of science fiction books. He'd never even read *Harry Potter,* and whenever we went to see a movie, I ended up wishing I could discuss it with Elli instead of him. Also, most of our non-movie dates consisted of me and Elli going to watch his band practicing. Which meant that, instead of admiring Liam like I was supposed to, Elli and I would just talk like we would have normally, except that we had to shout to hear each other above the music. Liam got mad about that, and Elli and I figured out it was easier to have a conversation if we ducked outside to the alley behind Jason Keil's dad's garage where the band held their practices. And then, because it was just me and Elli talking outside in the cold anyway, what was the point of being in the alley at all? So Liam and I broke up.

Elli dated Brendon Lee a little while after that, and I went out with Richie Martinez, and Elli went out with Nick Charles. None of them lasted long.

Basically, our no-dating pact was based on the simple fact that neither one of us had ever really wanted to date anyone in particular. If the boys I dated had kissed anything like Malcolm, it would have been a bigger problem.

Kissing Malcolm is a problem.

A big, big problem.

Malcolm's kisses are salt and vinegar potato chip kisses, sweet and savory and addictive.

I want to keep kissing him, and I'm not going to want to stop.

PART FIVE

Izzy
Leaving

Eventually, soon—sooner maybe thanks to the problems I'm causing between Malcolm and his father—I'm going to have to go home. Go to college. Go back to my normal life that doesn't have anything to do with Malcolm or Halford or Ian. I'm going to need to put the lid on my box of unfinished business, and the longer I keep kissing Malcolm, the harder that will be. I need to stop kissing him. I really need to stop.

Malcolm cups my cheeks with his hands as I pull away. We both breathe like we've run the Marine Corps marathon, and my heart beats out a drum solo from some insanely doped-out seventies rock band. Malcolm brushes my cheek with his thumb. There's wonder and tenderness and a question, a lot of questions, all tangled in that gesture.

I wish I had some answers.

Leaving would be wise. I should embrace wisdom. Lately, I haven't done much of that.

"Well, okay. Good night," I say. "Thanks for, um, everything. For today."

Malcolm's smile is honey slow and sweet. It spreads into his eyes. Then he leans forward and kisses me all over again, and I'm not leaving. Neither one of us is leaving. In fact, I am growing more enthusiastic about kissing by the minute.

"Wow," Malcolm says eventually.

"Wow," I agree.

"This could get complicated."

"I know." I grin, feeling absurdly happy. "Did I mention I'm very glad you're not my brother?"

It's a joke, an incredibly awkward joke based on an incredibly awkward day, but Malcolm goes stiff. I reach for his hand, and he turns away toward the window.

"About that," he says in a dead and quiet voice. "The reason Dad and I were arguing is because he admitted to me he and your mother did cheat together. Once. Only once, he said, as though that makes a difference, and he's not your father. Your mother told him that was some conductor she'd worked with, so maybe that can help you find the truth."

My stomach squeezes, then squeezes again. It rejects everything about that statement. Rejects more as the words sink in.

"When?" I ask. "When did they cheat?"

"After he and Mum were married obviously—"

"When?"

Malcolm looks blank, and I want to scream. I'm shivering, frozen in the draft of cold air that seeps in around the nursery windows, my lungs clogged on dry and ancient dust.

Because he still doesn't get it.

If I was wrong about Mom cheating, if she was willing to sleep with a married man—if Ian wasn't the man Malcolm believed his father to be—then how can we believe anything at all?

"Could your father be lying?" I ask at the same time that Malcolm says, "Would your mother have lied?" And we stand there, our faces bleached by the moonlight sifting in through the playroom windows, long shadows like enormous holes opening around our feet.

Malcolm
Locked Doors

Izzy vanishes into her room and the lock clicks behind her. I don't particularly care whether I wake up Dad and Anna as I pound my fist against the solid oak. "You can't shut me out, Izzy. We have to talk about this."

"I don't want to talk."

"But consider the odds. They're incredibly remote."

"Mom wrote the letters. She wrote the eleventh letter. You said yourself you would have thought the same thing I did if you didn't know your father. And you didn't know him, did you?"

"We shouldn't panic."

"You're the one banging on my door. *I'm* trying to go to sleep," she says, but her voice is still coming from just the other side of the wood.

I picture her standing there, arms wrapped around herself in self-defense, her face still tight and sick and confused.

God. Why did I kiss her? I shouldn't have kissed her.

I still want to kiss her.

"I'm not leaving, Izzy. I'll stay here the entire night unless you come out and talk to me."

I press my ear against the door, waiting, and I swear I can *feel* her on the other side. I feel the wood breathing between us and hear the thump, thump, thump of a heart beating, but I'm not certain if it's mine or hers. It's an angry rhythm, and that's the first moment I discover quite how furious I am—again. All over again. And I'm bloody tired of being angry.

Izzy
Possibilities

Someone slips a folded sheet of paper beneath my door. They knock faintly but don't say anything, and I scoot out of bed, pad over, pick up the note, and unfold it. Malcolm. I don't need to see his signature to know that. His handwriting is exactly like he is, full of contradictions, strong and precise, elegant and full of energy.

> *Izzy,*
>
> *Meet me at 7:00. We can go down to breakfast and face everything together.*
>
> *Mal*
>
> *P.S. Hope you slept.*

It's 6:30 in the morning, and I've spent most of the night wondering what to do, what to feel. I guess it's good that Malcolm will be there with me to confront Ian, but at the same time, I'd really prefer never to see Malcolm again. I want to go back to Elli, back to my used-to-be-normal life. Nothing about my present situation is normal.

How can I face Malcolm after we kissed last night? Just thinking about that makes me start shaking all over again.

People kiss after first dates. They kiss perfect strangers when they meet. A kiss is no big thing.

So why did this one feel so enormous?

I looked up kisses while I lay in bed awake last night, the history of kisses, words for kissing, the meaning of kisses. It's always humbling to find that, no matter how smart we think we are today, people have been smarter in the past. Something like 3,000 years ago, an anonymous Egyptian poet defined what I feel better than I could have said it.

> *Finally I will drink life from your lips*
> *and wake up from this everlasting sleep.*
> *The wisdom of the earth in a kiss*
> *and everything else in your eyes.*

I woke up to possibilities when Malcolm and I kissed, as if I'd been sleepwalking my entire life when it came to boys. Now I'm awake and I don't want to return to sleep. I have to, though. I have to make myself.

If Malcolm turns out to be my half-brother, how do I unfeel what I felt when our lips touched? How do I unremember?

———— ❖ ————

Birthday

A veil of silence has fallen between me and Malcolm. We barely look at each other as we walk down to the kitchen, and I'm relieved to discover Ian already at the table. He's reading a newspaper and drinking tea. Looking up, he smiles and asks how I slept, and there's a slight awkwardness to the question that makes me think maybe he's a little shy.

"Fine, thank you." I hide my face by saying hello to Gelert and the smaller dogs that loiter beneath the table.

Malcolm and I shouldn't pounce on Ian right away, I tell myself. This shouldn't be an ambush.

I sit down at the place set to Ian's left.

There's no full English breakfast of eggs, baked beans, sausage, and tomatoes in Anna's kitchen. Which I guess makes sense since Ian is a doctor. Instead, she sets down a beautiful salmon frittata and a platter of bread with another photon-eyed look in my direction. Actually, her weapons are getting stronger. The photons are nuclear-tipped this time.

"Will you be staying again tonight, miss?" she asks me. "Should I make up the room for you?"

"Of course she's staying." Ian folds the newspaper, sets it aside, and beams at me as though there can't be any doubt. "Malcolm and I need to show her Halford."

"I took all the tours yesterday," I object.

"That's only the beginning. There's a great deal more than what's available on the public tours. Mal and I can take you around together, which will give us all a chance to talk." He looks at Malcolm with a hopeful, tentative smile that makes me think of a dog offering a busy owner a toy to play with. A dog that's not used to having a lot of luck. When Malcolm doesn't respond, Ian turns back to his plate and stirs his food around. "At least I hope you'll stay," he adds. "I'd be grateful."

I don't know how to answer. I really don't know how to sit through the meal making polite small talk and pretending I don't know what I know.

"When exactly did you sleep with my mother?" I ask. This is not a decision. The words come out without intention.

Anna audibly inhales her outrage, and she turns to glare at me before whipping back toward the stove. I'm sure there's a protocol that says I should have waited until she's not around, that all this is too sensitive and private, but frankly, right now I don't care about being polite.

Malcolm isn't looking at me, he's looking at Ian. And Ian looks down at his plate. Then there's a sudden commotion from under the table and a scrabble of paws large and small. Gelert emerges and stands studying us, whining softly as if he feels the tension, then he ambles over and lays his chin on Ian's arm. Ian absently strokes the shaggy head.

"I'm sorry," I say. "I should have phrased that differently."

Ian sighs. "No, you're right, and I've been sitting here myself wondering how best to bring up the subject again. It occurred to me overnight that I took your mother at her word when she told me about your father. Perhaps I shouldn't have. Cella could be economical with the truth at times. When it suited her."

He raises his eyes without lifting his head, and there's something endearingly vulnerable about the way he looks at me.

He has a kind face, a sad one, but apart from the eyes and eyebrows, he doesn't look much like Malcolm. I wonder if that's the result of years of him being sad and years of Malcolm being angry. Emotions change people.

"It was August 14th, 1998," he says. "The night before the Feast Day of the Assumption of Mary in France. Your mother was playing a free concert at the *Fête de Tuileries*. Flis—that's Felicity, Malcolm's mother—had taken the twins to her family in Derbyshire for the week, and I had estate business in Paris. It happened quite by accident that we met."

"I'd like to see you accept the 'accident' excuse if I got some girl pregnant," Malcolm snaps.

They turn to look at me, both of them, and I'm quietly doing the math. The math is a problem. August to March doesn't add up, but it doesn't completely *not* add up.

"My birthday is March 18th." My voice sounds far away. "1999."

"Seven months." Malcolm sits very still.

Ian doesn't move.

"Babies can come early," Malcolm says.

"I don't think I did. Mom never said, but I never asked the question, either."

I was small, though. Small in the pictures, at least compared to Elli. And her dad always said she was tiny.

"This means you *could* be my sister," Malcolm says. "You could be."

"I'm probably not," I counter. Feeling queasy, I shake my head and turn to Ian. "Should we get a DNA test or something?"

"No. This can't be right." Ian's pale again. His forearms are splayed on the table on either side of his plate, and he leans against them heavily while Gelert nudges him, whining.

Anna, who I'd completely forgotten, comes to pour him a fresh cup of tea, adds milk and sugar—quite a bit of sugar—to it, and hands it over, studying him with her brows knitted. He nods an absent thank-you, takes the cup, and pushes back his chair.

"I need to sort a few things before the gates open," he says. "And obviously, this needs far more discussion." He glances in Malcolm's direction but doesn't really look at him—as if he can't bear to see what Malcolm's thinking. "Mal, would you bring Izzy to the office at 9:30, please? I'm sorry. I truly am."

He hurries from the kitchen. Malcolm is frozen. I'm frozen. How can Ian just leave like that? Again. *Now*?

"Bloody typical, that is," Malcolm mutters. "Ducks out without answering any questions."

Anna slams the door on the stainless steel refrigerator and whirls around to face him. "You think this is his fault? It was *her*. *Your* mother." She points at me. "Though God knows, there's blame enough to go around. I love you like you're my own, Malcolm Halford, but your father's borne the weight of raising you and saving Halford and running his surgery all these years without so much as a word of complaint. And what kindness or understanding have you once shown him for all he's done for you?"

She's turned the colors of an old English painting, bright pink cheeks and ash pale skin. Her lips go slack as if she's shocked herself by speaking to Malcolm like that, and she stands a long moment by the refrigerator holding a plate of yellow butter she just removed. Then she slowly opens the door and puts the butter right back in and turns and marches from the room.

———◆✳◆———

Safe Space

Malcolm pushes back his plate. "That went brilliantly."

"Are you okay?" I ask.

"I doubt it. You?"

The thought of eggs and salmon makes me queasy.

I don't want to look at food, much less smell it.

Malcolm stares at me, except I don't think it's me he's seeing. I don't think either one of us wants to see each other.

He could be my *brother*. And I kissed him in a highly unbrotherly way.

Please don't let him be my brother.

One night. Seven months. That's a really, really unlikely scenario. Almost impossible. Really.

He scrapes his chair back and holds out his hand. "Have you ever heard of Nicholas Owen? The priest hole builder?"

Maybe the stress has gotten to be too much for him.

"Priest holes?" I ask.

"Places to hide. Come with me."

I give a numb nod, because we're well out of the realm where things make sense.

We leave the kitchen with even more space and awkwardness between us. We know less than we knew before. We know nothing definite.

I want to tell Malcolm it isn't possible.

Except I can't. Not absolutely.

Ian was right the first time. Before his flat denial. My mother was fluent in the language of lies on occasion, both white lies and gray. She could tell me my hair looked fine even on a beanie day. She would tell me I was brilliant and beautiful and the best daughter in the word even when I'd been spiteful, mean, and ugly. She'd say she was too busy to go out to dinner with friends so she could have a movie night with me instead. She'd tell someone it was lovely to see them even if she couldn't stand them. Her music was perpetually almost finished.

People loved her for that. *I* loved her for that.

Could she have told Ian he wasn't my father to keep things from getting complicated? More complicated. Absolutely. I can see her doing it.

So now I really, *seriously* need to know.

I need to know before Malcolm and I spend another second together.

He leads me to a staircase behind the reading room, and he pauses, listening, at the top. Finally, he beckons me to follow as he descends. "After the Queen Mary scandal, the side of the family that rebuilt this place pretended to be Protestant, but they weren't. They built three hideaways into the structure of the house to hide their priests and Catholic friends."

"That wasn't on any of the tours."

"We do the priest holes on the Murder Tour, which is offered two nights a month. Even then, we only show a couple of them. This is the other one. Mine. I hadn't thought of it in ages until last night. I'm not even certain if what I want to show you is still there."

On the eighth step down from the landing, he stops and kicks the baseboard along the wainscoting that extends partway up the wall. The panel pops out, and he turns sideways and vanishes into the recess. A light snaps on inside, and then his hand reaches back out and beckons.

His voice is muffled. "It is here. Come in."

I duck through, and the panel falls shut behind us. We stand face-to-face in a space about three feet deep. Malcolm steps back quickly, but even so, the space is claustrophobically small. We look at anything except each other.

The stairs jut out a little inside, as if the wall was built on top of them, which forms small shelves that are stacked with books and toys. On the right, there's an area that's been built into a platform big enough for a futon piled high with blankets and pillows and a small reading lamp set on a narrow wooden table. There's also a wall of actual bookshelves populated with more books, Lego sets, toys, and puzzles. All of it, everything, is choked thick with dust.

"Those were some lucky priests," I say.

"Dad converted it for me after Ginny died," Malcolm says, and the lonely weight of his childhood hangs on his smile.

I swallow and look away. "Because you didn't want to use the playroom anymore?"

"I haven't been here since my mother's funeral. I didn't want to think about the place."

"It's where you were when you heard your parents arguing, isn't it?"

"Yes, that, too." He rubs a hand across the back of his neck as he looks around.

It's the perfect hideout for a little boy. Quiet and remote with just that hint of pretend danger that boys like best. At the same time, it's cozy, like being curled up in a basket that contains a private world. The shelves are carved with rosettes and scrolls and shells as if they were taken from somewhere in the house much grander, and they're filled up with things Malcolm must have loved back then.

I think about Ian making this for him, and about Malcolm walking away from it. Refusing to remember it. I think about how scared and angry and alone that small boy must have been.

"I've read how hard it is to lose a twin," I say, and it's only after the words are out that I realize I might once have lost a sister, too. A sister I'll never know.

Jesus, this changes *everything*.

"It was the silence," Malcolm says quietly. "That was the hardest to bear after Ginny died. As though I'd heard her heart beating along with mine from the moment we each had heartbeats. Then suddenly that was gone, along with the noise of her footsteps running and her laughter and the way she'd screech at me when I took something she wanted to play with. Maybe because she died so young, we hadn't quite formed our own identities yet. We were still more 'we' than 'me,' and without her I'd no idea who I was myself. I felt off-balance. Being here helped. It shrank the enormity of the world for me down to a space this size."

"Then why did you give it up?"

"Because Dad was the one who'd built it for me. Small boy logic. That was what I'd loved about it most at first, the fact that he'd restored the shelves himself and put it all together. I used to lie here and wonder about the people who had hidden here: who they were, who they were hiding from, how long they stayed, what happened to them. Whether Ginny would meet them in heaven. Henry VIII made up a whole religion so he could divorce Catherine of Aragon and get out from under the authority of the pope, and for centuries people used that as an excuse to do horrible things to each other. But this was one of the safe spaces where those people could survive. It made me feel like I could survive, too. Until it didn't."

"You must have been a strange child," I say,

because it's too heartbreaking, "if Henry VIII made you feel better."

His smile is rueful, as if he's laughing at himself. "Yes, I might have been a little odd."

Our eyes catch. He sits on one of the steps, and I lean back against the wall, well away from him.

"I've always thought normal was overrated," I say.

"It's rather a meaningless concept, the whole idea of normality. Like aspiring to be average." Malcolm offers a wraith of a smile, and then he sighs. "You know, I spent much of last night considering what you said about putting objects together with the people who'd lived here. It's similar to something Dad used to do for us when Ginny and I were small. He'd point out a portrait of an ancestor in the gallery, then we'd go back to the armory and he'd show us the man's regimental sword, or the drum he'd brought back from the battle of Naseby, or the poison dart blowgun he'd collected in the course of oppressing some indigenous people or other."

"Charming."

"Well, he didn't put it like that. And I was too small to know better, so I thought the stories were brilliant. People like collecting things, don't they? They always have, but I think it's the secrets we collect that define us. The things we're willing to do in public versus what we try to hide. If your mother kept your father a secret, she must have had a reason."

I trace a pattern in the dust of the wall, a rosette like the one carved on the bookshelf. "If she believed it would be easier, for her or for my father—whoever he was—if he didn't know he had a child, she might have lied. That's the kind of thing she would have done. Not maliciously. Just because the truth might have made everything too complicated."

Malcolm watches the motion of my finger and then he draws the same rosette on the floor beside him.

Dueling roses. The same but not.

The English fought a series of wars over roses, which eventually wiped out both the Lancasters and the Yorks.

Malcolm slants a look at me. "We don't need Dad to have our DNA tested. We could have it done ourselves."

The small room feels even smaller.

I hate not knowing. A few months ago, I was obsessing over college admission notifications. Only months ago, that was the worst thing I had to worry about.

"When he said 'no' earlier, do you think he meant he didn't want us to get tested?"

"I think he was denying that your mother would have betrayed him. He's in denial, but I don't want to wait for him to get over that. Do you?"

"I wish I'd never found the letters."

"Then you wouldn't have come. Do you regret coming?"

"I don't know," I say. And I don't. Not yet.

February 28, 1998

Dear Ian,

I've never minded birthdays before, and in principle I don't think we should mind them. Women develop grace and wisdom as we get older, an elegant sort of patience. But I find myself looking in the mirror today, searching for the changes in my face that I am certain must be there. Those new lines I saw between your brows must surely be reflected in me, too.

Would those lines be there if you'd never met me?

Is it me? Or is it her?

Today I think of the broken promise of us, and I wonder if it was ever a possibility.

Dreams turn to nightmares so easily, don't they?

I do love you. Still.

Always.

Cella

Interruptions

Ian shows me parts of the house I ha
the other parts of the family quart
on the Murder Tour, the dungeon. Malcolm is with
us off and on, but there's a torrent of interruptions
from the estate manager and the banquet manager
and the wedding coordinator and I don't even know
who else. A few times, he and Ian trade off, as if I'm
the baton in a relay race. Ian's nice, but I think the
thought of me hurts him, and I hate my mother a little
for that even though I don't have any right to hate
her. I'm not even sure if she did anything wrong.

Except *what if?* And if she lied to Ian, it means he
didn't *not* want me.

It means she didn't let him have a choice.

He swipes an access card to open a door that leads
from the armory out into the courtyard. He sneaks
looks at me while he talks about the things and places
we are seeing. I wonder if he would have loved Mom
all these years if he'd known what she had done. *If*
she did it.

"I don't think I can bear not knowing. How long
does a DNA test take?" I ask.

"That depends." We reach the courtyard and stand
blinking in the sudden light, and Ian shuts the door
behind us. "We'd have to send off for the test kit—I don't
keep them around my surgery. Not much call for it."

He's not impatient to know the truth. I wish he was.

"Was it hard for you, growing up without a father?" he asks. "I imagine it must have been."

"Mom did her best to be everything for me."

"I'm sure she was brilliant. I tried to be that for Malcolm after his mum died, but I couldn't manage it." Ian stops, and we stand in a bubble of silence while on the other side of the courtyard crowds of people with hot, glistening faces and hordes of chattering children rush past us like a river. Then he speaks again. "Izzy, this is hard for me. I'd like nothing better than to find out that you are my daughter. Just the idea of that brings me joy. But I'm afraid of what it could mean for Malcolm. There would be a lot of public questions, for one thing, and he may need time to get used to the idea before that happens. One way or the other. He's been through too much in his life as it is, and he's always been determined to push me away. I was afraid I'd lose him entirely if I tried too hard to hold on to him. I'm even more afraid of losing him now."

I can see that. How easily any remaining relationship between the two of them could break.

"I suppose I always imagined we'd find our way back to each other," Ian continues. "That there'd be time. Now I feel as though I'm at the edge of a cliff with him. One wrong step and I could lose him forever. I need to tread carefully, make certain he'll be all right. Can you bear with me a while until I think things through? Decide how best to proceed?"

His phone rings before I can answer, and it's the wedding coordinator again about the peacock-bride. Ian looks like he'd like to throw the telephone down and stomp on it, but his voice is mild as he tells her he'll be right there. Then he apologizes to me and makes a call to Malcolm arranging to pass me back over again.

I stand in the courtyard watching Ian rush away. Then he's gone, and I'm left watching impatient children being dragged from place to place by equally impatient parents, dropping crumbs from bribe-worthy pastries and ice creams to the waiting pigeons that waddle after them. Snippets of conversation float around me, everything from the quality of the food at the snack bar to the urgent need for buggy rides to take people around the grounds. They discuss the Halfords, too, past and present, much the way people talk about celebrities back home.

It hits me hard that I could be Ian's illegitimate daughter. His *bastard* daughter. In America, I don't think that means anything anymore. But I don't know about England. Does having a child outside of marriage still matter when you're an earl? Do people judge you for it?

Being illegitimate has never bothered me. Mom never made me feel like I was less. But now, I can't help wondering what all these people would make of that—how they'd talk about Ian and about my mother.

Can you do an anonymous DNA test? Really anonymous? Based on the news recently about police trolling through DNA databases on genealogy sites, I'm not so sure. The companies that do them don't seem to be big on privacy. These days, you can find anything on the internet except the right to keep people from prying into things that aren't their business.

Stubbornness

Apparently, the peacock returned to the scene of the crime through the broken window this morning. And he brought some girlfriends. Apparently, the carefully set table for the reception is a mess of peafowl droppings, and the bride and her mother are in hysterics that can only be calmed by an actual member of the Halford family.

"On the bright side," Malcolm says, "Dad's brilliant at soothing hackles. Comes of being a doctor. And while he's busy soothing, Pricilla will get the staff to replace the china and scrub the floor and change the tablecloths. Fix the flower arrangements. Of course, if the bride's mother hadn't insisted on inspecting everything last night so she could have a lie-in this morning, the tables wouldn't have been set yet and there wouldn't have been a problem."

"There wouldn't be a problem now if the bride hadn't broken the window. Or let the peacock into the building in the first place."

"Or that."

"Poor Olivia, though. Imagine having your wedding ruined by peacock poop."

Malcolm and I look at each other, which is a huge mistake. It's awful—I know it is—but neither of us can help laughing. Maybe it's nervous laughter, but it's freeing.

I can't imagine there's much more of Halford that I haven't seen. We've been to the butterfly sanctuary and skirted the lake where Malcolm and his sister used to race the wooden boats his father carved for them. Now we're walking through the walled garden where a team of gardeners grow most of the "herbs and veg" that are used in the Halford kitchens. The Pavilion where the peacock disaster is unfolding is just visible at the end of a long, ornamental walk surrounded by decoratively laid out beds of edible flowers and herbs and vegetables and vines.

The new greenhouses—which Malcolm calls glass-houses—have been moved to the corner of the garden out of the way, but the Pavilion is the original Victorian structure with hundreds of panes of glass in wrought iron frames soaring up to a two-story-tall room with a triple dome. They've removed all the plants from the center of the building to create an event space, but as we draw closer, I can see that they've left some of the original exotic fruits: banana trees and pineapples, oranges, and great, twisted grapevines more than a century old that twine overhead. It looks like the Garden of Eden. A perfect place to have a wedding.

Malcolm steps inside to check with his father, and I hang back and watch the choreographed dance of waitstaff and managers scurrying in and out with carts of china and cutlery and linens. It really is all a bit too *Downton Abbey*.

And it makes me feel very illegitimate. In so many ways, I don't belong. But I'm glad I've had the chance to see it.

"What are you thinking?" Malcolm asks when he comes back to me.

I shoot him a cautious look. "Why?"

"Dad's going to be a while yet. He says he'll meet us at the stables."

He leads the way through a side gate into another private section of the grounds. Everything on the estate is controlled by swipe cards and security systems, and there are cameras and security guards and even motion sensors in parts of the house, which really does make it like living in a museum. Or a glasshouse.

"Do you feel like you're always on display when you're here?" I ask.

"I'm not here that much. I haven't been since I went off to boarding school a year after mum died. But it's part of the price, isn't it?" He gives me a grin that falls about midway from shy to embarrassed. "And I do love it. All of it. The house, the history, the stories. Family stories."

He sweeps his eyes over the lawn edged by trees and shadowed by the side of the house. His expression reminds me of the way my mother would look when she was giving birth to a piece of music.

"It makes me feel part of something living here, and it gives me purpose," he says. "The one thing I've always appreciated about my dad is that he's included me in every decision he makes that impacts this place. It's not easy keeping it going. My great-great-grandparents turned it into a hospital for wounded soldiers during the First World War at their own expense. The government took the house over for the military in the next war, and one of the reasons I want to encourage craftsmen to set up workshops here is that we're still trying to repair the damage from that. Then taxes went from six percent to sixty percent, and death duties were eighty percent. Most of the men who used to work the estate had gone to fight, so everything changed overnight. Very few of the big country houses survived."

"You could argue it was a way of life that wasn't worth saving."

"Not as it was, but it could become relevant now. To the whole community. We already provide more jobs than anything else for miles around, and it might sound mad, but with robots and automation and globalization and climate change, I think we'll need more jobs away from the cities. Places like this can help bring back local farming and small industries and craftsmanship. Jobs where people can take pride in individual achievement without having to be engineers or architects or lawyers or footballers."

"It's too expensive to fix things or make them by hand. Which is a shame." I'm smiling at Malcolm again. Probably a goofy kind of smile, because he always manages to surprise me. "Is that what you're trying to do with the workshops?"

"Something like that." His cheeks have gone red. "A way to bring back a new generation of craftsmen. There are things people don't even know how to do anymore."

We're standing close. Too close. I feel the moment when Malcolm's embarrassment turns into awareness between us. Into something we can't have.

"So. Right." He waves toward the buildings we're approaching. "These are old carriage houses, which is a whole other debacle in the appalling Malcolm history."

He crosses the remaining few yards of cobblestones outside, pulls the door open, and snaps the light on.

In addition to a couple of old horse-drawn carriages, there's a collection of Aston Martins, none of them close to working order.

"The cars were one of Dad's brighter ideas. He bought them to restore as an attraction for the tourists."

"You said it was your history?"

"He thought we could restore them together. By which I mean tinker together, really, because neither one of us knows the first thing about cars. He had visions of us researching and pottering around and finding people to do bits and pieces for us."

"And not even James Bond cars could win you over?"

"I'm quite dangerously stubborn." Malcolm's voice is subdued. "I suppose the harder he tried, the more I shut him out. I didn't see that then, and I'm not sure how we can find a way back from it. *If* we can." He runs a hand over a graceful swoop of dusty, rusting hood and then snaps off the overhead lights before we exit.

We stand blinking in the sunlight, and I want to reach out to him, but I force myself to stop.

He nods, looking around, though not at anything in particular. Then he walks back toward another building nearby and lets us in. Yellow light spills through high windows onto a wide center aisle that runs between two dozen empty stalls. There's a plastic trash can standing near the door, and Malcolm removes the lid to reveal that it's filled with carrots floating in fresh water. He hands me a few and takes some himself to feed them to the three remaining horses. Technically, it's more like two and a half horses, if you count the fat gray pony named Jane who greets him with an insistent whinny.

Malcolm rubs her ears and shows me the scar on his forearm where she threw him when he was six. I show him the scar on my elbow where I got thrown off at camp—which is why I'm perfectly content to admire horses from the safety of the ground. He sneaks Jane a couple of extra carrots when he thinks I'm looking the other way, which I see only because I turn back to sneak her a carrot of my own.

I blow a stray curl out of my eyes. Malcolm smiles, and the light is suddenly too bright, even though it hasn't changed.

"I wish we knew the truth," Malcolm says.

"It's a lot for your dad to process, too. He's probably thinking about you and what people would say and what I'd want from him—"

"What do you mean, what you'd want?" Malcolm asks.

I was thinking about what I'd expect emotionally from a father I've never known. That's hard. But a cold mask has slammed down over Malcolm's features, shutting off any sign of warmth. And I can see what he is thinking.

I hate what he's thinking. I don't want anything from either him or his father.

I don't want to take anything *away* from him. It hurts that he could think I would.

"Nothing. I don't want anything," I say with only a hint of wobble in my voice. "Nothing that belongs to you."

Illusions

Text to Elli:

Me: So change of plan...

Elli: What plan? You've been winging it.

Me: Don't go all sciencey and I-told-you-so on me.

Elli: Planning isn't science. It's planning.

Me: Well, I'm planning to come home.

Elli: You all right?

Me: I will be.

Elli: Good. Can't wait to see you.

I'm back in my room, and packing takes about ten seconds. Most of that involves glaring at the shoebox of letters surrounded by T-shirts and underwear. Then I shake my head, and zip up the suitcase. Voilà. I'm done. And I'm already carrying it to the door when someone knocks.

Ian stands in the hallway. His eyebrows float upward in a very Malcolm expression when he sees the luggage. "What are you doing?"

"I need to get home. Sorry."

"Did something happen? Did Malcolm say something?"

"He's fine. I just…" I shrug. I don't even want to come up with an excuse.

"Then it's me. Don't go yet, Izzy. Give me a chance."

I shift the suitcase in front of me and grip the strap with both my hands. "I don't want to cause trouble between you. That's not why I came."

"I know that." He steps closer, and his eyes are dark and bruised looking, and there's defeat written in his shoulders. "In any case, leaving won't make the trouble go away. It will only leave us with unanswered questions. You don't want that any more than I do."

"That wasn't how it seemed."

His jaw clenches briefly. "I know. I've handled this very badly. None of this is fair to you. It's just that it isn't fair to Malcolm, either."

He steps past me into the room, and the silk wallpaper and the sheer voile curtains surrounded by thick falls of embroidered brocade cast his skin in a greenish light. He crosses over the miles of carpet until he stands at the window looking down at the view: park and fields and pastures and rolling hills, which all belong to Halford as far as the eye can see.

"I've made too many mistakes. With Malcolm, with your mother, and with my wife. Looking back, it's so simple to see where things went wrong. It feels as though I ought to be able to reach back through the years, shuffle a few things, and save all the misery. But that's wishful thinking. And logic. Emotions aren't logical." He sighs. "It's not fair that you've been dropped into any of this, but I have to ask you. I doubt I'll have another opportunity to set things right with Malcolm. He'll duck out the moment he has an opportunity, and that will be the end of it. That's why I need you to stay."

"He'll duck out that much faster if I do. Trust me."

Ian studies me until my cheeks get hot under his scrutiny. "So you *have* argued?"

"It doesn't matter."

He stares out the window again, and I don't know why, but I go and stand beside him. It feels right, somehow. Just standing there.

"I'm going to beg a rather enormous favor of you," Ian says. "I don't expect you'll agree, but I hope you will. I hope you and Malcolm will both take a trip with me."

My eyebrows rise, because this wasn't at all what I was expecting. "What kind of trip?"

"Your mother and I had planned to go to India on our honeymoon. We never had a chance to go, and I've never had the heart to go alone. I'd like you two to come with me. It would give us all the opportunity to get to know one another without the constant distractions we have here."

I can't help smiling. "No peacocks?"

"No peacocks." Ian looks relieved. "More importantly, it would be harder for Malcolm to escape back to Oxford. Give me the chance to repair things with him. I know this isn't fair, my asking you this. And of course, it's all awkward for you. But I'm desperate. I love him, and you two seem to get along. I don't want to lose him, and I don't want to miss out on the chance to get to know you, either. Will you consider it?"

He's right. It's totally unfair for him to ask. And if he had any idea how hard it would be to be stuck somewhere with Malcolm, he wouldn't even think to ask.

I want to say no. That's the knee-jerk reflex. Only I do want to know him, don't I? And he isn't wrong about Malcolm, either. If I leave now, I'm not sure the two of them will ever be fixed. Which isn't really my responsibility, except it is. Mine and my mother's, because I dropped Mom right back between them by bringing her letters here.

In the end, though, it's Ian himself who makes me decide.

Standing there dwarfed by the eighteen-foot window, with his shoulders stooped and his head bent slightly, he looks even more alone than Malcolm. Thanks to Mom, they've both always been alone.

These past months, I've gotten to know how hard being alone can be, how hollow it makes you inside, as if nothing in the world will ever be enough to fill you up. As if you're swallowing all the laughter that other people release so carelessly around you, and it's just echoing in your hollowness.

"I'll go if you can get Malcolm to agree."

Ian grabs me by both shoulders and beams down at me. "You're wonderfully generous." He shakes his head, and the white strands salted through his dark hair disappear in the sunlight behind him and the shadows melt away the years. "I'll speak to him as soon as I can and hopefully make arrangements. It doesn't need to be for very long."

In that moment, I see what my mother must have seen in him. It's an illusion, I know that just like she must have known it. Illusions can be more powerful than reality, though. They draw us in like whirlpools, gently at first, then deeper and deeper, until we drown inside them.

Halford and this world Ian and Malcolm were born into seems like an illusion to me, a dream world. But to Ian, this is real, and it was my mother who was the dream. He gave himself to her, and she never fully allowed herself to love him back. To adapt herself. To let go.

Letting go requires courage. That's what she regretted.

Maybe I'm much more like my mother than I suspected.

Malcolm
Request

My father pulls me aside in the corridor out of earshot of the people passing by. I listen to what he says and gape at him. Clearly, he's lost the plot.

"We can't all run off to India on a whim. I've a project to finish and there's Halford and your practice."

"The *locum* doctor's already there to cover the surgery anyway. And we could get there and back in five days. Surely, we can all manage that."

It seems like a waste of airfares, but five days isn't long. The trip would give me a chance to square things with Izzy as well, now that I've made a bollocks of everything between us.

Dad studies me, then stuffs his hands into the pockets of his trousers. "I don't know what you said to her, but she had her suitcase zipped when I knocked on her door. I had to beg her not to leave immediately."

The way he looks at me, I feel like I've just spilled juice on the Louis XVI armchair again. Damaged feelings can't be repaired as easily as furniture, though.

"And Izzy agreed to do this? You're sure?" I ask.

Dad nods and pushes his hands deeper. "As long as you agree."

"Five days?"

"We can leave from London tomorrow. You can head back to Oxford the night we land, if you insist."

His phone rings in his pocket, but he ignores it and waits for me to answer. In the end, I give in. "I'll agree on one condition—whatever you're still hiding or trying to think through, you'll tell us before we get back here. And you'll send away for the DNA kit."

"Agreed." He holds out his hand for me to shake, as though we've struck a bargain.

I feel as though I'm somehow conspiring with him against Izzy, and that feels wrong. On the other hand, I don't want her to go back to the States. Not until…I sigh. I can't finish that thought. Some thoughts are better left unfinished.

Izzy
Travels

Text to Elli:

Me: Changing plans again. I'm going to India with Ian and Malcolm.

Elli: India?!!? Why? Also. Stop calling things a plan. You do not plan.

Me: This is Ian's plan.

Elli: What do you even know about these people? They could be murderers. They could hide a LOT of bodies on 17,000 acres.

Me: Are you reading Stephen King again?

Elli: It's better than living Stephen King.

Me: This is only a mystery caused by death. It isn't horror.

Elli: So go, then. Jetset off to see the world without me. See if I care. Only are you sure you don't want me to come with you?

Because I could come with you and be sensible when you can't.

Me: I'm always sensible.

Elli: I laugh. So hard. You don't know what that word is supposed to mean.

Pandemonium

It's barely light outside, but the flight to India leaves from Heathrow at 9:30, so Malcolm and I are ready to go. Anna marches into the reading room after Ian, and her dislike of me has shifted into downright hatred overnight. The look she throws me as she follows Ian in there and slams the door could kill at twenty paces.

"She's shouting at him," Malcolm says. "That isn't like her."

"Is it like him to run away to India?" I ask. "It does seem a little irresponsible."

"On the other hand, I can't remember the last time he had an actual vacation."

"When did you?"

"I've gone off with friends."

He comes to stand beside me in the gallery as I scowl up at a portrait of a small girl in a wispy dress that reminds me of a painting I've seen somewhere. I can't remember where.

"That one's by Thomas Lawrence. He did the *Pinkie* portrait that hangs opposite Gainesborough's *Blue Boy* at the Huntington Library in California. This one's nothing like as well known, but then *Pinkie* is mostly famous by association. The Gainesborough nearly caused riots in the streets of London when Huntington bought *Blue Boy* and dragged it off to the States. We Brits considered it a piece of our national heritage. Which is ironic considering the vast chunks of other peoples' treasures we've carted off and can't or won't give back."

"I'm not sure we'd want to look too closely at how any of those were originally made or paid for, either," I say. "Like the Taj Mahal. I can't believe that I'm actually going to get to see it."

I turn to him, moving a little too fast. He's got blue smudges beneath his eyes, and his hair is still damp from the shower. He smells clean and spicy, and he's dressed in layers, which is very practical since it is currently 111° F in Agra, India, but only 65° F in London. I don't think I have enough clothes to take off for 111° F. And I should definitely not be thinking of removing clothes anywhere near Malcolm. Mine or his.

I'm staring at him and he sucks in a breath. I turn away.

"You do realize there's more to what my father's doing than he's telling us?" he asks me. "He's up to something."

"Any idea what?"

"Whatever it is, I heard Anna say she'd never forgive him if he didn't tell me."

I shift back around. "Maybe he knows more about me than he's saying."

"Impossible to guess." Malcolm gives a slow, considering shake of his head. "Look, Dad told me you had packed. Can you possibly forgive me for what I said? I was an idiot. Anyone who knows you for five minutes can see you're not here for money. It's only that people always seem to be wanting something from us."

I know that. I knew it almost as soon as he'd said it, but that didn't make it hurt any less. "Conditioned response. It's fine."

"Still. I am sorry."

I shouldn't be relieved. I shouldn't be happy at the thought of not saying goodbye to him yet. But I'm neither of those things, which makes me a little angry at myself.

Standing there with my suitcase, I feel as if I've packed the me I used to know away, folded her into unfamiliar shapes pressed into compression bags so that she takes up a fraction of the usual space inside myself. A wave of *missingness* rolls over me, and I want my safe life back. I want to smell Mom's skin and be folded into her music, and I want her to be part of all the rest of my firsts.

I want her to tell me who I am now that she's gone—who I am, where I came from, and who I'm turning into.

Scared Brave

On the plane, Ian offers me the window, but I'd rather have the aisle. Malcolm takes the middle. It's not like I'm going to sleep anyway. The shade is down. Ian lifts it and glances outside before he stows his briefcase. Malcolm tucks his backpack under the seat in front of him, then I hand him the end of my charger and ask him to plug it in.

He straightens and turns to me. "Are you nervous?"

"Not about flying." I dig through my purse for my earbuds, chewing gum, and the little clear bag that has my toothbrush and toothpaste plus my wide-tooth comb. I've already wedged my scarf and travel blanket in the seat pocket, and I've got hundreds of books on my computer tablet, at least one for every mood or need while we're in India.

Malcolm has a thick book on the cultural history of furniture on his lap for light entertainment. Ian has a stack of medical journals he plans to read and throw away. They're very different, the two of them, but they're both serious and determined. Determined is sexier than I imagined it could be.

I need to stop thinking things like that about Malcolm.

"What's your favorite book?" I ask in an attempt to change my mental subject.

"The Canterbury Tales," Malcolm and Ian say simultaneously. I think it surprises them because they glance at each other, but for an entirely different reason, it also surprises me.

I start to smile because that's on my list of bests as well, then I remember that genetics can make people like similar things, which isn't anything to smile about. And I don't want to think like that.

"What's your favorite story from it?" I ask.

"'The Nun's Priest's Tale,'" Ian says.

Malcolm smooths his book where there's a tiny crinkle in the dust jacket. "I prefer 'The Knight's Tale.' Chivalry, mythology, and a bit of trickery. Also, the language."

"Definitely the language," I say, delighted in spite of myself. "And favorite movie?"

Ian clicks the buckle on his seatbelt. *"The Shawshank Redemption."*

"Far too easy. Everyone loves that," Malcolm says.

"Am I meant to dislike it simply because too many other people don't?"

"That isn't what I said," Malcolm says.

"So give us your favorite, then," Ian counters.

Malcolm's lips twitch, and his lids partially hood his eyes. "*Gladiator*."

"Hypocrite."

They're both laughing, and I like hearing them laugh together. But their movie choices say a lot about them. *Shawshank* is about survival and escape, about patient endurance, hope, and redemption. *Gladiator* is about revenge and warped versions of family. Pretty much on point. But both the characters are inherently *good*. They're both on my list of best non-Disney movies.

"All right. Next," I say. "Favorite food?"

"Dessert," Malcolm answers. "And why aren't you having to answer questions?"

I shake my head. "I don't do favorites, only favorite-in-the-moments. It's all about the context."

Malcolm leans back against the seat as the plane lurches out onto the runway. Beneath the dark, sharp curves of his brows, his green-ice eyes are darker in the low glow of the cabin lights. Apart from the eyebrows, we don't look at all alike. My eyes are brown like Mom's. My hair is a frizzy mess. I see almost nothing of myself in either him or Ian. Nothing at all except maybe my eyebrows.

But now I've lost my train of thought. Malcolm's said something, and I haven't heard it.

"Earth to Izzy," he says. "I asked what happens to your in-the-moment-favorites once they're over.

Some of them must turn into all-time favorites. It only stands to reason."

"You can't repeat a perfect moment. I can have the perfect *Sachertorte* somewhere else, but it's never going to be as good as the night Mom and I had it at the café Sacher after seeing *Aida* at the Vienna opera. We sat with the cake and a cup of cocoa and the snow started falling in fat, drifting flakes outside the window, and we made up stories about all the people walking by. If I say that *Sachertorte* is my favorite, what I'm actually saying is *that* moment was my favorite, and I'm limiting myself because no *Sachertorte* could ever taste as good as that one."

"Opera and *Sachertorte*. Your mother did love that." Ian's smile is as hard to pin down as the taste of apricots and chocolate. "She once brought us a dessert picnic, with tiramisu for a starter and *Sachertorte* for mains and Danish princess cake for dessert. She brought a CD player—they still had those back then—and we listened to Mozart's *The Abduction from the Seraglio* on the small knoll at the top of the Halford lake."

He doesn't seem to realize that what he's sharing isn't something I want to hear. I force my face still, force myself to breathe through the pain. Maybe it shouldn't hurt to discover that my traditions with Mom aren't mine alone, but it feels like I've just lost another piece of her. As if these last months keep chipping pieces of my childhood away. I picture Michelangelo chiseling at a block of marble, which gets smaller and smaller and smaller until all that remains is dust, until a breath lifts that into the air, too, and then it's gone.

I search for another memory, something to give back to him but maybe also to reclaim my mother for myself. To push the world of *them* a little further back from the immediacy of having Ian talking about her when I'm not ready. I'm not sure I'll ever be ready.

"She decided we should go skiing last year," I say, and I tell Ian and Malcolm about going to Aspen, which is a fairy-tale-perfect town full of shops and restaurants, Hollywood celebrities, cowboys, and Olympic champions surrounded by ski slopes on steep, gorgeous mountains. Virginia has ski resorts, too, and so do Pennsylvania and West Virginia. We could have gone to any of those places more easily, but that's not how Mom liked to do things. Instead, we flew to Colorado, booked into a condo within walking distance of the runs, and started with a few lessons before hitting the bunny hills.

By the second day, we were skiing the intermediate runs, and so, on the third day, in Mom-logic, it made sense for us to progress to the expert slopes. We took the chairlift up, perfectly confident, but what from the bottom had looked like small bumps on a reasonable grade turned into giant moguls on a hill so steep we stood at the top and laughed in panic. Mom laughed so hard, she slipped and slid until she lost her poles and both her skis. I hiked them down to her, and then slammed face first into a mogul myself when I tried to take a turn. By the time she had picked *me* up, we were halfway down the hill already. We couldn't go up and didn't dare go down, so we crawled off to the side and lay there with our eyes closed and the sun on our faces.

"We told each other Edgar Allan Poe stories until we scared ourselves brave enough to clip our skis back on," I say, remembering.

"Are you scared brave now?" Ian's eyes smile at me. "If so, pass me a little courage, would you?"

"Are you afraid to fly?" I ask, and I can feel Malcolm watching the two of us, as if he's surprised.

"It's never been my favorite thing, but no. When you get to be my age, it's not leaving the ground that scares you, it's the things and the people you leave behind." It feels like an admission, something much larger than the words, and Ian turns toward the window as if he's embarrassed by what he said.

The plane takes off. I adjust the overhead knob that controls the cold flow of air. "I think I've been scared brave ever since Mom died," I say. "I'm scared of everything: the future, the world, my life. Loneliness. Too many questions. Not enough answers. I'm so scared of everything, I can't be afraid of anything in particular."

That's a lie, though. I'm suddenly afraid Ian will turn out *not* to be my father, and I'm afraid Malcolm could be my brother, and I don't want—I so, so very much don't want—either one of those things to be true. One of them is bound to be, though. And that's the problem, isn't it?

Human Contact

Malcolm and Ian fall asleep. Malcolm encroaches on my armrest, and his bicep brushes my shoulder now and then. I let myself take the opportunity to watch him. Really, he's so attractive it's annoying. His hair falls over his forehead, but I can still see the faint crease between his brows. His blanket has slipped down his chest. I tuck it back up, pretending that I don't want to touch him. But we all need human contact when we're frightened. That's what I tell myself.

> Imagined Text to Elli:
>
> Me: If a boy wanted to build you the Taj Mahal as a memorial, what would you think?
>
> Elli: I think I'd be flattered, but I'd tell him someone beat him to it.

Me: If it was the right boy, I'd be flattered.
If it was the wrong boy, I'd be creeped out.
Either way, I'd give him a list of better ways
to spend 55 billion dollars.

Elli: Oh, oh. Don't go getting images of "the
right boy" stuck inside your head. Ideas like
that are bound to mess you up.

Malcolm
Symmetry

My father is still asleep and Izzy has finally drifted off. She's leaning against my shoulder, and I feel her with every breath she takes. My own breath strains with the effort of not pulling her closer, and I don't want to move away for fear I'll wake her.

That's what I tell myself.

I wonder if Dad used to watch her mother sleep. If he used to try to parse what made her particularly beautiful to him. There's more to it than symmetry, and it's more than Izzy's expressions or the way she watches people or her generosity or the stubborn courage she doesn't even know she has. It's as though every girl I've known before Izzy is the rose that Joran Masterson carved during the workshop whilst Izzy is the finished masterpiece.

Being here with her must be bittersweet for my father. Bittersweet and painful.

For me, it's getting more difficult by the moment.

PART SIX

Izzy
Agra

I was reading *The Goldfinch* the night before my mother died. I haven't finished it. The thing about reading other people's words is that they can fly at you unexpectedly, burrow in, and leave holes that shake your world. I've read books that made me cry for hours. Some books make me cry for days.

I'm still waking up unexpectedly at night to find I've been dreaming of Mom, my throat sore and my pillow wet, so I don't need any help with crying. For now, I'm not reading any books that I haven't read before. No books that aren't safe.

Does that sound cowardly? Probably. But when life's unstable, I at least need certainty in my literature.

Who was there for Malcolm after his mother died? Who did he turn to when he couldn't turn to Ian? Were there books that gave him comfort? I can't imagine boarding school was much help.

And who was there for Ian? Who's ever been there for him? That's what I can't help wondering as the cabin lights come back on for landing and he wakes up. It's strange, because obviously he's nothing at all like the general-reduced-to-slave in *Gladiator* or the innocent accountant locked up in *Shawshank*. Maybe he isn't even entirely innocent. But still, there's something about him that makes me feel like he's been wronged, that makes me want to believe in him.

We land in Agra, and the airport runways shimmer gold in the sunlight. I bump against Malcolm as I lean to look out the window.

"Sorry," I say.

"Is that an apology for bumping me or for snoring the last three hours?" he asks, doing that sexy eyebrow lift thing again.

Dying of mortification is a real possibility. But I give him a blinding smile instead.

"I do not snore, and remind me to accidentally whack you with my bag as I get it down for even suggesting it."

"Remind me to make a recording of you *not* snoring next time you go to sleep."

There's a beat where he looks at me and I look at him, and then he grins with his entire face. Which makes it impossible to be mad at him.

Imagined Text to Elli:

Me: What's stronger than brain soap? Because I think I desperately need some.

Elli: Did you bring hand sanitizer? Maybe that could work.

Brilliant

Why is it that a day on a plane can make me feel like I haven't showered in a week? We've changed planes three times, but I'm still wearing the same clothes, and that just feels so, so wrong.

I follow Malcolm and Ian and stumble into the terminal. Miraculously, there's a driver standing by baggage claim with a printed "Ian Halford" sign. He's a thin, stiff-backed man, with glasses and graying tufts of dark hair ringed around a shining scalp, who introduces himself as Mr. Chandra. Between him and Malcolm, they heave my carry-on suitcase and all the other bags into the trunk in two seconds, and we slide into a beige Mercedes that knows its way around air conditioning. Which is a relief because the outside temperature could make a self-respecting oven blush. The air is hazy and smells of exhaust as cars, trucks, and scooters whiz by on the wrong side of the road. Which is, for Malcolm and Ian and everyone in India, actually the correct side of the road, and I'm the one who's wrong.

Ian climbs into the front and Malcolm sinks into the seat beside me and leans back as the cool air hits him. "This is brilliant. Thank you for picking us up."

I love the way Malcolm says "brilliant." Okay, I love his accent, period.

Mr. Chandra's accent is harder to decipher. I assume my ear will adjust, but so far in India, I've felt like I need a translator to help me decode the English, which is really an accent on top of the British accent. Which for me is a double whammy. Mr. Chandra lurches out into traffic where he slots us like an IndyCar driver into a space barely large enough to fit between two trucks, both of them decorated with paintings, jewelry, and assorted religious icons. They're also dangerously overloaded with extra goods piled on the roof and hanging by ropes on either side. This, Mr. Chandra explains, is partly the reason most of the cars we see around us have icons on the dash or hanging from the rearview mirror. He personally keeps an icon of Ganesh, the elephant-headed god of wisdom and learning, on his dashboard. He says Ganesh is also the remover of obstacles.

There are millions of deities in some traditions of Hinduism. The belief in one God is non-exclusive. Most Hindus believe in one supreme being, but also leave room for minor gods, including—sometimes—Jesus. I wonder if that kind of non-judgmental approach is how they've managed to have not only Hindus but Muslims and Christians and Buddhists and Sikhs and Jains all living relatively peacefully side by side for centuries. Except there was also the caste system, so I shouldn't romanticize. People are people everywhere, and underneath the skin, we're all capable of being ugly.

Watching the traffic as we approach the city, I decide that praying to everyone and anyone you can pray to suddenly makes perfect sense. But I have to agree with Mr. Chandra: deity of removing obstacles for the win.

India is not the calm, relaxed place of my yoga-influenced preconceptions. It's the opposite of relaxation. It's a kaleidoscope of color with beauty, ugliness, opulence, poverty, noise, motion, and unexpectedness all thrown together like it's been mixed up in a blender and fighting for attention. In front of us, there's a scooter occupied by a man, a woman in a bright green *saree*, a stack of hay, two milk canisters, and a chicken. The woman is riding sidesaddle with a briefcase on her lap, the bale of hay is strapped to a rack above the scooter's rear wheel, and the milk canisters are hung on either side. The chicken is in a crate.

"What do you suppose the hay is for?" Malcolm asks me, leaning closer.

I shake my head, but I'm more interested in the engineering required to make all that work. "Maybe it just makes extra room for the chicken crate."

"People in India are very good at solving problems," Mr. Chandra says, laughing and looking back at us over his shoulder. "We are also very good at making room. Room to pass other cars, room for extra passengers, room for extra cargo."

He points out a bicycle rickshaw with a load of crates stacked so high I can't actually see the driver. I'm not sure how much the driver sees, either, or how he can possibly carry that much. No wonder people standing at the side of the road seem to be praying while they wait to cross between gaps in vehicles of every possible decade, continent, and income bracket. Not to mention motorcycles, scooters, bicycles, bicycle rickshaws, the three-wheeled *tuk-tuks*, overloaded trucks, tractors, ox-carts, and donkeys. Mixed in around the fringes there are also goats, pigs, monkeys, and random chickens milling around and an occasional sacred cow with a death wish strolling down the street.

I stare out the windows until the traffic zooming at us gets to be too nerve-inducing, and when I look around the car again, Mr. Chandra and Ian seem to be chatting as if they've known each other for weeks. Malcolm reaches over and squeezes my hand. He doesn't say anything. He doesn't even look at me in that smug way boys do that makes them feel superior. Which makes me like him even more. And since I don't want to sit here having unbrotherly thoughts about my maybe-brother, and I definitely don't want to watch the traffic, I turn back to the window and concentrate *really* hard on watching the women in bangle bracelets and jewel-colored *sarees* who are working on a road crew wielding shovels and pick-axes and carrying buckets of gravel on their heads. Everywhere I look, *sarees* and the long tunic, scarf, and trouser combinations called *salwar kameez* make bright spots of color that draw the eyes.

India is the definition of brilliant, if brilliant means vivid and alive and unexpected and thought-provoking. There are stories everywhere in the world, obviously, but here they are packed into every square inch of space, and the more I look around, the more I want to spin like a top with my arms wide open and soak in every sight and sound and experience.

Time

The hotel gates are draped with yellow hibiscus and bright purple bougainvillea, and the structure itself looks like a palace complete with arched windows and walkways, marble statues, and dozens of fountains outside the lobby.

At least fifteen people greet us in the traditional *namaste* greeting I know from yoga. Palms together, a valet bows when he opens the door to the car, a bellman bows on the steps, a doorman bows at the door, porters and reception workers bow in the elaborate jasmine-scented marble foyer beneath its high gold dome and crystal chandeliers. A woman in a *saree* paints our foreheads with a sandalwood *tilak* for auspiciousness and prosperity. Everyone stands palms together, bowing slightly, smiling, which seems to be what they do for everyone. But Mr. Singh, the general manager, comes to meet us at the reception desk himself. That might not be quite as normal.

He's gesturing and suddenly everyone in the place has taken on a whole different level of attentiveness.

"We are very pleased to be having you stay with us, Lord Mortimer, Lord Halford, Miss." He bows to Ian and Malcolm and me in turn.

Ian coils in on himself and his eyes don't blink. Then he smiles with exquisite politeness. "I thought I'd made the reservation simply as Dr. Halford."

"It is not very often that we receive a reservation for someone with the same name as both the address and the city," Mr. Singh says, smiling. "Our employees are vigilant."

"They certainly are," Ian says. "Well, thank you. We're very pleased to be here, but perhaps we could keep all that a little quiet? Would that be possible?"

"Incognito? Certainly Lord—*Doctor* Halford." Mr. Singh smiles widely, as if the idea amuses him.

With a nod that inclines his entire upper body forward, he escorts us to the elevators, past an oil diffuser that makes the corridor smell of jasmine, and takes us upstairs himself. Instead of unlocking the door, he knocks, and the suite is opened from inside by a man in a traditional long tunic in white and red with a red turban that drapes down his back. He introduces the man as Ravijeet, our private butler.

I never even saw the butler at Halford Hall. Which I guess made it easier to ignore the fact that, even though Halford needs repairs and has to pay its way, doesn't mean that Ian isn't stinking rich. Rich-rich, just not grand house in the country rich. How did that not sink in? Malcolm—*Viscount* Halford—is probably totally used to three-bedroom hotel suites with private butlers.

I most definitely am *not*.

It's not that Mom and I didn't have money, or that—in classical music circles, at least—she wasn't treated like a celebrity. She was, but this is a whole different level. She was the basement of celebrities and Ian's the floor below the penthouse.

He and Malcolm apparently think my reaction to all this is funny. The two of them watch me as I look around, both of them wearing these matching indulgent grins as though they're watching a kid eating an ice cream cone for the very first time.

Ravijeet shows us three separate bedrooms and four bathrooms, plus a kitchen, television room, dining room, and living room, all of which have marble or teakwood flooring carpeted with beautiful throw rugs and wall-to-wall windows that open out onto a terrace that overlooks the garden. He walks without so much as a squeak of his shoes as he takes us out there to show us the views of the Taj Mahal.

Through a faint haze that lends everything a magical sort of shimmer, the Taj looks close enough to touch, its high dome rising above the smaller domes and four minarets that float like a mirage above the trees.

"Is this how you expected it to look?" Ian asks me, pausing beside me as I stare.

I think about the fact that my mother was going to come here with Ian on her honeymoon, and my breath hitches and my chest hurts because she didn't, and now she never will. It seems so wrong to be doing something that my mother never had the chance to do. To be here when she isn't.

I wonder if Ian feels that, too. He must, but he's worried about *my* expectations.

I want to tell Malcolm he's lucky that his father is still alive, that they're both lucky they have time to mend whatever is broken between them.

They have *time*.

"It's all so much more," I say in answer to what he asked. "What about you?"

He glances from me to Malcolm and back, and there's a suspiciously bright gleam to his eyes. "More than I've dared to hope for in far too long." He pauses, breathlessly, and I can see pain written in the shuttering of his face and hear it in the tightening of his voice as he says more quietly, "Thank you both for coming with me."

Shock

I'm dressed in a soft, patterned robe, drying my tangled hair in the bathroom. It's not until I turn the dryer off that I realize someone is pounding on the door. I run to answer.

Malcolm is pale, his eyes wide and laced with the kind of panic that is very anti-Malcolm. "Something's wrong with Dad. We have to go to the hospital—the ambulance is meeting us downstairs."

"Go. I'll be right behind you."

I hold my robe closed with one hand and run to the bed to grab my clothes, and by the time I turn, Malcolm's gone already, his feet thudding on the floor.

I dive into my clothes and don't even bother

putting on my shoes before racing after him. He and Ravijeet are just helping Ian into the elevator as I round the corner, so I don't bother going after them. I charge down the stairs instead, but there's no ambulance outside yet. Mr. Chandra pulls up with the car as I race out the door, and I'm just in time to catch up as everyone bundles Ian into the back seat. I climb in front and all the doors slam at once, and Mr. Chandra is talking on his phone as he pulls away.

Ian's face is sweaty and pale, and he's gripping his arm. He's breathing hard and fast, and his eyes are closed. He slumps against Malcolm's shoulder. Malcolm keeps telling him to relax, that it's going to be all right, but I can see by the look on Malcolm's face that he doesn't believe it.

He glances up at me, and my chest squeezes, and this is what I'm thinking:

1. Ian can't die. He can't.
2. I jinxed him—I caused all this by thinking there was time.
3. I don't want Malcolm to feel the way I feel.
4. I should have seen this. The clues have been here since the moment I met Ian. He hasn't been feeling well.
5. I gave him a shock by showing up out of the blue, so this is all my fault.

6. Ian's a doctor, so why didn't he know he was sick?

7. Ian's a doctor. He knew. He knew, but this time with Malcolm matters so much that he ignored what he knew.

8. This has to be what Anna wanted him to say to Malcolm. So Anna also knew.

9. Please God, don't let Malcolm realize any of this, because he'll feel awful.

10. Please God, don't let Ian die.

Malcolm
Broken Hearts

I should have seen this coming. Dad should have seen this coming.

Of course he must have, but this time with Izzy clearly mattered more. Either that or he's ready to give up like a coward and die of a broken heart. Or all he cares about is reliving some mad fantasy of his time with Marcella Cavalera. Or both.

His breath is hot, and his skin is clammy and cool as he turns his head and tugs my sleeve. "Malcolm," he says. "Listen to me."

"Don't try to talk. Save your strength."

"This is important. Critical."

I ache to shake him. I want to take back every spiteful, selfish, and blistering thing I've ever said to him or thought about him, but instead of saying that, instead of saying that I love him, I hear myself spilling more bitterness into the air between us as though I cannot help myself.

"Can't you do the sensible thing for once and bloody well shut up? There'll be time enough to say whatever needs to be said."

He closes his eyes. I swallow hard and wish I could take it back. If I could, I'd rewind the past eight years of my life.

"Sorry, Dad," I say. "Of course, I'm listening."

Instead of my father's voice, though, I hear the wail of the ambulance siren as we swing around a corner, its lights flashing toward us, winding between the cabs and cars and precariously laden *tuk-tuks*. Mr. Chandra screeches the Merc to a stop and flings his door open to jump out and wave his arms until he flags it down.

The medics strap Dad onto a gurney and try to fit an oxygen mask over his mouth and nose whilst he struggles to push it away.

"Whatever happens," he says to me, "you're my son, Malcolm. Remember that and know I love you. Never forget it." He catches my wrist and fights to draw me closer.

The medics try to hold him still so they can run their tests. They separate us forcibly, and I stand aside until they load him inside the ambulance. Buttons pop on his shirt. The men work in tandem attaching electrodes to Dad's chest, and he lies back with the mask in place. His eyes watch me, wide, worried, and urgent.

I feel far away and helpless. *He* looks helpless with his thin chest bare and the wiry hair on it sparse and gray. I don't know when that happened. How did I not see that he was ill? How have I missed so much?

He's still watching me. Tears leak from the corners of his eyes. I'll never get used to seeing my father cry. How can I bear to see it?

Izzy
Longing

There's a moment as Ian and Malcolm are forced apart where the realization that they can't reach each other is etched on both their faces. This is what longing looks like, the kind of longing that's written in regret and lost opportunities and broken hearts.

Mr. Chandra waits with me at the hospital until Malcolm comes back to us, and it's a long wait that feels infinite. I fill it with conversation and questions, both spoken and silent, and the kind that can be answered and the kind that probably can't.

I jump to my feet when Malcolm comes through a double door. It seems odd that he can look five years older in the space of hours. He's still himself but also *not*, and I try to imagine what it would do to him to suddenly not have Ian, to have no more time with his father the way I suddenly had no more time with Mom. To have the full weight of Halford and all that responsibility crash onto his shoulders.

It sinks in for the first time that Ian had that happen when he wasn't much older than Malcolm is now. At Malcolm's age, Ian kept Halford from becoming a hotel filled with elegant and impersonal rooms and people who had no connection to all the stories and history and life that had taken place within its walls.

I wonder if my mother really understood that.

I wonder if it made any difference. To either of them.

Malcolm and I meet in the middle of the room. We pause, awkward and unsure, and our hands reach out and then our arms. I'm not sure which of us needs it more, but now we're holding each other and holding tight, our hearts turned to wild creatures clawing at our chests in fear.

"It's a heart attack," Malcolm says. "Obviously. He knew he had some blockages, and he was supposed to have a procedure in London—that's why he was there."

"But he came back because I showed up," I say. My tongue feels too thick to fit inside my mouth, and my throat is parched.

"He came back because I called him. He thought the procedure could wait a week. I should have seen it. I should have said coming here was a stupid idea."

I wince at that. "He begged me to go along with

it. He wanted to make sure the two of you were all right before we figured out DNA tests and whatever. He didn't want you running back to Oxford."

"What?" Malcolm stares at me. "He said he wanted to get to know *you* before you could escape to America."

We stare at each other, and I say, "We're idiots. All three of us."

"Possibly runs in the family," Malcolm says, which is like a cold splash of water poured over both of us, and we step quickly back to a safer distance.

"So what happens now?" I ask.

He crosses his arms, creating a physical barrier between us, and the dark whirl of confusion in his eyes is hauntingly familiar—I've seen it in the mirror every day since the moment Mrs. Gupta interrupted my English class. I sigh and steer him over to the chair beside Mr. Chandra and tell him to sit and breathe. When he finally relaxes, I thread my hand through his because he needs someone. I had Elli and her parents, and he has no one.

It's not dangerous to touch him, I tell myself. It's a gesture to offer comfort, pure and simple. But his skin is electric and rough on mine, and he stares down at where our hands are pressed together and then we both look away as if we don't see it, the contact won't be there. Neither of us moves.

Waiting

The hospital looks the same as any other hospital, except some of the floors are made of marble instead of linoleum or tile, which makes it echo differently. The coronary care unit reminds me of intensive care where my mother died. Where I let her die. There's the same hospital stench of lemon cleaner that can't completely mask the odor of the things they tried to clean away. The nurses wear the same ominously sympathetic expressions, and they speak in the same hushed voices.

There's a nurse at the station by the doors to the surgical ward. She's small-boned and short, with long hair rolled in a bun and a blue uniform buttoned all the way to the neck. Each time we check in with her, she taps a keyboard and peers at a computer screen and says Ian's surgery hasn't finished yet but Dr. Asrani will come out whenever they're done.

We go back to the waiting room again. It's crowded and loud, and it smells faintly of curry spices. A couple dozen people look up every time the door swings open, their faces eager and afraid. The tenth or eleventh time this happens, Malcolm snatches my hand and drags me out to the corridor where he gulps air as if he can't breathe. He steps aside, bumps into me, and swings around to brace his back against the wall.

"I can't stay in there." He stares at the floor a moment, then pushes away from the wall and starts to pace. "It's taking much longer than Dr. Asrani said. Something had to have gone wrong."

I shrug, because I don't have an answer.

Malcolm does a lot more pacing. I prop up the wall and watch him, but the walking doesn't seem to make him feel better. Eventually I go to him and grab both his hands, rooting him in place.

"Stop it," I say. "You're not going to outrun what's happening by wearing a path in the floor."

His breath hitches. "What if he dies, Izzy? What if I never get a chance to say all the things I should have told him?"

"He's your father. He already knows all those things, and he's not worried about whatever happened in the past. Trust me. That's not what parents care about. He just wanted to see you. He wanted you to know how much he loves you."

I wish I'd been able to give that to Mom. A few last words. Last moments together. Did she even know I was there with her?

"He wanted to tell me something, and I didn't let him. No different than all the rows we've ever had before—all the arguing we've done, I never truly listened to him. Never given him a proper hearing."

Malcolm slides down the wall into a crouch, forearms draped across his knees. His hands look strong but also helpless, and he stares at them as if he realizes they have the wrong kind of strength.

I lower myself beside him. "That's part of being a kid. We think parents expect too much from us, but maybe we expect too much from them. We don't think of them as people with dreams and human failings; we expect them to have the answers. Maybe they don't."

Malcolm casts me a sideways look. "I've been sorting through my memories these last few days, ever since I read your mother's letters. I find myself wondering what I missed whilst I was growing up. What I didn't see. I was too filled with rage when Mum died, as though all her anger had transferred itself to me on top of my own. All the anger over Ginny, anger over what Mum had said. I accepted every accusation she'd made, and each time my father played your mother's music all these years, it felt as though he was killing Mum all over again."

"It can't have been easy for you."

"No." Malcolm shakes his head. "He used to sit in the reading room, staring into the fire and playing her recordings. He had them on albums, the old vinyl kind in the sleeves. I hated them so much that I went in and smashed every one of them when he was called into the hospital one night. After that, we were both happy for me to go off to school. It was easier after that. English boarding schools were invented specifically so parents and children can avoid ever needing to have actual, meaningful conversations. I was gone most of the year and when I came home on hols, all we ever spoke about was sports and Halford."

His profile is as sharp as a knife, and I can see the regret that's slicing him open. I look away.

"You know," Malcolm continues, "he told me the other day that Mum knew about your mother before they were married. She knew what she was getting into—knew he could never love her—and she agreed to marry him anyway. It was only supposed to be about the money. Hers was supposed to help him save Halford, but then she fell in love with him and she spent all those years watching him wish she was your mother. Knowing she never could be."

Hot tears make my eyes blur, and I blink them away. Hearing that makes it somehow even worse: I think of Malcolm's mother longing for Ian, him longing for my mother while doing his duty to Halford, my mother longing for him but choosing her gift instead. All three of them living with the bitterness of their choices and paying the price, day in and day out.

I can see why Malcolm was angry. And even if she knew going into the marriage, it doesn't change how hurt his mother must have been.

For the first time in years, I think of Katie Pearson, who moved next door to Elli in seventh grade. She was fun—nice—at first. She followed us everywhere, sat with us at lunch, asked herself to the pool. Elli and I didn't mind at first. We both invited her for sleepovers a few times, and we went to the Snowflake Dance together that year. But Elli and I were still Elli and I—we had each other, which was all we needed. The more Katie saw that, though, the more she resented that she didn't have it with Elli herself. She started hating me, and I walked into school one day and found the word "slut" scrawled on my locker in magic marker and rumors being whispered. Katie had known Elli and I were best friends the whole time, but she'd convinced herself she could make Elli her own best friend instead. When she couldn't, it made her hate us both.

Hope is the one thing you can't guard against when it comes to relationships. Hearts are built for hope.

My Katie story feels too seventh grade to share with Malcolm, but I want him to know I understand. And there's another example right in front of us.

"Have you heard the legend of the Taj Mahal?" I ask.

He gives me a slanted look and leans his shoulder against the wall. "Are you trying to distract me? I'm sorry. I'm being a self-indulgent wanker."

"No, you're fine. It's just something I was thinking."

I can see the effort it takes for him to smile. "All

right. Tell me about the Taj Mahal. I'm sure you have a version I haven't read."

Izzy's History of the Taj Mahal

In 1606, the son of the Mughal emperor, who ruled what is now India, Pakistan, and Bangladesh, fell in love while walking through a bazaar in Agra. The boy was only fourteen, and his nickname was Khurram, which meant joyous, and before he was born, the soothsayers had predicted he was destined for greatness. The girl was a Persian princess with long dark hair, smoldering eyes, and a gift for making intelligent bargains.

Khurram trailed her through the market, watching as she haggled over ruby silks and carpets as soft as a breath, over glowing lamps, and engraved gold bangles. Their eyes met again and again from distances that grew ever smaller as Khurram rushed to catch up. His thoughts of the girl became a fire inside him that he could not quench. But she was rushed away before they could spend time together, and he returned to the palace scheming about how soon he could see her again. He haunted the bazaar until she appeared. And very quickly he told his father he intended to marry the girl he came to call Mumtaz Mahal, his jewel, his chosen one. Khurram's father eventually agreed, but that was not all that was required for a wedding. The occasion needed an alignment of the stars. Wise and holy men toiled to divine the date that would be the most auspicious, and so the two lovers waited five long years to marry.

In the meantime, his father reminded him, Khurram could not remain unwed. He had his duty to perform, and so he was given other brides to fulfill the obligations and alliances the Mughal empire needed. For the sake of his people and their future, Khurram did as he was bidden, and his wives all lived in the palace in great luxury with their families elevated in status. But it was Mumtaz who remained his only love while he waited to wed her, the one who heard his secrets and kept them safe.

Poets wrote about Mumtaz, about her beauty, grace, intelligence, and generosity to the poor. Khurram's wives saw none of that. Some grew more bitter with every poem. Every word spoken in favor of Mumtaz Mahal became a dagger that pierced their hearts, and there were many such wounds through the years, both before Mumtaz and Khurram were wed and after.

Mumtaz only grew more and more beloved. Khurram set about to fulfill his destiny, and he entrusted Mumtaz with the great seal of the realm, giving her a role in governing. She helped him design and build many of the most beautiful structures in the empire, advised him on military campaigns, and traveled with him wherever he went. With her help, Khurram soon became known as Shah Jahan, the King of the World, and in his reign the

Mughal Empire was the most productive of any nation on the globe.

But after seventeen years of marriage, Mumtaz died giving birth to their fourteenth child. Since they had so rarely been apart, she was afraid that Khurram would follow her into death as well, so, to give him purpose while he grieved, Mumtaz asked him to make her three promises as she lay dying. First, that he should be kind and mindful of their children. Second, that he should try to find love again. And third, that he should build her a monument more beautiful than any they had already built together, one more beautiful than any other in the world, and that he should visit her there each year on the anniversary of her death.

Khurram grieved so deeply that his hair and beard turned white almost overnight. For twenty-two years after Mumtaz died, he dedicated his treasury and 20,000 of the finest craftsmen in the world to building the Taj Mahal from translucent white marble inlaid with flowers and scripture of carnelian, jade, obsidian, turquoise, lapis, and precious gems. He made the Taj as perfect as his love for Mumtaz, as subtle and balanced and full of unexpectedness. And when he was finished, he began work on a second, identical monument for himself across the river, and the two were to be connected by a bridge that symbolized the way his soul and hers were two sides of one great love.

This, however, was not to be.

Khurram fell ill before he could finish, and through those long years of his happiness and the madness of his monument to love, the bitterness and jealousy his other wives felt had become a poison throughout the palace with even some of his own children resenting the love he bore Mumtaz Mahal. With Khurram weakened, the youngest of his sons seized power and locked Khurram in the Red Fort of Agra. For nine long years, Khurram lay in his bed by the tower window, tended only by his loyal daughter and gazing over the city at the Taj day by day and night by night, knowing he could never visit again or fulfill the promise he had made to Mumtaz. Not until the day he was ready to join her in death himself.

So great was the jealousy and hatred his love of Mumtaz had awoken that in his final hour even a funeral procession befitting a Mughal emperor was denied Khurram. Despite his many achievements, the King of the World was laid to rest quietly in the mausoleum built for his beloved bride, with no one but his daughter to mourn him. Those who hated him soon forgot him, and even the great Mughal empire crumbled into dust. Thanks to the Taj Mahal, though, the love between Khurram and Mumtaz survived beyond them all. It survived the death of the empire and the birth of one century after another. And still today, the Taj Mahal remains the most beautiful testament to love that was ever built.

Brown Sauce

Malcolm sits cross-legged on the cool, white marble in the corridor beside me, his head tipped back against the wall, his hands draped across his knees. "I don't come across very well in that story, do I? Is that how you see me?"

I hug my own knees closer to my chest. "That was Khurram's story, not yours. It's all about point of view. I could have highlighted different facts and made the son the hero of the history instead. In that version, Khurram spent too much money building monuments while ignoring his subjects. He killed the architect who designed the Taj Mahal and cut off the hands of the finest craftsmen in the realm so that no one could ever make a building more beautiful than his. In that version, his son was only saving the empire from his father's grief."

"I don't like either version very much."

"The point is, the heart wants what it wants. Love can make anyone blind, selfish, and cruel when it comes to how much suffering we inflict around us. Your father loved your mother as much as he could and tried to do right by her, the way Khurram tried to do right by his other wives. There are degrees of love, I think. Maybe grand loves come along once in a lifetime, if we're very lucky, but most people settle for smaller loves out of loneliness or convenience.

Unless you've had the other kind and know the difference, that's probably enough to make a happy life. But our parents knew. They knew, and your mother saw that, and she changed the rules by falling in love with Ian, too, and they all trapped themselves a fury of love and hate and longing."

"I could forgive him if he hadn't cheated."

"We can't know how hard it was. And your father is only human. They all were. It's human to make mistakes."

Malcolm's silent. Then the door to the surgical suite opens and a doctor in blue scrubs emerges, his steps too slow. He passes us and pauses at the door to the waiting room as if he's gathering strength.

I have a theory about people delivering news. There are basically two types: the kind who hurry to get bad news over with, and the kind who try to put it off. I'm not surprised to hear the burst of crying that erupts a moment later. Malcolm's hand reaches back out for mine. I feel every inch of warm skin, every point of contact.

What if the doctor comes out with bad news for Malcolm, too?

"You have to forgive Ian," I whisper. "Right now. Right this second. You have to let everything go. If you don't, you'll hurt yourself more than you hurt him."

"He tried to be a good father. I don't think I let him."

"The priest hole and the cars?"

He nods and his brows knit together. "Brown sauce. Jesus. There's another thing I haven't thought about in years."

"I don't understand."

"Brown sauce is something we eat with chips. Like ketchup, although you'd probably think it was more like American steak sauce." Malcolm rubs a hand across the back of his neck, shifting toward me. His body angles around until the knees of his jeans nearly touch my thigh.

He tells me the brown sauce story, and I can picture them so clearly, Ian and a twelve-year-old Malcolm, his jawline softer, his cheeks rounded, and his hair just darkening from blond to brown. Malcolm is standing at his mother's funeral, wearing a navy suit with the sleeves too long. It's raining and his father tries to hold an umbrella over him, but Malcolm wants nothing to do with that. He stands by himself, his shoulders tight and his fists clenched against the world.

He is soaking wet when the service is over, and when they leave the chapel, he runs off by himself, all the way back to the Hall and straight upstairs to his room, water streaming from the tips of his shoes. He slams the door and huddles on his bed, knees drawn up while he shivers. Ian brings up a tray with cake and a bacon sandwich and sets it down where Malcolm can reach it.

"He tried to talk to me, but I covered my ears and

shouted at him to leave," Malcolm says. "He sat on the floor with his back to the wall and read a book, neither of us saying a word for hours. It drove me insane, but I was determined I wasn't going to be the one to break the silence first. Of course, I did. I told him to go away. Yelled that I didn't want him. He said that was fine, but that even shouting was better than silence, and he wanted to be sure I understood that he'd always be there, to yell at or talk to or anything else, whenever—if ever—I changed my mind. He said he'd be right outside the door for as long as it took. Then he pointed to the bottle on the tray beside me and said fathers are like brown sauce. Sometimes you want it with your bacon sandwich, and sometimes you don't, but it's always good to know you have the option."

"What did you do?"

"Nothing. I tiptoed around my room all night, peering beneath the door to see if I could spot his shoes outside."

"And they were always there?"

"Yes, until Anna dragged me down for breakfast. Izzy, what if I've left it all too late?"

I pick up both Malcolm's hands and hold them until he looks at me, ignoring the sizzle of energy between us. I won't say it's going to be all right.

People die. Parents die. I've sure learned that the hard way. I hope Malcolm doesn't have to learn it yet.

"My mother once told me Hindus believe the ideas formed in the mind or heart power the whole karmic structure of the universe," I say. "Maybe we have to believe in the outcome we want to happen. Believe as hard as we can. Harder than we've ever believed before."

"I want to believe."

"Faith is faith, Mal. You believe or you don't. Either way, the kind of man who tells you he is brown sauce wouldn't want you sitting here feeling guilty. Stop it."

Malcolm looks at me and gives a rueful smile. "Did anyone ever mention that you're bossy?"

"You should meet my best friend, Elli. You'd see what bossy really looks like."

"I'd like to meet her," Malcolm says. "Since she's your best friend."

We become aware at the same time that we're sitting very close and staring into each other's eyes, and Malcolm clears his throat as we pull our hands apart. I didn't think it was possible to feel as connected to anyone as I feel to Mom and Elli, but Malcolm has slipped in while I wasn't looking. I wonder if that's because he's my brother, or because he's something else.

Tipping my head back against the beige wall of the corridor, I watch the people coming and going in the waiting room, watch the procession of street shoes or rubber-soled hospital shoes. The corridor is full of people, but I feel like there is only me and Malcolm and, somewhere on a surgery table, a man I desperately want to know better.

I hope the universe is listening.

> Text to Elli:
>
> Me: Is there a limit to how many emotions a person can hold all at once? Or do you eventually just pop like a balloon?
>
> Elli: Your skin is tougher than you think. But I'm here any time you need to vent.

Recovery

Accompanied by a middle-aged nurse, Dr. Asrani, the surgeon, comes to speak with Malcolm. The doctor's blue hat is puffed awkwardly over graying hair, and his surgical mask is pulled down below his chin. I try to convince myself that the stoop of his shoulders is due to fatigue and not defeat as he comes toward us.

He directs a quizzical look at me before he speaks. I don't know how to introduce myself.

"This is Isabelle," Malcolm says, slipping his hand in mine and dragging me forward. "She's family."

Dr. Asrani gives a distracted nod. "I am sorry

to say there were complications with your father's surgery."

He goes on to explain the technicalities, but words like "bypass" and "damaged muscle" are basically the only words I understand. Malcolm's grip on my hand is painful when Dr. Asrani mentions that Ian could possibly need yet another surgery. I extract my fingers and loop my arm through Malcolm's, not sure which of us I'm trying to prop up, knowing only that we're stronger together.

"Another surgery for what?" Malcolm asks.

"We will know more in the next several days," Dr. Asrani says, "and then we can discuss the options. You could consider donating blood. Your father will be in the recovery room for some time now, and it will be several hours before you can see him. You should always rest and eat while you can. It will be a long recovery."

Malcolm and I stand in the corridor looking at each other after the nurse and Dr. Asrani walk away. The silence contains relief and gratitude, uncertainty and fear.

"You should go back to the hotel for a couple of hours and take a nap," Malcolm says. "There's no point in both of us hanging around."

"I'd like to stay with you."

We walk to the waiting room side by side. We're not touching, but I feel as if we are, as if there's a thread that ties us together, that makes our arms swing in unison even when there's a foot between us. I wonder if Malcolm feels it, too.

Only a few days ago, I learned Ian might be my father. I can't bear the thought of losing him, of losing the possibility. On the other hand, the more time I spend with Malcolm, the more I feel conflicted.

The heart wants what it wants, though. I want Ian to be healthy. Beyond that, I want what I shouldn't more and more with every passing minute.

———◆❋◆———

March 18, 1999

Dear Ian,

I gave birth to a perfect little girl today. I didn't know I could make so much room in my heart, but when I held her for the first time and she looked at me, love filled me like the fiercest, most insistent music. How I wish you could hold her for yourself.

You looked so dispirited when I left you. So little of this situation is as it should be. It is not the two of us, together, holding our children, looking forward to more children. Yet when I see this beautiful child, I can't regret a thing.

Don't be sad. I hope you aren't. I hope you are finding it in you to have joy in the life you've chosen. I do not blame you for your choices. Not anymore. Looking down at Isabelle when the nurse settled her in my arms, I vowed to find joy in life outside of music, too. To find joy in Isabelle's every moment.

I hope you listen to joyful music. That will help.

Love always,

Cella

—◆❈◆—

Izzy's Playlist of Joyful Music

1. Pitney/Tchaikovsky: The Nutcracker Suite for Piano
2. Haydn: Symphony No. 94 in G 'Surprise' Menuetto
3. Rossini: Barber of Seville Overture
4. Strauss: Blue Danube Waltz
5. Chopin: Raindrop Prelude
6. Dvorak: Symphony No. 8 Scherzo

—◆❈◆—

Malcolm's Playlist of Joyful Music

1. Beach Boys: Good Vibrations
2. Redbone: Come and Get Your Love
3. U2: Beautiful Day
4. Edwin Hawkins Singers: Oh, Happy Day
5. Queen: Don't Stop Me Now
6. Counting Crows: Accidentally in Love
7. Billy Joel: Uptown Girl
8. George Ezra: Blame It on Me

Izzy's Playlist of Joyful Music Version 2.0

1. The Zombies: Care of Cell 44
2. George Ezra: Paradise
3. Redbone: Come and Get Your Love
4. Cheryl Crow: If It Makes You Happy
5. Hanson: MMMBop
6. Katrina and the Waves: Walking on Sunshine
7. Abba: Dancing Queen
8. Lauryn Hill: The Hymn of Joy

Outside

We listen to music on Malcolm's phone, sharing a single set of headphones, and sometimes we talk. Mostly we wait and watch people come and go around us. It's three and a half hours before a nurse pushes through the doors and looks around. I didn't realize how much we stand out until she walks straight toward us in the crowded room.

She's fine-boned and beautiful, with huge eyes and long lashes and dark, dewy skin. Malcolm jumps to his feet and goes to meet her.

Her smile is wide and it includes us both, but when she speaks she looks at Malcolm. "Your father is awake now, if you would like to go in for a moment."

Malcolm starts to follow her, but I hang back. "I think I'll wait here," I say, feeling awkward and in the way. "You go see him. Say whatever you need to say to him—don't miss out on the opportunity, Malcolm. I mean it."

He stiffens and then, with a visible effort, makes himself relax. "He isn't going to die—he won't. And you're part of this now as well."

The coronary care unit is a single room with glass doors that open onto a nurse's station fiercely guarded by a nurse with a stare that could slay dragons at fifty paces. That doesn't match the rest of her appearance, which is short and thin and fragile with long hair is rolled into an enormous bun. Beyond her, the beds are arranged in a horseshoe with curtains that are all pushed back. No one has any privacy. The nurse lets in visitors two at a time, so there are family members waiting in the corridor. Inside, they sit or stand beside their loved ones, the reds and yellows and greens of the women's *sarees* like small rebellions against all the white and beige of the walls and beds and curtains. A determined beauty.

The machines are too familiar, emitting the same weird rhythmic sounds that remind you they seem more alive than the patients hooked up to them, the hushed steadiness of the ventilators punctuated by beeps and the rattle of instruments, the faint squish and squeak of the nurse's rubber soles in constant motion. We thread the gauntlet of overflowing family members, and Malcolm's hands are in his pockets so that his shoulders are hunched as if he's expecting to receive a blow. Another one. Then he lifts his head and smiles at me.

That's all it takes. My heart twists.

Which is awful.

It should be wonderful to feel this swirl of emotions, this sense of falling. But what if I was right? What if the takeaway from Mumtaz and Khurram's story, from Mom and Ian's story, is that you only find your someone special once in a lifetime, and that only if you're lucky? What if it turns out that Malcolm is supposed to be that person, and I can't let myself feel anything for him?

I should stop myself.

I'm trying. I don't know how to try any harder.

Malcolm and I approach the bed together. Ian is weak, but he holds out his hands for both of us. "I'm sorry about all this. Clearly, I'm more prone to miscalculating than I'd care to admit even to myself."

"You're human," Malcolm says, "and maybe it makes sense you'd have a broken heart."

Ian's eyes widen and lock on Malcolm's. For a long time, they look at each other, then Ian's eyes fall shut, and they're liquid with tears when he opens them again. "Could you forgive me, Mal? For all of it?"

Malcolm stands tall and straight, and then he drops to his knees so that he's not looming over his father. Very quietly he says, "There's nothing you need to ask me to forgive."

Falling

I've never done this before
Never caught myself falling
Feelings so deep
I can't see the bottom
I could fall with you
Fall into you
So deep that
I'll disappear into us.

Isabelle Cavalera

Trouble

Text to Elli:

Me: Hug your parents and your brothers.
Tell them you love them.

Elli: Have you been drinking?

Me: I had some tea. Chai. It tasted nothing
like Starbucks. It didn't taste like much.

Elli: Acquired taste?

Me: The chai may be the only thing under-
whelming in all of India. I wish you were
here.

Elli: Me, too. Can I do anything for you?

Me: Remember that Kleenex you offered
me a while ago? Have it ready.

Elli: Hurry.

Coward

It's not quite dark when Mr. Chandra drives us back
to the hotel, but the nurses suggested that both we
and Ian need to rest. I passed out giving blood, which
made me feel like an idiot. The nurse told me not to
look next time. She said that nine times out of ten, as
long as the person doesn't see the blood, they won't
faint even if they're squeamish. I hate the idea of a
next time, because that implies that Ian will need
more blood. More surgery.

Out in the city, the traffic is dying down and the
monkeys are out, dark silhouettes scampering along
the tops of the walls and buildings. Women hurry
home with sacks of food, children in tow behind
them. The blare of horns seems even less patient
than before, and a taxi driver gets out ahead of us
to help someone push a broken down *tuk-tuk* from
the road.

Malcolm's unusually quiet, looking out the
window.

"You all right?" I ask.

He glances over, and his expression softens. "Relieved mostly. And sad that it took Dad having a heart attack to make me fully confront the fact that I'm a bloody ass."

"Really, you're only an average ass," I say, "considering what you heard your mother saying. You were too young to process all that."

"Which doesn't excuse all the years in between."

"He didn't have to send you off to boarding school."

"You don't know me well enough to know that yet."

The word *yet* hits me hard, and I think it hits him, too. The smile freezes on his face.

"I do," I say. "I think I know you already."

The braziers lining the driveway at the hotel are burning, and oil torches flicker throughout the grounds, sending up sooty smoke. Malcolm's eyes reflect that fire and his face reflects the darkness. "There's knowing facts and knowing the core of a person. They're not the same."

I turn away. "That's what scares me."

Our hands rest on the seat beside us, and we both move them simultaneously until our pinky fingers are only a half inch apart. That fatal half inch that feels like contact even when it isn't. Then we stop. Maybe we stop together, or maybe it's me reacting to him, or him reacting to me, but now there's an invisible barrier between us, as if acknowledging even this small piece of what I feel has turned possibilities into probabilities. Into disaster.

I'd go home right now, if I could. I'm a coward and staying is only going to destroy me. This is what Ian saw coming, though maybe—hopefully—he didn't foresee the reason. He must have realized that, at some point, I'd want to head for the nearest airport. Being here in India makes it harder.

Him in the hospital makes it impossible.

Malcolm and I return to the suite, and Ravijeet sets our supper out on a table on the terrace overlooking the fountains and the terraced pools that reflect the flames. A trio of Indian dancers twirls to music punctuated by their ankle bells. The sun turns the white marble of the Taj to gold and pink and crimson before the sky deepens to an indigo haze and the stars emerge.

"This is surreal," I say as Ravijeet leaves us. "As in it can't be happening. None of it."

The table overflows with dishes of *saag paneer*, which is spinach with Indian cheese, tandoori chicken, and tender crepe-like *masala dosas*, accompanied by plenty of *naan*, *raita*, and chutney.

Malcolm concentrates on holding the serving dishes for me, but as good as the food all looks and smells, neither of us is hungry. We're going through the motions. I can see that in the flatness of Malcolm's eyes.

"What will you do if it turns out we *are* related?" he asks.

, I swallow a bit of the soft *naan* bread, pretending that's what's responsible for the dryness in my throat. "I'll go home."

"No." The word comes out sharp and loud. Then he shakes his head. "You'd break Dad's heart all over again. And Halford would be your home. Literally. I don't know about the estate and all of that—but you'd be entitled to something."

I bite my lip, remembering the last conversation we had that touched on this, and I wonder if it's been in the back of his mind ever since. But I meant what I said at the time. I still mean it. "I don't want anything from you or Ian. I don't need it."

"You might change your mind. Money has a tendency to do that to people."

I look up, feeling as if he's hit me. "Is that what you really think I'm like?"

We stare at each other, and Malcolm slowly shakes his head. "No, but it's how other people are. Partly because estates like this are inherently unfair. If Ginny was still alive, we'd have been in the same situation, and I'm sure Dad would have sat us down and explained that it would all have to come to one of us, because that's the only way Halford can survive. The same person has to get the estate and the money and the title. The estate needs the money for upkeep, and these days, the title helps to bring in the tourists, which at least partly keeps the money from running out. Ginny couldn't have inherited the title, so..."

"So inherited institutional injustice."

"That's true, but it doesn't change anything."

I dig down to see if I can find resentment among the too many things I feel. I should feel resentful on Ginny's behalf. Why should it make so much difference that someone was born a girl or that she was born a few minutes or a few years later?

"If a woman can be queen, why can't she be an earl?" I say. "Or a duke, for that matter. Britain has had queens most of the last three centuries. You'd think they'd have changed the rules."

"Maybe there aren't many husbands who'd fancy themselves being called 'countess.' Much less 'lady,' in the case of a baron's other half. I don't see that's likely to change."

"Doesn't mean it shouldn't." I'm more than halfway serious, and I think we both know I am.

"It's hard work feeling like we should be outraged all the time, isn't it?" Malcolm says.

"What do you mean?"

"There's so much in the world that's unfair, and I want to change at least my corner of it—I'm trying to make it better. But half the people I meet want to be where I am and the other half are furious that people like me exist." He's very serious now, and even though what he said isn't anything I probably couldn't have figured out myself, there's something about the way he looks at me over the candles, as if he's forcing himself not to look away, that makes me feel like he's trusted me with a confidence that's precious and easily broken.

It's hard to know how to answer.

"Outrage can be addictive, can't it?" I manage finally. "It's easy and it binds people together, makes them feel as if they're not alone." Then I close my eyes, because if I let myself, I can be swallowed by my own outrage all too easily. By the need to voice a protest because I don't know how to really solve the problem, *a* problem, any problem. By *this* problem—the one that sits between me and Malcolm like a river of electricity.

"When my mother died," I continue, "it didn't seem right that the world hadn't changed as much as my life had changed. School was still school, and there were still people laughing, walking around enjoying themselves, being oblivious. People— even my friends—were still texting while they were driving. I'd see cars weaving on the road in front of me, and I'd know what they were doing. At every traffic light, I would notice girls with their heads bent, or men typing with the phone propped up against the steering wheel. And I'd want to snatch the phones out of their hands and see what was so damn important that they were willing to risk killing someone else while they were typing."

Malcolm reaches across the table and picks up my hand. I twitch back, skin burning, but he winds his fingers through my own. "Did you consider going to the media? People might listen since your mum was famous."

His touch is heat and ice all at once, like physical therapy for a sprain that's a deep-down ache. Only I doubt this ache will go away.

"If Mom had been a pop star or a lifestyle celebrity, maybe that would have helped. She was famous, but not famous enough. Who someone *is* will always matter to some people—it's how humans are wired. My point is that it isn't fair, but I understand what you're saying. You and Ian and Halford matter, though. People are fascinated by royals."

"There'd need to be an epidemic to make us that."

"There are only twenty earls in England. You could make a difference."

"You can make your mother's death matter, too. I'd help. And Dad."

"I'd like that." I smile, and then we look away, driven apart by uncertainty. By reality. Malcolm pulls back his hand.

I say, "He's going to be all right, Malcolm. He is. That's the part you have to remember." I say that, even though I don't have any right to say it.

Even though I've no idea if it's true.

Malcolm's fork clinks against the porcelain as he picks it up again. "Don't tell him you want to go home. Please? You can't tell him that."

I shake my head, not knowing what I mean by it, and Malcolm doesn't ask me for a clarification. We sit on the terrace in what's possibly the most romantic spot on earth, breathing in the heat of each other's breath, the incense and the spice of the food, the scent of night-blooming jasmine drifting up from the garden. We listen to the music and the dancer's bells.

The Taj Mahal glitters in the moonlight under a pincushion sky, and I feel closer to Malcolm than I would have thought it was possible to feel to anyone this fast. I also feel alone.

So, so alone.

Nutella

> Text to Elli:
>
> Me: I think my heart has gotten bigger and left more room for emptiness. And I don't know what will fill it up.
>
> Elli: I don't suppose Nutella would work?
>
> Me: This is even beyond Nutella. I wish you were here.

Elli: I wish you were here. I'd give you a
bathtub full of chocolate.

November II, 2011

Dear Ian,

Izzy asked about falling in love today. How one tells.

It made me remember the long, soft sigh of falling into
love with you. Poets speak of lightning bolts and the knowl-
edge of a single glance across a crowded room. I fell in love
with you between one poem and another, between one walk
and another. I fell in love with your thoughts, your touch,
your questions, your compassion.

Izzy and I are fine on our own. She is self-contained,
my darling Izzy. Even now her question is more curiosity
than personal interest. She will always be fine.

Me? I'm fine, too, mostly. But I miss you a hundred
times each day when I encounter a thought or an image or
a piece of music I want to share with you.

So many things I want to share. It's been too long since
I've seen you.

Always,

Cella

Malcolm
Moonlight

Moonlight is deadly, especially when the night carries all the scents from which perfumes are made. Drops of water from the fountains turn to prisms that tremble in the air, and the stars are glitter dust sprinkled across the night above the gleaming ghost dome of the Taj Mahal. The hotel gardens are draped in the kind of silence that doesn't require words.

I made the mistake of saying I didn't think I could sleep, so Izzy suggested walking. Our hands gravitate toward each other, and I try to tell myself that's only us being two frightened people in need of comfort. Still, I wonder whether any moment in my future will withstand the memory of walking here with her. Can I ever love someone else deeply enough to forget the magic of this place, this minute heavy with uncertainty and expectation? I'm beginning to understand how my father felt, and that's something I never thought I'd understand.

"I've been so caught up in myself I haven't stopped to ask you how you're doing with all of this," I say. "How do you feel?"

"Shocked," Izzy says. "A little numb."

We descend the steps to the pool and sit side by side, dangling our feet in water that's still as warm as a bathtub. I look up at the Taj and the stars, and Izzy stares down at the torchlight reflected on the moonlit water.

"I probably shouldn't have dragged you out here," I admit to her. "The truth is, I can't imagine doing any of this on my own, and I can't imagine anyone else I'd rather have here with me."

She studies me, and I can see she doesn't know whether I mean *here* in the garden, or here in India. I'm not certain myself.

Firelight glimmers on the water that runs off between her toes as she kicks her feet. She's only inches away, and I've never been so aware of skin and distance. I push my hands beneath my thighs and sit on them to keep from reaching for her.

"Was it like this with your mother? The waiting?" I ask. "How did you get through it?"

Izzy glances over, and I realize I've phrased the question so badly she can't possibly understand.

But she does somehow.

"Mom was brain-dead when they brought her to the hospital," she says. "I had to choose to let her die."

My every muscle twitches in reaction. "Izzy! Oh, Jesus. I can't imagine."

Her chin trembles, and then suddenly she's crying. I'm holding her, and both of us are shaking. Her head burrows into my chest and my chin rests on her hair, and she's warm and real and alive and so very deeply present I can't make myself pull away. Izzy is always very present.

She tilts her head up to look at me, her eyes turned to liquid honey and fire by moonlight, and in that moment, I know the meaning of faith. Because I know, I *know*, there is no force in the world cruel enough to make me feel this way about my sister. I couldn't. It would be a different sort of connection entirely. Something would warn me away from madness instead of whispering an invitation.

Blood

Blood speaks to blood. I'll swear that until my dying day.

I knew the instant when Ginny died, and though I hadn't suspected why, I'd felt an uneasy *wrongness* since waking up that morning. There was a village fete later, and Mum was in charge of organizing. But Ginny had a cold and a horrid cough, and when she said her head hurt and she felt tired, Mum couldn't cancel. I felt an echo of Ginny's pain myself, a twinge so muffled I was able to ignore it by pushing it far away. I didn't have any sympathy for her, or any patience. What was a headache when there were cakes and races and a bat-a-rat stall with prizes? I said she was only being a baby, and she said I was being a big fat pig, and I was glad when Mum and Dad left her with Anna and took me by myself.

I waited twenty minutes in line for the coconut shy, and I'd scarcely thrown the first of the wooden balls when I suddenly felt as though someone had thrown the ball directly at my head. I clutched my temples, and my father swears I screamed Ginny's name. He and Mum both came running, and when he'd pulled me to my feet, I insisted we needed to go home because something was the matter with Ginny.

He and Mum both told me I was wrong. I wasn't.

Human infants are born with a flap between the right and left atriums of the heart. In seventy-five percent of babies, that flap seals itself and never becomes a problem. Twenty-five percent of children, though, end up with a hole in their heart or a flap that never completely closes. Twenty-five percent. Almost none of them ever notice. It's only occasionally that the flap can open when people are straining hard. When they cough, and blood that hasn't passed through the lungs can carry blood clots out into the bloodstream. Sometimes, a blood clot can travel to the brain.

By the time Anna checked on her that afternoon, Ginny was unconscious and paralyzed, and she died before the ambulance reached the hospital.

We weren't identical twins. Perhaps if we had been, I'd have had a hole in my heart as well. That was what I kept asking everyone with various degrees of indignation and regret and accusation. Why didn't I have a hole in my heart instead of Ginny? Why her instead of me?

We weren't identical twins, but our blood was identical enough for me to feel her death.

I'd know if Izzy were my sister. I would.

I'd know.

Izzy
Freedom

There's music spun into the still moonlight of this garden, music and beauty and tragedy. The water sighs and birds cry softly in the trees. I look at Malcolm, and I want to pretend, I need to pretend, just for a moment, an instant. Is that so very wrong?

He turns me toward him until our knees touch at the edge of the pool, and then his hand is on my cheek. We stare at each other as if we're both trying to make enough memories to last for the rest of our lives. Just in case. At least that's how I feel. The human sounds of the hotel behind us recede into the background, and there's only the electricity I've been trying to keep grounded suddenly sizzling free and crackling between us.

"Whatever happens," Malcolm says, "promise me we won't stop being friends."

I think of feeling like this for the rest of my life. Having him close enough to touch while trying to pretend I don't want to touch him.

"No," I say. "Being friends with you might not be possible."

"Not being friends would be even more impossible." He releases a sigh that whispers across my skin. "This can't be wrong, Iz. Not the way I feel. I won't believe that fate or God or a million gods are cruel enough to make me feel like this if it could be wrong."

"Fate is cruel to a lot of people. All you have to do is look around to see that."

He draws me toward him, tipping my chin so that we're looking straight into each other's eyes. "If you don't feel what I'm feeling, that's one thing. If you choose not to be friends with me after we find out, I'll understand. If you eventually fall in love with someone who can give you a better, fuller life, I'll understand that, too. But if growing up with my father taught me anything, it's that feelings aren't convenient and they don't always go away. I can't imagine feeling this much without it rewiring something inside of me. And I refuse to consider hurting someone the way my mum was hurt. I refuse to hurt someone because of you."

A shiver brushes along my skin like the wake of a brush fire, and I shudder, then shudder again.

What do you say to a guy who tells you something like that?

How do you know what you feel unless you allow yourself to feel it?

I believe in stories. I believe in words. But these words I cannot say. They require action.

I catch Malcolm's face between my palms and claim his lips with mine. This might be the only time I'm ever going to get to kiss him again. Now, while I can still let myself believe that how I feel about him is all that matters. All that's true. That my interpretation of Mom's letters was wishful thinking driven by fate and loss and hope.

I no longer hope Ian is my father.

With all of my heart, I hope he isn't.

Most of my heart.

Well, part of it.

Time disappears, falls into the spaces between us while Malcolm and I are kissing. Everything I've tried to deny, all the electricity and loss and ache and want and need and *life* that poured into me through my open wounds bursts back out again and makes every nerve ending in my lips work overtime.

There are roughly 10,000 nerve endings in human lips. Kissing dilates blood vessels, sends extra oxygen to the brain, and releases an avalanche of different hormones and chemicals that change how we feel.

In German, there are more than thirty words for different kinds of kisses, including *nachküssen*, which is a kiss to make up for the kisses that haven't happened.

If Malcolm and I will never have another kiss, I want to be sure this one will be enough.

German Words for Kisses

1. Abschiedskuss: farewell kiss
2. Begüssungskuss: hello kiss
3. Bruderkuss: brotherly kiss
4. Bussi: buss
5. Busserl: peck
6. Elternkuss: parental kiss
7. Engelskuss: angel's kiss
8. Eskimokuss: nose kiss
9. Französischer Kuss: French kiss
10. Freundschaftskuss: friendship kiss
11. Geworfener Handkuss: blown kiss
12. Gratulationskuss: congratulatory kiss
13. Gutenachtkuss: good night kiss
14. Handkuss: blown kiss
15. Intimkuss: intimate kiss
16. Judaskuss: Judas kiss
17. Küsschen: little kiss
18. Kuss Zurück: kissing back
19. Lauter Kuss: hearty kiss
20. Lippenkuss: lip kiss
21. Luftkuss: air kiss

22. Mundkuss: mouth kiss
23. Mutterkuss: motherly kiss
24. Nachküssen: kisses that haven't happened
25. Raucherkuss: smoker's kiss
26. Schmatzer: smacking kiss
27. Schmetterlingskuss: butterfly kiss
28. Seelenkuss: soul kiss
29. Tiefer Kuss: deep kiss
30. Todeskuss: kiss of death
31. Verräterkuss: traitor's kiss
32. Vakuumkuss: vacuum kiss
33. Vaterkuss: fatherly kiss
34. Wangenkuss: cheek kiss
35. Wachkuss: kiss awake
36. Zungenkuss: soul kiss

Reminder

Text to Elli:

Me: I want you to find a bottle of steak sauce at the grocery store and put it on the shelf in your bedroom.

Elli: Why steak sauce? Why the bedroom?

Me: Just trust me. Put it somewhere you'll

see the bottle every day, and every time
you do, I want you to remember that you
can't take love or happiness for granted.

Elli: I'd be happier if you were here and not
talking like you'd been brainwashed by a
yogi.

Me: I miss you, El.

Elli: No offense, but your texts are getting
weirder. Tell me what you need! What can I
do to help?

———◆✹◆———

Beneath the Masks

I sink into bed, and the mattress is deep and soft, full
of cushions and luxury. My mind drifts to Malcolm
when I should be thinking of anything but him.

How do I stop thinking? The moment you tell yourself not to think about something, that's the moment
you only think about it more. I never knew feelings
were like that, too.

I look around this enormous room in which I'm
supposed to sleep, and I think of all the people in
the world with much bigger problems: Ian lying
in his hospital bed hooked up to machines, and the
people who live in some of the places we saw today:
doorless, windowless huts roofed in tarps or thatch

with cow-dung patties stacked up outside to use as fuel. There are people who string blankets on sticks as makeshift tents on the center dividers of the roads or under billboards with ads for expensive jewelry shops. Bathrooms here are a luxury for a lot of people and some have to relieve themselves in the street and take bucket baths outside.

My problems are so very small. I hate that they feel so big.

Outside beyond my window, the domes and minarets of the Taj Mahal shimmer above the tree line. The moonlight is still and beautiful, and slender fountains play among the marble statues of the garden so that the place and people make me think again of Verlaine's masks and masqueraders:

> *Playing the lute and dancing and almost*
> *Sad beneath their fantastic disguises.*
> *All sing in a minor key*
> *Of victorious love and the opportune life,*
> *They do not seem to believe in their happiness*

It was a mistake to kiss Malcolm tonight. Not because it could be epically wrong, but because if it's wrong, I will spend my life as a masquerader, too. I'll be doomed to pretend not to feel what I have felt, pretending I never had the potential for magic within my grasp before I had to let go and leave it behind.

I think of Shah Jahan, imprisoned in the Red Fort

of Agra, condemned to spend years looking across the Yamuna River as the sun spilled gold and crimson through the translucent marble of the Taj Mahal. And all the while, he himself couldn't get past the walls that kept him locked away.

My mother's walls were constructed of music, but in their own way, they were just as strong and high. She wore a mask her entire life, pretending to be happy. Maybe on some level, she was happy. She had her gift. She had me. She had fame and purpose and money, but if I'd been able to ask her at the end of her life whether that was enough, what would she have said? She'd had the kind of love people long for and dream about, and she pushed it away.

Her letters speak of the regret beneath the mask. Would she have been happier if she had made different choices? I wonder if Ian would be lying in a hospital bed right now.

What scares me most, I think, is that I can't help wondering if maybe she *tried* to protect herself from what she felt. Was there a part of her all along, as she and Ian were falling in love, that was telling her not to let herself fall too far? Was she aware of heading into heartache?

I'm afraid she tried and it didn't work.

I'm not sure it *can* work. How do I live with that?

Malcolm
Awakening

The Taj Mahal is a specter above the trees outside, and I lie in bed thinking about the shadow it has cast. My father is confined in hospital, unable to reach it, just as Shah Jahan couldn't reach it in the last years of his life. I think of Dad collecting his replicas, his small mausoleums for the love he couldn't have.

It can't have been wrong, that kiss between myself and Izzy. Something that feels so right can't be wrong.

But what if that kiss is the last and there are no more between us?

How does a kiss turn from awakening and potential into goodbye?

PART SEVEN

Izzy
Monuments

We head back to the hospital in the morning, and rush hour traffic is heavier than it was last night. Literally heavier. How the *wallahs*—this is the term for vendors—can possibly carry so much, I don't understand. The physics seem impossible. We pass a family, a mom and dad and two little girls about four and five years old, all squeezed onto a single scooter along with a full-grown goat. A man zips past us on a motorcycle strapped with eight milk cans of varying sizes. In front of us, there's a bicycle rickshaw with at least fifty boxes of shoes stacked up around him and held together by a mummy wrap of clear plastic sheeting.

A new carefulness has settled between me and Malcolm, and he tries to hide it by peppering Mr. Chandra with questions: Why is the overloaded cargo so often held together by plastic wrap? Why do the women wear such beautiful *sarees* to work in the fields and to do their laundry by the river? Why does everyone stop at yellow lights but line up in the zebra crossing as if there's going to be a race to get across the intersection?

Mr. Chandra laughs more often than he answers, maybe because there's a new "why?" everywhere we look. Or maybe he doesn't feel like encouraging more questions. The most common answer seems to be, "Because it works." India has its own logic and its own rhythm.

"You have to admire the philosophy and patience behind it all," Malcolm says.

"Patience?"

"With everything. Traffic. Hardship. Karma."

"We are a very tolerant people," Mr. Chandra says.

He's taken his eyes off the road for only a second to look into the rearview mirror, but a truck barrels at us head-on, packed so high with plastic-wrapped mystery bundles that it threatens to topple over. Mr. Chandra swerves at the last moment, and we scrape by with inches to spare.

"That and we believe we have many lives." Mr. Chandra laughs. "There is an old saying here. A man needs only three things in India: good luck, good brakes, and an excellent horn. You are fortunate we have all three."

I hope our luck continues.

I looked up heart attacks last night. Only twenty-five percent of patients survive the first attack or the first day after. Fifty percent of those that survive are dead within ten years. That sounded bad until I thought it through.

The heart is the core of the human body. The fact that so many people live ten years or longer tells me there's more to the heart than muscle and blood and tissue.

Maybe some people want to live more than their hearts want to die.

Ian needs a reason to fight. Over breakfast, Malcolm and I decided maybe the letters can help get him through the next few days. But it's a gamble. There's a fine line between filling a heart and breaking it.

Unanswered Questions

Dr. Asrani confirms that the attack left Ian's heart too weak to pump enough blood through his body. "The heart it is like a person," he says. "Over time, it grows tired and weak, but there are many treatments. Many medications and implantable devices. Many options. We shall see tomorrow, maybe the next day. I hope he will be stronger very soon."

He glances at the shoebox that I'm carrying, and I can see the questions he isn't asking.

Malcolm raises his eyebrow at me, and I nod. "My

father was in love with a woman—Izzy's mother—for many years, but they couldn't be together," he says. "The shoebox is full of letters, love letters and notes and reflections, that Izzy's mother wrote to him but never sent. He's never seen them, and Izzy and I thought it might keep him interested if we read him a few at a time."

Dr. Asrani is in a green shirt and tie and a long white coat today instead of his surgical scrubs, and without the hat and the mask he looks younger. Less certain. I keep expecting doctors to have all the answers, but thanks to Mom, I've already learned that isn't true. Where the science of medicine stops, the art begins.

He rubs his chin with two fingers and pulls out his cell phone from his pocket because it's vibrating. "Read him one or two and then we will see how he is feeling," he says a little absently. "I shall ask Mahadevi, the ward nurse in charge, to check on him."

"Thank you," Malcolm and I say together, and Dr. Asrani hurries through the swinging doors, leaving us to follow.

The ward nurse is short and plump, with a wide, gentle smile and masses of dark hair lightly threaded with gray and coiled into a bun that has to make her head hurt beneath its weight. She assesses us as Dr. Asrani speaks to her, and then Dr. Asrani hurries out of the CCU again, leaving us to visit Ian.

Malcolm's hands are in his pockets as we follow Mahadevi across the room. The posture makes his shoulders curl in on themselves, and the line between his brows has grown too deep. I watch him instead of looking around, because the room reminds me too much like the intensive care unit that already tore my world apart. Now it's threatening to take Malcolm's, too. The thump and hiss of a nearby ventilator sounds like a monster approaching, coming for Ian step by step.

I shove the thought away, assuring myself that this isn't the same as with my mother.

Ian isn't brain-dead. He's forcing a smile as we approach the foot of his bed, which is at the apex of a horseshoe of identical bays with heart monitors and chairs and IV poles and breathing machines. I try to tell myself that he doesn't actually look worse even though he's meant to be getting better.

That's what I tell myself. But logic and whatever part of my brain processes emotion are disconnected. My mind has turned to dust, blowing around in circles inside my head.

Maybe the mind, like the heart, wants what it wants. It plays tricks of desperation.

I have been kidding myself in thinking I didn't hope that Ian was my father. I want him to be, and I want him not to be, but mostly I want—I need—him to be all right.

Malcolm walks up to the bed, and we both sit down as Ian gestures for us to sit. "How was the hotel?" Ian asks, his voice soft as if speaking louder would require too much effort. "Were you able to get some rest last night?"

"Never mind us. How are you?" Malcolm asks.

"They're doing a gallant job putting up with me." Ian shifts and his eyes slide toward the box I'm holding. "I can't imagine that's a new pair of shoes, somehow. Especially as it's a rather old box."

I gather up every scrap of courage I possess and lean closer, as if I'm the one who can't get my vocal cords to work at full capacity. "I didn't tell you the whole truth before about why I came to see you. Mom never told me about you, but after she died, I found this shoebox full of letters she wrote you."

His eyes have grown brighter, and he lifts his head. "She never wrote me any letters."

"She didn't send you any." I let the answer sink in before I continue. "I read them, not knowing what they were at first, and then once I started I couldn't stop. I think you should know what they say, but they might make you sad."

Ian turns his head away on the pillow. Mahadevi stands at the foot of the bed, watching him and watching the machine that monitors his heart. I don't know what the waves on the monitor mean, but the shrug she gives me is so small it's almost imperceptible.

"Can I read you the first letter?" I ask Ian. "Then maybe you can decide if you want to hear any more."

Ian's voice is even softer. "Thank you, Izzy. I think I'd like that very much."

I remove the first letter from its envelope, and I wonder how many times a letter can be read. Is it measured in years, or decades, or centuries? When do words lose power?

Ian drinks in every sentence I read, and I imagine he looks less deflated by the time I finish the first letter. I wonder how I would feel in Ian's place. Would I want to hear any more?

"Can you read the next one, please?" he asks.

The CCU is nearly empty while patients sleep or lie there with the monster sounds of machines punctuated by the faint, incessant alarms. Three beds over, a woman in a deep pink *saree* with a nose ring as large as some of the biggest hoop earrings I've ever seen sits with a man about her own age, her husband probably. He's asleep, or in a coma, or on too much medication, and he doesn't seem aware of her. She talks to him quietly, clutching a photograph of two children in a frame on her lap. Farther on, two young women sit talking to a man who must be their father, their faces over-animated as if they're trying too hard to seem happy. Nurses move from one machine to another, rehanging IV bags or readjusting this tube or that.

I read the second letter.

The nurses pause to listen beside us as they pass. Mahadevi is writing something in Ian's chart, and she shoos them off, then tucks the pen back inside the clipboard and hangs the chart at the end of the bed. She doesn't walk away, though. Her head is tilted as she listens, her face exquisitely sympathetic.

Ian's eyes don't leave my face except now and then to look at Malcolm, who sits with his muscles like piano wire.

"I think that is enough for now," Mahadevi says. "Give the patient time to rest."

"Do you want me to read more later?" I ask Ian.

"Very much," he says, but then he turns back to Malcolm. "Are you all right with all this? Would you mind?"

Malcolm shifts forward in his chair. "I don't suppose you remember Aunt Clara's wedding? I was fifteen and furious that you'd dragged me there, and I told you it was dead embarrassing for Aunt Clara to think she was falling in love in her fifties."

"You were a proper devil when you wanted to be," Ian says.

"You told me love has nothing to do with age. That people can fall in an instant so hard it becomes impossible for them to see the world through a single pair of eyes. You told me you hoped—if I was ever lucky enough to have that happen to me—that I'd have the good sense Clara showed in grabbing love with both hands."

He glances over at me, and I can't look away. Then he clears his throat and speaks to Ian again. "You said," he continues, "that maybe the louder and more often and more publicly we tell someone we love them the more real love becomes. That saying it makes us and everyone else believe it. At the time, I didn't understand what you meant. But I do love you, and I haven't told you that nearly enough. I want to have years to tell you. I want to make up for the time I wasted being angry, and if that starts with all of us hearing how much Marcella loved you, I'm grateful to have the chance to listen."

Little Things

The street in front of the hospital rumbles and blares with the toot of horns from cars, scooters, and *tuk-tuks*. And though it's an entirely different world from some of the poor areas we've passed through, even here the exhaust-heavy air gives off a faint stench of urine. Down the block, a pair of the feral mixed-breeds that Mr. Chandra refers to as India dogs looks up at us hopefully then puts their heads back down again.

India dogs are skin and ribs and paws and ears and

pleading eyes, and they've all interbred until, with their short tan fur, they look like they're all related to each other. Someone has put a bowl of water down for them and another empty bowl presumably held food at one point. Mr. Chandra says people feed them, however poor they are themselves, because they like to start off the day with a good deed for the sake of karma.

Karma, according to Mr. Chandra, is both simple and complex. The basic idea is that if you do good things today, they will eventually come back to you, though not necessarily in your current lifetime. In other words, today's bad luck may be a payback from bad deeds in an earlier life.

Faith, more than hope, seems to be at the heart of many things in India. Even darting across the road is a leap of faith. Several men are already in the process of crossing, which really means they're standing partway across and waiting for a chance to dart a few more feet between the cars that careen along too fast.

Malcolm grabs my hand. Calculating the timing, he drags me along and we make it across the road in three short, terrifying bursts. Fear amplifies the usual electricity between us and my heart thunders. Neither of us lets go, and our palms are illicit and hot pressed up against each other as we maneuver around a crowd that has spilled into the street and jockeyed into position around the nearby chai stall.

The *wallah* swirls a boiling pot of the spiced tea an inch above the flames of his stove before lowering it until it nearly bubbles over and snatching it up to start all over again. The stall smells of ginger and garam masala powder, reminding me of the chai lattes I love to drink at home. But I already know I'll be disappointed with the taste, possibly because the overly sweet chai at home has burnt out my taste buds for the real stuff.

It doesn't matter. I love everything about this moment, and I concentrate on nothing but this, this stand on the corner, the way the *wallah* turns tea into an occasion, the bloom of spices in the air, the feel of Malcolm's skin on mine.

Maybe that's the lesson I'm learning from Ian and Malcolm and England and India and Mom's death: life is full of moments you can either mark or dismiss. Living fully isn't about doing big things. It's about doing the small things, all the things, as fully as you can.

I look over at Malcolm and he smiles. We stand there, breathing while we wait. I think I can feel his heart pounding. I wonder if he can feel mine, too.

Broken Open

For the next couple of days, Malcolm and I mostly

shuttle between the hotel, the waiting room, and the CCU. The waiting room is like a giant game of musical chairs for the people visiting patients. An older woman in a delicately embroidered saffron *saree* and a worried expression sits between her two daughters in the soft plastic chairs while her son and eldest daughter visit with her husband. Boredom and fear make everybody chatty, and before I know it, I'm sitting with my hands on my knees hearing all about how Mrs. Mittal's daughter, Laksha, the youngest, is getting married. Mr. Mittal was supposed to go to the groom's family with gifts of sweets, clothing, coconut, rice, and turmeric, and unless he does that, the groom won't officially be off the market.

"Then what will she do, if another girl steals him from her?" Mrs. Mittal asks, but I think it's a rhetorical question, because judging by the way Laksha rolls her eyes and laughs, that scenario isn't likely.

Laksha's hair is cut shoulder length and layered, and she wears a Western-style navy dress, but there are glass bangles on her arm and a small diamond pierces her left nostril. "My parents are traditional, and so are Darshan's," she says. "He and I met at university and fell in love, but our parents wish to do things the way they did them."

"Is it wrong that your father and I want you to be happy, *beti*? Our parents arranged our marriages, and *they* have lasted," Mrs. Mittal says with a speaking glance at her other daughter, Panya, who wears a long *kurta* over skinny jeans and high-heeled sandals.

That look of faint disappointment is universal. So is the angry blush that stains Panya's cheeks.

Mom and I never argued much. The only time I remember her really being disappointed was when I told her I didn't want to go to Oxford, which was what she'd always wanted for me because it was where she'd gone. That was my rebellious stage—okay, not so very rebellious in the scheme of things—but I had just finished reading *Gatsby* and decided I wanted to go to Princeton.

I wonder if Ian was the reason why Mom was disappointed. Had she been secretly hoping I would meet him if I went to Oxford? Was she looking for an excuse to see him again?

Malcolm and I sit and listen to Mrs. Mittal, who has cheeks like drying apples and eyes that are meant to shine with laughter. I want to shout at Laksha to listen to her mother while she can. I want Mr. Mittal to get better quickly, and for Ian to be all right. I want so many things that my heart feels wrung out from wanting.

It's hard and surprising to feel so much. I've probably cried and laughed more at books and films in my life than I have about anything real, but since Mom's death, it's like my skin has broken open and left me exposed. I've cried more, bled more, felt more, wanted more, hated more, loved more. The world is both uglier and brighter.

Kumquats

Reading the letters has become a group activity. A couple of times every day, Malcolm and I take turns reading one or two, and in between Ian has to rest. He says he wants to savor them, give himself something to look forward to. But I think in a way they exhaust him.

Mahadevi and Gauri, his favorites of the nurses, come to listen whenever they can. Soon, most of the others start watching for the readings, too. Whenever I come in with the shoebox, there's a sudden flurry of activity on the phone and in the corridor, and one or two nurses come in and report to all the others who wait outside. Even Dr. Asrani stops by now and then. Gauri and the other nurses have also started playing Mom's music at the nurse's station twenty-four hours a day. The doctors objected at first, but Mahadevi produced articles from medical journals that showed how playing music in the recovery room could improve patient outcomes and reduce the need for pain medication. Whether the doctors didn't want to argue the science or whether they were just scared of Mahadevi, the music stayed.

Mahadevi runs the CCU, but she's only been nursing since her husband died of cancer. Sita, who is still in her twenties, has a brother who's studying to get his master's degree in foreign relations at Johns Hopkins University not far from my house, and Gauri's sister invented an iOS app to help women who are stuck in abusive relationships and marriages. Mrs. Mittal brings us homemade vegetable curries or flaky, sweet *balushahi*, now that she's happier because Laksha's fiancé, Darshan, and his family came to visit her father and he was able to complete the ritual acceptance and blessings so that they could all get down to the intricate business of planning the engagement and wedding ceremony.

Time here is like eating kumquats, the first burst of sparks on breaking the sweet, delicate skin, then the shock of sour fruit, the two mingling together with every bite until each intensifies the other. Malcolm and I spend most of our days in the waiting room or exploring Agra when Ian forces us to go outside. We visit the Red Fort where Shah Jahan was imprisoned, and the tombs of Emperor Akbar and his wife. We walk through Katchpura Village to the Mehtab Bagh, the Moonlit Garden, on the banks of the Yamuna River opposite the Taj. Malcolm discovers there's a conservation center not very far from Agra and arranges for Mr. Chandra to drive us there so I can bottle-feed a baby elephant. I make a donation when Malcolm isn't looking, and when I come out of the bathroom later, I find that he's made a big one, too.

It feels like we're playing hooky, though, every time we leave the hospital. Malcolm and I both tense up whenever we enter the cardiac care unit, in case Ian's gotten worse since we left him. And my heart pounds uncomfortably every time Dr. Asrani comes, until he finally smiles and says that Ian is doing well.

"But not too much excitement, eh?" he says. "Not so much with the Bollywood letters yet."

That's gotten to be his favorite joke.

Everywhere we go in the hospital, nurses and doctors and people we've never seen before come up and talk to us about Ian and Mom and the letters as if what happened between Mom and Ian is one of the Bollywood love stories that are often playing in the waiting room.

Malcolm and I have gotten in the habit of watching them with Ravijeet back at the hotel, too, and we usually stay up watching and talking long after Ravijeet goes to bed. Most nights, we end up falling asleep together on the couch with the TV still running. Malcolm likes that Bollywood villains seem to represent the biggest problems in Indian society—in any society, really—and I love that the scripts are basically modern-day Charles Dickens with musical numbers. But, like Dickens, it does sometimes seem like they're torturing the characters unnecessarily before they get to the end.

"It is *vipralambha shringara*," Mrs. Mittal says. "I could see Shah Rukh Khan playing Dr. Ian. Shah Rukh Khan weeps so beautifully."

"What's *vipralambha shringara*?" I ask.

"Love in separation. It is wonderful." Mahadevi dabs her eyes. "Films are best when you can't help crying."

Laksha shakes her head. "I like when people are happy."

"You are young, *beti*." Mrs. Mittal pats her arm. "It is good to dream of happy endings while you still can."

Ian doesn't love this speculative, gossipy side of the discussions, but he claims he can't object that people want to hear the letters.

"I fell in love with your mother because her mind was beautiful and full of wonders. I like watching people falling in love with her words. It's bringing her back to life for me."

I don't know if that's dangerous or helpful, but reading the letters aloud, watching people reacting to them—watching Ian smile and catch his breath and shed tears over them—makes me feel as if Mom's here, whispering into my ear. And I feel like I'm seeing her through Ian's eyes as well.

———❋———

April 14, 2013

Dear Ian,

   I find myself thinking often about the places that became the vocabulary of our time together. The walks we took in Paris along the Seine, the meal at Le Train Bleu, the monuments of the Trastavere in Rome and our picnic of cheese and bread and wine on the Spanish Steps, the gondola in Venice where you and the gondolier did a duet of "O Sole Mio" along the Grand Canal in your terrible tenor and I laughed until I cried.

   I took Izzy to Paris this week. I wanted to show her the magic, but I realized halfway through that I was so busy showing her what you and I had thrown away that I wasn't letting her discover her own magic for herself. She will have her own Paris someday, I hope, her own grand love, and being here with her brings our sacrifices to life. I hope the boy brings you as much joy as Izzy brings to me.

   Regret is pointless, but if she ever asks, I will tell her not to make the mistakes I made. I'll tell her to risk anything for love. Risk everything. But Izzy isn't me. She has a balance and an inner peace that I will never find.

It is interesting how much our children teach us.
Yours forever,
Cella

Mona Lisa's Smile

My mother once told me that regret doesn't change anything. Only actions can make a difference.

She took me to spend spring break at the Hotel George V in Paris. For once, she wasn't working, and she wanted to show me all her favorite places. We climbed the 704 steps up the Eiffel Tower and stood in the wind, her hair whipping as wildly as mine, our arms entwined while all around us lovers leaned against each other. We took a baguette, cheese, and a bottle of wine to the banks of the Seine with an itchy wool blanket. The wine was bitter, but I felt too grown up to refuse a glass when she offered, and we watched lovers strolling and boats passing by. A little boy in a blue jacket lost the dragon kite he was flying and started to cry, and his father bent down to dry his tears.

Mom said that kites are more emotional than physical anyway, that you keep them in your heart as a reminder that people can learn to fly. Then she charmed the chef at *Le Train Blue* in the *Gare de Lyon*, who brought us tasting portions of his entire menu, and then after dinner, we went to see *Don Giovanni* at the Paris Opera where the *Phantom of the Opera* was set.

On the third night, Mom woke me at midnight with lemon soufflé and cocoa from the restaurant kitchen, and we sat cross-legged on the bed blowing into our steaming cups and looking out the sheer white curtains at the silhouette of the lighted Eiffel Tower.

"We've finished doing what I needed to do," she said, "so tomorrow, the city is yours. What shall we go and see? Anything at all."

"The Louvre," I said.

"What part? I didn't bring my running shoes."

"Near Eastern Antiquities, Greeks, Egyptians, Etruscans, Romans, and modern Near East."

"Only if you tell me a story in every wing. I'll need an excuse to stop and catch my breath."

"Deal."

"*And* we have to see the *Mona Lisa*."

I agreed, but Mona had always been a disappointment up to then. And after inching through the line to the glass display, I still didn't see anything special in her famous secret smile. All I saw was a woman who looked a little smug and guilty.

"Look deeper," Mom said. "You're the one who always says you have to look beneath the surface."

I felt the impatience of the people waiting in line behind us, and all I wanted to do was walk away. My mother slipped an arm around my shoulders. "You can only see what you expect to see, Izzy. Look more carefully at Mona Lisa's mouth."

Someone behind us coughed, and I started to edge away. Then either because of the change in angle or because I was focusing on Mona's lips instead of at the painting as a whole, I discovered she wasn't actually smiling at all.

I think about the trip in a new way after reading Mom's letter aloud to Ian. After having been to Halford and Joran Masterson's workshop.

The appeal of the *Mona Lisa* is partly in understanding the technique. Leonardo da Vinci took years to create something that the world had never seen before, and he sacrificed time and love and other things in his life until he had made it as perfect as he could make it. My mother sacrificed everything to bring her music into the world.

Ian is crying again as I put aside her letter about Paris, and I think it's because of her regret.

I tell him about our trip, and he looks over at Malcolm as if weighing what to say before he says it. He slides his pale, veined hand along the rough cotton of the bedsheets and closes his fingers around mine. "My heart aches hearing her use the word 'mistake,' but I am glad she shared that evening with you in her own way. Showed you the things we did together when we met again."

"I think it was more about her than me," I say, which is just another thread of the tapestry of my childhood unraveling and being rewoven into something new. "She told me I should always have the courage not to regret the things I sacrifice. But obviously she did regret."

Ian reaches for the cup of ice at his bedside and gives himself time to crunch and swallow before he asks, "Is that all you get out of that letter, Izzy?"

"What else is there?"

Malcolm leans forward. "She said you both sacrificed. 'Our sacrifices,' she says, and she refers to me. Why was I a sacrifice?"

Ian sighs deeply, and he avoids Malcolm's eyes. "I've never considered it as a sacrifice, Mal. But that night in Paris, Cella offered to find a way to make things work between us. So that we could be together. That would have meant divorcing your mother and potentially losing you, though, and I'd made a commitment. I couldn't—I didn't want to—break it."

"So you chose Mum instead of Marcella? That's what you're saying?"

"Your mother and I were friends. We shared a deep affection. I did love her, in my own way," Ian says. "As much as I could. But if I'm honest, it was you and Ginny I chose that night. Cella understood that eventually, though it wasn't easy for her."

Malcolm
Rearranging

I've come all the way to India only to have my life reshaped at the side of a hospital bed. It feels as though I've taken apart a photograph, shuffled the pieces, and now I'm watching as they reassemble themselves into a different picture. There's no pleasure at all in knowing my father chose me over his own happiness. Worse yet, he didn't tell me that—not until I'd put the pieces together for myself.

This picture of my father that emerges letter by letter and day by day is of a person I do not know, but I do admire him. Which only makes me more aware of what a selfish sod I've been.

I hang back as Izzy folds up the latest letter and heads back to the waiting room. "I'll catch up in a moment, Iz."

She nods and walks away, and Dad stiffens as though he's afraid of what I'll tell him. He's still weak, and he tires easily, his breath straining against the thin sheet, the sound of it drowned out by the louder, mechanical breathing of the machines around us and the cacophony of beeps and squeaks and rattles that seem implausibly loud.

There's no privacy in the hospital. Perhaps that's why Dad pretends not to mind that everyone is gossiping about the letters. I loathe the intrusion of it all.

"I haven't been a very good son, even without taking into account what you went through," I say.

Dad raises his head and adjusts the pillow behind him so that he can look at me more easily. "The mistakes are mine, not yours. That's the bargain we make as parents. And I am very proud of you—I don't tell you so nearly enough."

"Proud because of Halford?"

"Proud because of the way your mind works. Like Izzy's mother." He sighs again, still fragile. "Even now medicine has no answer for love, no idea how much of it is chemical or biological. I fell in love the moment I first saw Marcella, but that love bloomed and ripened and grew richer over time. I suspect that first part is down to fate or the universe or chemistry—alchemy, perhaps, because the same held true of my love for you. I loved you the instant I saw you, but the rest came from a thousand and one small moments: the way your fist curled around one of my fingers, the way you studied everyone so solemnly, the questions you asked as a boy, your thoughtfulness, generosity, and involvement in the world, the person you've become."

The way he looks at me, there's no denying he's telling the truth, and I think it's the one word—generosity—that brings me the greatest amount of shame. When have I ever been generous with him? When did I ever give my own father the benefit of any doubt?

He's the one who is generous with everyone. Even me.

"I've never stopped loving you," I say, "even when I pretended otherwise. That's why the letters trouble me most. Their honesty makes me feel naked and ashamed," I admit, though I think we both know that has little to do with the letters themselves.

"I suppose I felt that sharing the experience of reading them with you and Izzy would be worth the necessity of sharing them with strangers."

I can't argue that. If it gave him even an ounce of strength to fight, it would have been worth it. But hearing Marcella's words, watching my father's reactions as he hears them, has been a different, more personal experience than reading them myself. "It's only that it's more attention than I bargained for, and I worry it might become more public. What if someone sells the story or the press picks it up?"

"The hospital's been very good about our privacy. So far as anyone knows, the letters are about Dr. Halford and Marcella Cavalera. In any case, I'll be moving back to the hotel soon, so it will all be over."

There are days yet before that can happen, although Dr. Asrani says with a bit of luck Dad can leave the CCU tomorrow. Still, I nod as though I'm agreeing with my father's optimism, and I reach out and squeeze his hand, silently telling him all the things I wish I had the words to say. His eyes are fever bright, and he places his other hand on top of mine as though he hears my thoughts. As if he knows.

"Would you send Izzy back to me for a moment alone?" he asks eventually. "I suppose I had better apologize about the letters to her as well."

Ian
Hope

Every breath I'm taking these days feels as though it's borrowed, as ephemeral as magic. And in the sweetness of having Malcolm and Izzy here beside me, it's easy to ignore the stakes and the danger these letters pose. A blink of an eye, that's all it would require to bring disaster. Discovery is always around the corner, so Malcolm isn't wrong. One word in the wrong ear, and every choice I've made, every sacrifice, could prove to have been for naught.

I should have stopped Izzy reading the moment I understood what the letters were. I should have had her leave the letters for me to read myself, or at the very least asked for privacy when the nurses first began to take an interest. But hearing Cella's words in Izzy's voice, having the chance to watch her reading... She's so much her mother's daughter. I can hear Cella speaking her thoughts to me, and all the aching years fall away again.

Reading the letters is binding us all together. They're a miracle and a precious gift, and until now, I couldn't bring myself to turn my back on that. Now I must be stronger. I must confess the truth and hope Izzy will understand.

I can only hope she'll be as generous as her mother.

Izzy
Revelations

Ian asks me to draw the curtain around his bed, which he never does. He usually goes out of his way not to separate himself or ask for special treatment. The narrow hooks rattle on the tracks attached to the ceiling, and the scrape is raucous, like the shrill of a crow in a quiet meadow. Everyone in the room looks over, their faces shining with curiosity.

"Pull the chair closer. Here," he says, his voice pitched so low it's barely audible above the overture of medical machines and the low rustle of conversation.

I rock the chair closer and shift in place until my knees are sideways to the bed.

"I haven't any notion of how to begin." He reaches for my hand, and his skin is warm and papery, but the grip is tight. His eyes are wide, rimmed in white that makes the beautiful green shine very bright. I think he's wary and holding on to me so hard in case I suddenly run away.

"What is it?" I ask.

"I suppose it's best to tell the truth. That feels very difficult after all this time."

I brace myself, but it's hard since I don't know where the blow is coming from or what kind of pain it will bring.

"That night in Paris with your mother," Ian says, "was a few hours in a bubble of time. She and I set everything else aside in the joy of seeing each other. It was as though we were falling in love all over again but even more easily because our hearts had traveled that same path once already. Neither of us wanted the day to come to an end, so she coaxed the kitchen to send up one of her dessert picnics at midnight. She said she'd made a terrible mistake leaving me and that we needed to be together. She took my hands, and her expression was so hopeful, so certain, that for a moment I let myself dream with her."

"It must have been hard for her to admit it," I say.

"Yes. And it was a wonderful dream. A magical one. We lay on the bed hand in hand and whispered of all the things we could do together. She'd worked out all the possibilities of it for us. But I'd made promises to my wife and to Malcolm and his sister. They were still little more than babies then, still so little, but I loved them. And if I'd gone back on my responsibilities to them, I wouldn't have been the man your mother had fallen in love with. Do you see? Whatever I did, I was going to hurt someone. Break someone irrevocably. Either my family or your mother. I couldn't have them both."

His expression reminds me of the beggar children here in India, the ones who make my heart break. Mr. Chandra says we shouldn't give them money because the adults who send them out to beg will only find more children to send out, and they burn and cripple the kids on purpose so people will feel more sorry for them. Some of the kids have these horrible dead expressions as if they're not expecting anyone to give them anything, as if they've stopped hoping for it, which makes it impossible not to open my wallet and give them every bit of money I have with me.

Ian has that same air about him now. He doesn't look like he expects me to understand, as if he's bracing himself for rejection. For punishment.

But I can imagine how he felt.

"I see," I tell him, and I can't blame him for choosing his family. For being honorable.

The tightness around his mouth and eyes softens just a little. "Your mother didn't. She was unhappy at first, and angry," he says. "I told her I hoped we could at least remain friends and stay in contact—I needed that desperately. But she packed her suitcase and left a note on her pillow while I slept. I woke in the morning and she was gone."

I imagine my mother slipping out into the Paris rain

in the early hours, lamplight blurring in the puddles on the sidewalks around the dripping café awnings like a Renoir painting. I don't know why I imagine rain, except that teary goodbyes should always occur in rain.

She would have been crying. I can see her as clearly as if I'm looking at a movie.

My throat aches for her, and my heart is hollow.

Ian removes a folded sheet of paper from beneath his pillow and presses it into my hand. "I want you to have this," he says. "But you must promise never to show it to Malcolm—or anyone else."

Farewell

My Darling Ian,

This last chance to be with you was magic, but our Paris can't last forever. Tonight must be our last good night in a string of long good nights.

Our diverging paths were chosen long ago. And you're right. Thinking it over logically, I can see you have to keep the promises you made to Felicity and her children when you agreed to make them yours. If you broke those promises for my sake, you would eventually come to hate us both.

I would come to hate us both.

Goodbye, my love. My heart. I will look for you in the audience at my performances. I will always look for you, but I hope you'll honor my wishes in at least one thing—don't try to contact me.

I'll hold this unexpected blessing of this last time with you in my heart, and that heart will belong to you forever. Be well. Be happy.

Yours ever,

Cella

———◆❊◆———

The Long Lie

The letter is folded small, as if it's been kept in a wallet all these years, and the creases are soft from being refolded many times. The ink is smudged and the paper is stained by tears. I wonder if they are hers or his.

Then I wonder something else. Once I get past the words and the grief and the tragedy, more of what my mother said jumps out at me. The questions settle in.

My lungs stop working and the room begins to swirl. I force myself to take a breath. Two breaths. I make myself count to ten while I try to process, to make sure I've got it right. But I only get to seven before I blurt out what seems so unfathomable.

"Is she saying Malcolm isn't your son? That the twins weren't yours? Is that why you don't want him to see this?"

Ian's so pale that the sheets on the hospital bed threaten to erase him. "When your mother left—the first time she left me—it felt as though she'd carved out my heart and taken it with her to America. Felicity, Malcolm's mother, was not only my second cousin, she was one of my closest friends. She helped me pick up the pieces, but in truth, we helped each other. She had fallen pregnant by a soldier who'd been killed, someone her parents wouldn't have found suitable anyway. So she was rather desperate for a solution."

"And marrying you, that solved her problem."

"I knew I could never love anyone the way I loved your mother, so marriage would have been out of the question otherwise. But I still had a responsibility to produce an heir for Halford. Making a home and a place for Flis and her children seemed like the solution to both our problems. She was a Halford herself. We didn't think we were harming anyone. At the time, we were too young, heartbroken, and impetuous to know any better."

He picks up my hand again and holds it tight enough to hurt, though he doesn't seem to realize that. He's studying me as if he wants to look straight through the skin and bone into the tangle of feelings knotting themselves inside my heart.

"You must understand, Izzy. It never mattered that the twins weren't mine. I loved them. And I suppose because they weren't truly mine, there was always a fear at the back of my mind that I might lose them. That I didn't have an honest claim. Of course, ultimately, I did lose Ginny, which made it even harder to watch Malcolm drifting away from me."

"But that was years later."

"Yes. You can't hold tight to children, though. The harder you try to hold them, the more they struggle to get away. I've always thought I'd have time to repair the damage with Mal—whenever he was ready to let me. I can't lose him completely. You do see that, don't you? And he's had enough hurt in his life without having to cope with not knowing who he is. Without losing the one constant he's ever had."

"Of course."

"That's my main worry, but there's something more immediate as well. What Flis and I were too young to consider at the time is that there would be questions about the inheritance. Parts of the estate are entailed, and the issues are complicated. This is why I couldn't agree to a DNA test when you arrived. Do you see? It would open Pandora's box if anyone found out. The situation would require investigation and arbitration, and with so much at stake, things like that can get terribly ugly. It would have been hard enough for Malcolm if I'd ripped it all away from him as an infant, but now, after all he's put into Halford, to risk him losing it—he's strong and resourceful and rather brilliant in his own right, so he'd survive. Halford might not survive losing him, though, which is the one thing that Mal couldn't bear."

I pull my hand away, skin sliding over skin. My palm is damp, and I feel as though I've taken part of Ian with me and left part of myself behind. I don't know where I begin or stop anymore.

"So what are you asking me to do?" I say.

"I'm afraid I need to ask you to decide. I see how you two are together. Everyone sees it. The nurses all assume you're Malcolm's girl, and to them, the two of you are a contrast to mine and Cella's story. A possible happy ending. But, of course, they haven't grasped that you could be my daughter."

It sounds so old-fashioned and sweet when Ian says this, when he calls me Malcolm's girl. There's a moment—a shiningly possible moment—where I think it could happen. Where I think I could have Ian *and* Malcolm both.

There's the problem with assumptions.

They're too often wrong, and there's a very real reason why Ian said I have to choose.

My body goes cold and numb.

I fell into the Potomac River in the middle of winter when I was fourteen, and the water was thick with ice. I came out stiff and shivering, and it took hours to feel warm again. That's how I feel now, only I don't know if I'll ever feel warm again.

"If I'm your daughter, people would assume Malcolm and I must be brother and sister—even though we aren't." I lean closer. "Everyone would think that. Including Malcolm."

"That's why even the DNA testing could lead to problems. None of it is as anonymous as we think, and there aren't many safeguards in place. You never know what they're going to do with the information, or who has access. This situation would be gold for some ambitious journo or the paparazzi, and they'd pay well for the story. Malcolm's already expressed concern about the interest the letters have stirred up among the nurses."

"No one here would say anything."

"Probably not. But the point is, we're vulnerable." Ian shakes his head and rubs his palms together as if he's trying to wash them clean. The look he gives me is heavy with regret.

"I truly am sorry about all this, Izzy. When I found out...I never thought I'd have a child of my own flesh and blood. The thought that I might have one, that part of my parents might live on...I didn't know how much that would matter to me. What I'm asking—what I'm afraid to ask—has nothing to do with how much I want you to be my daughter. But until this morning, I couldn't think of any way to avoid Malcolm finding out that he is not my son."

I suck in my breath. "And is there a way?"

"Dr. Asrani gave me some information that suggested an option." His voice shakes, and he stares down at his hands.

"What option?" I ask, raising my chin.

He lets his eyes drift closed. "It would require a sacrifice. One more lie on top of all the others."

Mismatch

Malcolm and I both gave blood in case Ian needed to have another surgery. But Ian's blood is type AB. His children could only have type A or B, or type AB like mine. Malcolm is a type O universal donor, which rules out him being Ian's son.

"We could pretend to reverse that," Ian says. "So long as we don't give out too many details and Malcolm doesn't ask too many questions, it's the only way I can think of that would allow Malcolm to accept that you and I couldn't be related without a DNA test. If you'd be willing to go along."

"So we say I'm type O?" I ask.

It's simple, really. In the context of how hurt Malcolm would be if the truth came out, this would only be a little lie.

"Of course, I won't try to force you into anything." Ian's watching me, his face ash grey in the harsh hospital light. "I've no right to even ask this of you, and I'll certainly understand if you want to have the DNA tests done. We can try to manage it discreetly. Take out a post office box in London, send the swabs in anonymously. Believe me, I'd like nothing better than to be able to claim you as my daughter, but whether we have results to confirm it or not, I can honestly tell you that you're already family. It won't change anything. Not on my end."

He reaches for my hand again, and I can see that he really believes what he's saying. Maybe that's because he's always had a family. He's always known who he is and where he came from.

I've been an adopted part of Elli's family all my life. They always did their best to make me feel like that. But it wasn't the same. It's never the same.

Every part of my body hurts. "What about Malcolm's biological family?" I say. "Does he have brothers? Sisters? Grandparents?"

The shake of Ian's head is an epitaph, infinite with sadness. "His father was in care—foster care, you'd call it—as a child. He grew up rough and joined the army to get away from all that. Getting involved with him was a show of rebellion for Flis at first, but they fell in love in the end. She was honest with me about that, and we looked into the family situation before making our decision. I didn't want to risk costing Malcolm any blood connection he might have had."

He doesn't seem to realize he's only making matters worse for me. But then, how could he?

I've spent my whole life living with the sense of something missing, clinging too hard to the family I'd cobbled together to compensate for the father I didn't know. What's worse, looking at Ian now, I realize he's exactly the kind of father I would want. One who cares so much for Malcolm that he'd give up everything for him. Even if it means he's choosing Malcolm over me.

That's the real choice, isn't it? Malcolm or me.

One of us doesn't get to have a father, and if I don't agree to lie, then it will be Malcolm who'll have to learn to live with the kind of missingness I've always felt. Missingness and nothing that can fill it.

Ian raises his head off the pillow to study me. "Don't try to decide now, Izzy. I can see you're struggling with all this. Give yourself a day or two. However long you need. Consider all you'd be giving up. I could never publicly acknowledge you as my daughter, and if whatever's between you and Malcolm didn't work out—"

"I'd have to leave. Either way, I'll have to leave," I blurt out, because I can't stand the idea of waiting to lose them both if anything goes wrong.

"Stay for the rest of the summer at the very least."

Ian smiles, a kind smile with only a hint of reproach, as though he deserves the pain. "Please, Izzy. Stay for Malcolm's sake if not for mine. It's clear how much he cares for you—and how much you care for him."

I care too much to stay.

I hate decisions where someone is going to lose, but I hate this kind of lie even more than that. It's the sort of lie that becomes corrosive, the kind that eats away at the honesty in a relationship until someday, someone finds themselves peering back through time and wondering if anything was real at all.

"I should bring up the question of inheritance as well, I suppose," Ian says, his eyes slipping away from mine. "The elephant in the room, so to speak. Being American, you're accustomed to the idea of equality between children, but—"

"I don't want a title or money," I spit out. "You don't know me at all if you think any of that matters."

I hate this conversation. I hate the lies. I hate that Ian doesn't know me, and I hate—more than anything else—that he's still thinking about dying, thinking about it as if it isn't years away.

The idea of losing him before I've fully found him hits me all over again, and money and acknowledgment and secrets and none of those things matter.

If we do this, if I agree to live a lie, then there's no chance I'll ever have a father of my own.

And I'll never *know*. How do I live with that?

Contrasts

I sit on the terrace late that night after Malcolm goes to bed, and I miss having Elli beside me. I can't say all this in a text or even in a call or video chat. Too much of what we say isn't in the words we speak.

For the first time, I wonder if Elli will still understand me as well when I go home. I feel like I've absorbed so many new thoughts and feelings since the last time we saw each other that the change can't help but create a sliver of space between us. If it were anyone but Elli, I would worry that it would make us drift apart. So many friendships are about convenience and shared experience. But this is Elli. I know we'll eventually be all right.

> Text to Elli:
>
> Me: I'm about to do something you might say is stupid.
>
> Elli: Prince Charming stupid?
>
> Me: Father and Son Charming stupid.
>
> Elli: There is no stupidity we can't fix. Just don't let yourself get hurt too bad.

I think it's too late for that. Or maybe it just doesn't

matter anymore. I'm not worried about protecting myself. I don't want to.

I've been protected from unpleasantness all my life. It took going to Halford and meeting Ian and Malcolm and coming here, too, to this place where life is loud and messy and hard and full of color to understand why people say you can't understand the value of life without seeing death, or feel true joy without having experienced suffering. Maybe that's the reason women here wear gorgeous *sarees* even while doing dirty jobs, because life requires contrast.

I want to live in contrasts. I want to find life in the spaces in between.

> Text to Elli:
>
> Me: I think sometimes we have to take off the armor.
>
> Elli: They don't make armor for self-inflicted wounds.
>
> Me: We should invent some. Self-inflicted wounds hurt the most. We could make a fortune.

Anachronisms

I don't know what makes me turn around, maybe just a sense of being watched. Malcolm's standing at the terrace door, and he gives a guilty little tip of his head because I've caught him.

"Do you know that you smile when you text?" he says. "It's cute."

"It's Elli. She makes me smile."

He drops into the chair beside me. "How long have you known each other?"

We've talked about Elli and his friend Percy and his other friends from Eton and Oxford a lot these past days, but now I tell him Izzy and Elli's Origin Story. He says he and Percy are a bit like that, though they've drifted apart lately at Magdalen, which is the one out of the thirty-eight colleges that make up Oxford. It has the dining hall that inspired the one at Hogwarts. It's also where Oscar Wilde went to school.

"Is Oxford hard?" I ask.

"Not terribly, unless you're put off by the prospect of having to churn out 10,000-word essays in a matter of hours."

"I'll take that over multiple choice any day of the week. I can always fudge an essay."

He laughs. "You and me both."

"I hate multiple choice," both of us say at once. And then we laugh again.

"There are almost always reasons why at least two answers could arguably be right."

"Exactly," I say, nodding. "Arguably. But you can't argue multiple choice, can you?"

Only maybe I've just never been good at choosing.

Malcolm and I are smiling at each other. For a moment he falls quiet, and then he says, "Do you mind about Princeton? Truly mind?"

I consider the question and then, reluctantly, I have to nod. Somehow sitting here with him in the dark makes it easier to see what I've been hiding from myself. "A little, I guess. But Columbia's a good school, and after losing my mom, I couldn't stand the thought of losing Elli as well."

"Were you at risk of losing her?"

"Probably not—not really—but I wasn't in an emotional place where I could risk it."

We fall silent, and as so often happens, neither one of us is ready to go to bed. I watch the water ripple in the empty pool downstairs, all still and lit up and golden. The night feels immense and full of things I cannot see.

"More Bollywood?" Malcolm asks.

I shake my head. Tonight, I need an ending I can count on.

"*A Knight's Tale*?" I suggest.

His brows knit together. "They made *The Canterbury Tales* into a film?"

"Not exactly, but Chaucer's in it. You've never seen *A Knight's Tale*? Really?" I jump up and rub my hands together. "Wait right there. Don't go anywhere. This is great, and you're going to love it. Jousting, chivalry, courtly love, villains you love to hate—all the Chaucer*ish* basics."

I run to retrieve my tablet, and the two of us settle on the floor in the living room, our backs braced against the sofa with the tablet and my earbuds shared between us.

The movie starts with Sir Hector in his armor propped against a tree. William and his two friends with tissues in their noses slowly realize that the stench means their boss is dead. Hungry and desperate, William proposes to impersonate Sir Hector for the last part of the jousting tournament.

Instead of watching the screen, I watch Malcolm's face. The dialogue and physical comedy are brilliant, but up to that point, it could still be just any cheesy historic movie. Then Queen's "We Will Rock You" changes the jousting scene from fourteenth-century Renaissance fair into twentieth-century English soccer stadium.

Malcolm's smile is wide with surprise and delight and anticipation. "The 1370s as the 1970s?" He pauses the movie and turns to me. "Is it like this all the way through?"

I love him for that. Because instantly he gets it.

He gets *me*.

A Knight's Tale is the perfect rags-to-riches story because it's not about getting rich at all. It's about being noble no matter where you come from. Yes, there are definitely plot holes and the romance isn't my favorite, but seeing the arrogant, ruthless Count Adamar get his comeuppance will never, ever get old.

That's what's supposed to happen, isn't it? The good guys are supposed to win.

Malcolm laughs in the same places I do all the way through, and when the movie ends with the stop-motion of Adamar falling in defeat, both of us are grinning. Malcolm's voice is almost hushed, as if he's gone to church.

"How have I never seen this before?" he asks.

"You've obviously had a childhood deprived of culture. But you loved it, right?" I roll over on my side to look at him. "I hoped you would."

"I did."

"Tell me why. Specifically. Not generally."

He shakes his head, as if I'm kidding or only mildly curious. Except I'm not. His answer *matters*. My whole world suddenly hinges on how he answers. Because in a weird way, I realize his response will be a sort of litmus test.

If I decide to keep Ian's secret, it will mean I'm keeping Malcolm's secret, too. And Halford's. What if Malcolm *isn't* the one who is legally meant to inherit the title? Never mind that there could be an entire family he doesn't know exists lurking somewhere in his DNA. This affects them, too.

I'm about to make decisions for a whole lot of people, and if I do that, then I need to know Malcolm's worth it. Worthy of Halford and Ian and sacrifice. Worthy of the lie. If he doesn't understand honor, justice, and loyalty, then maybe he's not the kind of person who'll deserve it.

Elli would say it's stupid to decide my future based on his interpretation of a movie he's only seen once, but people make decisions for all kinds of reasons. Gut instinct. The flip of a coin. A Magic 8-Ball. Tarot cards.

A Knight's Tale is as good a reason as any one of those.

Malcolm leans in toward me. "If I have to choose right this moment, I'll start with the Chaucer character. I loved him. I liked the anachronisms, too: the clothes and music and Kate the blacksmith making pseudo-Nike armor. Most of all, though, I have to say I loved Edward the Black Prince because he saw that William was more noble than Count Adamar had ever been and risked his own honor so that William could compete. And I loved William, because even when he had changed his stars, he didn't forget where he came from. My only regret is that he didn't fall in love with Kate instead of Jocelyn. If Jocelyn really cared for him, she'd never have asked him to prove he loved her."

I feel like my whole body has filled with air.

"Jocelyn had men tell her they loved her all the

time," I say, "even when all they really wanted was her title and her face and her father's fortune. But she was willing to run away with William and be a pig farmer instead of a princess."

Malcolm rolls over on his elbow to look at me. "I suppose that's true. If someone loves you, really loves you, though, I think you know it. Don't you?"

"Do you?" I can't help asking.

Our faces are inches from each other. I feel his breath against my lips. My heart pounds so loud I swear he has to hear it.

His eyes are dark as they slide down to my lips, and he inhales sharply. Neither of us moves. Not much at least. I feel us pulling toward each other millimeter by millimeter by millimeter, and I know we need to stop. We both know.

His forehead falls gently on to mine and we stay like that, forehead to forehead, skin to skin, breathing hard and otherwise not moving. Every neuron in my body is electrified and urging me to just give in, tell the lie, and kiss him.

"I've never believed in love before," he whispers raggedly. "Or at least I suppose I've never believed it can cause anything but heartache."

"I hope it can," I whisper back. "I'm sure it can."

I desperately need to believe it.

Somewhere since I met Malcolm, my lack of armor has turned deadly. I have only to close my eyes, and I see every millimeter of his face as if he's etched on the back of my eyelids. But it's more than just the surface image. I see the inside Malcolm. Not just the Malcolm I've spent every waking moment with all this time, the now-Malcolm, but also the past-Malcolm that he has let me glimpse, the Malcolm that turned him into who he is. I see the small, laughing boy who sailed boats with his sister. The bewildered boy who lost his twin and retreated into a priest hole lined with books. The boy who hid while his mother screeched accusations she knew weren't fair. The teenager who blamed his father for his mother's death. I see the Malcolm who stands on the terrace every morning watching the sun light up the Taj Mahal as if he wants to memorize every shade of pink and rose and crimson that makes the marble blush. And the one who is willing to admit when he is wrong—the one who wants to do things better. The one who's beautiful when he reads and the one who gets my favorite film.

Love isn't one size fits all, even though everyone thinks their own experience defines the boundaries of it. Some people step into love one movie date and football game and concert at a time, and they think that true love only happens slowly. Others claw their way in faster through shared pain and hope, while still others fall instantly and convince themselves that means their love is special.

However love happens, once you're there in the

place where love exists, it's impossible to get out again without leaving half your heart behind.

Whatever I decide about the DNA, and whether I stay or go after that, I have no doubt I'll carry Malcolm in my heart for a long, long time. He'll be impossible to avoid, impossible to forget, and unless I make the right decision, he'll always be impossibly out of reach.

Caring about someone, it turns out, is all it really takes to make decisions easy. When you care, it's not about sacrifice or deserving something. It's about needing to make the other person happy more than you need anything yourself.

I could tell Malcolm the truth about us right now. Tell him we're not related. I want to. I could tell him the truth, and then I could kiss him.

It's only a handful of words: *Malcolm, I'm not your sister.* But they're words I cannot say.

I'm not the one who needs to say them.

Climbing Up

Imagined Text to Elli:

Me: I don't know why people say you fall in love. You climb into it. The fall comes later.

Elli: Maybe it's a heaven or hell kind of thing. Depends on the path?

Me: I don't think so. Maybe speed is the only variable. You can run or jump a few steps going up. Going down all you can hope for is a parachute or a slow descent.

Sacrifices

It's morning rush hour, and we're stuck in traffic caused by a cow in the middle of the road while a milk *wallah* serves customers at the roadside next to us. Buyers walk up to the thigh-high metal canister planted in the dirt and dip a finger in to taste the milk and make sure it's fresh before they purchase. Behind the milk vendor, bushels of oranges, mangoes, pomegranates, and every possible form of vegetable are displayed beneath a giant billboard.

We're late arriving at the hospital, and Ian has obviously been worried—it's like someone switched on a light beneath his skin when he sees us. He searches my face and says, "You're here."

"Where else would we be?" Malcolm asks. Then as if he senses something is off, he turns to look at me.

It's no less dangerous to look into Malcolm's eyes now than it was last night. They're constantly changing color. When he's sad or worried, they're a darker green, and when he laughs, the light bounces off of them and burns its way inside me like a laser. The invisible string of energy that never seems to go away between us tries to snap me toward him like a rubber band.

That's not why I'm doing this, though, I remind myself. It's not about the two of us being able to be together.

Ian and my mother both sacrificed their happiness for something bigger than themselves. That's what I finally decided last night. They sacrificed, and Malcolm is a good man. He deserves good things.

That all needs to mean something. I want to make sure it continues to mean something.

Every emotion in the world is balled up inside my throat. Love and hope and fear and sadness and pain and regret and grief. Outrage, too. Outrage for all the pain and longing. All the things that were missed these last twenty years.

I do my best to swallow the lump of heartache, and when Malcolm looks away I nod at Ian. "Protect him," I whisper soundlessly. "That's what I want."

Ian
Gratitude

Izzy holds the box of letters on her lap, her hands splayed tightly on the lid as though she imagines the pages will become birds and fly away. She's so much like Cella I can scarcely bear it: gallant and kind and impetuous. That same undercurrent of unpredictability and wildness runs through her veins. Seeing her sitting here beside Malcolm, gratitude breaks my heart open, and pain crumbles it into dust.

The more I know Izzy, the more a selfish, irrational impulse wants to claim her no matter the consequences. If I could have a daughter like her, I'd love nothing more than to shout that from the rooftops. Whatever happens, I want to know her, to spend every last moment I have getting to know her.

What if saving Malcolm breaks her? I've no right at all to ask her to do something this difficult.

On the other hand, the more I watch her and Malcolm together, the more certain I am that I will have Izzy as a daughter one way or the other. I close my eyes and see myself walking her down the aisle of Halford chapel and giving her hand to Malcolm, and I can imagine Cella smiling at that. Because what she and I couldn't have, Izzy and Malcolm will. No two people were ever more perfect for each other.

Malcolm
Confusion

Izzy and my father are both behaving rather oddly. Dad reaches for her hand, and for a long awkward moment she ignores him, clutching the shoebox containing her mother's letters instead. Finally, she places her palm in his. Dad's fingers tremble with the strain of holding still so long, or maybe it's something else. Maybe his heart is getting worse.

Moisture leeches from my mouth and leaves behind a bitter taste on my tongue, but then common sense kicks in. If Dad had taken a turn in the night, he would be concerned about me, about both of us. Not just Izzy.

Still, there's something going on.

"I'm uncertain how to say this," he begins, and sensing it's bad news, I take Izzy's other hand in mine. "Dr. Asrani mentioned you and Malcolm had both given blood, so even though it was a long shot, I asked him about compatibility."

"If our blood types are compatible with yours, you mean?" I ask at the same moment Izzy asks, "And are we?"

He shakes his head. "I'm afraid not."

Izzy seems to grasp it faster than I do. "Well, that's it then, isn't it?" she says. "If my blood's not compatible, we can't be related. Is that what you meant?"

Science and Maths have never been my best subjects, but I can vaguely remember learning about blood types in primary school. I know parents with certain blood types can only pass on specific types of blood, so the wrong combination would rule out paternity.

Dad takes a breath as though to regroup himself. The answer is clear in the pale tightness of his features. "That's right."

I squeeze Izzy's hand. It's cold and tense, and I want to pull her out into the corridor and hold her. I want to kiss her. Because I can.

She and Dad are still looking at each other, and she hasn't even glanced at me.

I watch her profile, the way the corner of her mouth trembles as she fights to achieve a smile, the way the light accents the sharp angle between the end of her brow and the blade of her cheek, the hundreds of planes that make up something I can't stop watching. I grew up learning to see the beauty of Halford in unexpected places: the pattern of a floor and the curve of a banister, the symmetry of a garden. Somehow, until I met Izzy, I was never as aware of that in people.

She was always destined to lose in this situation. Either she was going to lose a potential father, or we would lose the potential between us. Feeling the tension in her now, I realize which one she wanted more. Maybe even she didn't know that until this moment when the chance to be part of a family again was snatched away from her.

Having a father is important, and I've thrown mine away. Done my best to ignore him. Seeing Izzy longing for something she's never had and never will have makes that realization even worse.

Dad still hasn't said anything else. He's crying silently, his chest shaking.

"Dad—" I begin.

Izzy pushes herself out of her chair and leans over to kiss his cheek. "It doesn't matter," she says with tears thickening her lashes and her voice. "I'm all right. Honestly. I never expected anything when I came—I just wanted to know, that's all. And now I do."

Oddly, Dad looks like his heart is breaking all over again at that. "You're still Marcella's child," he says. "That's all the blood connection I'll ever need."

Izzy smiles and slides her eyes away, and there's a wistful lostness in her expression that says it's not the same.

How is it that we so often forget to value what's right in front of us?

I want to tell my father I'm sorry for all the time we've lost. But I won't do that in front of Izzy. She's just lost even more.

Ian
Unspoken Lies

If I'd never met Izzy until this moment, I would still have fallen in love with her for taking the lie away from me. She never even allowed me say the words.

Poets know the value of falling in love, how quickly it can happen and for how many different reasons. We discount that in our modern world, and I wonder if we don't doubt love right out of existence. It's such a delicate, ephemeral thing.

William Blake fell in love with Catherine Boucher after telling her he'd had his heart broken by someone else. He asked if she pitied him for his pain, and when she admitted she did, he said, "Then I love you."

That was it. He decided to love her, there and then in that moment, and they were together until he died.

It truly doesn't matter whether Izzy is or isn't my flesh and blood. She's every inch the best of her mother, but more than that, she's special in her own right. Kinder than either her mother or I have been.

PART EIGHT

Izzy
A l o n e

We open the curtains and ignore the speculation in the way the nurses study us. Dr. Asrani comes walking toward us, the long white coat he wears on rounds flapping open over his surgical scrubs. He has a habit of sniffing as he reads the chart, running his finger over log entries the nursing staff have made. This morning, it seems to be taking him longer than usual. Mahadevi comes and they speak together softly, and Gauri and Aashi, the relief nurse we've seen the least, keep glancing over as if they know something's different about this visit compared to all the others.

I push myself out of the chair and stand behind Malcolm. He's leaning forward, elbows on his knees.

Dr. Asrani puts down the chart and studies the heart monitor then warms the stethoscope and stoops to listen to Ian's heart. Eventually, he looks up and bobbles his head from side to side in the Indian equivalent of a nod.

"It is time," he says. "This afternoon, we can move you to a room."

"If you are finished reading all the letters," Mahadevi says, smiling as if she's joking. But her eyes aren't smiling so maybe she isn't trying to be funny—the nurses are deeply invested in their daily dose of drama.

There aren't many letters left to read, and Ian doesn't have the excuse of needing time to rest in between them anymore. I pull out the shoe box and sit down in the chair by Ian's bed again, feeling a wave of gratitude at the prospect of having something to do. It takes me a minute to find where we left off, and Ian and Malcolm watch me the whole time with furrowed, worried expressions.

The more they stare at me, the less all right I feel.

"Stop it," I hiss at them. "I'm fine. I'm happy."

"Are you?" Malcolm asks, his brows arching. "Is it selfish that I'm actually happy about it?"

"I have nothing to be unhappy about." I glance at Ian and smile as I realize how that sounds. "Well, you know what I mean."

Ian laughs and points to the envelope I'm holding. "You had better start reading, then, because as much as I like the nursing staff, I've no intention of letting them keep me here any longer than absolutely necessary."

Two beds away, where she's hanging a new IV bag, Mahadevi blushes, but she doesn't protest.

———— �֍ ————

October 24, 2015

Dear Ian

Izzy is out on a date tonight. The boy is older but he seems reasonable, especially for a boy who plays in a band. At least he is musician or charmer enough to have listened to or read about a few of my recordings so that he could say intelligent things when he came to pick her up. But I hid at the edge of the window and watched him slump into his own seat and leave Izzy to open her door, and I don't know if that's acceptable now, or whether it's a sign of disrespect. I feel out of my depth. She is growing up. She's grown. All too soon, she'll be applying to college. Not Oxford, she's adamant about that because she's already set her heart on Princeton.

Is it wrong for me to want her to have the same happy memories that I had? I suppose the problem with happy memories is that we often end up looking back at them with regret.

I want so much for Izzy, but I have to be careful to let her find her own dreams. I feel the magic inside her, but I'm never certain if she wants it enough to reach for it. I'm giving her room and time, which are gifts that my talent never gave to me. I'm not telling her to avoid this boy. She's smarter than I ever was. Maybe she'll find a way to have everything she wants. Boys and gifts and magic. She'll write the world the way she wants it to be, and her vision will be one of a better world than we are leaving to her.

I think of you alone in the Hall with your son away at school, and my heart breaks for you, for him. For us. I find it difficult to be enough for my child when I am so alone myself.

As always,

Cella

Courage

It's hours later, and I finish reading the last of the letters. And I can't help thinking how the meaning of the last one has changed for me since I first found it. The last paragraph especially haunts me.

I find myself thinking more and more often about possibilities. Some day soon, maybe I'll find enough courage to reach for joy again. To reach for you again.

Ian has gone pale, and I can see it will haunt him, too. "Is that all? That's the final letter?"

"As far as I know. I'm sorry."

"Don't be." He reaches for my hand as I fold the letter back into its envelope. "Thank you, Izzy.

I can't tell you how much this has meant. Finding you. Hearing her thoughts."

I clear my throat and nod. "I wish she'd found her courage sooner."

"I wish *I* had," Ian says.

———❖———

Instructions

Ian refuses to let us help him when they move him to his new room. They're going to let him use a walker to get there, and he claims he will be too tired for company after the exertion. I think he mainly wants time to process the letters. He's asked me if he can borrow them to read over again.

"I won't keep them long," he says.

"Of course." My voice is shaking and on top of everything else I'm feeling, now I have to pretend there isn't something that squeezes hard down inside me at the thought of handing them over. Would it have made Mom happy to know how much her words have meant—not just to Ian, but to me and Malcolm, too?

The universe is so strange and unexpected. If Mom had lived, I might never have found out about the letters. I might never have met Ian or Malcolm at all.

The thought destroys me all over again, but I still refuse, *refuse*, to cry in front of them.

I won't.

"All right, the pair of you. Time you did something besides sitting around here all day again," Ian says. "Have Mr. Chandra take you out to the deserted city. Or go shopping. Make a night of it. I'll be perfectly all right until tomorrow."

The last thing I need is a long car ride with Malcolm and time in empty spaces. But maybe a crowded bazaar isn't a bad idea. A chance to let the embarrassment and self-consciousness die down between us. And I'd like to get the nurses something as a thank-you, anyway, for taking such good care of Ian. I want to find Laksha a wedding present, too.

I look around at Mahadevi and the other nurses who are still talking to each other about the letters. They sneak shy, smiling looks at Ian, and their eyes are red from crying. He's working hard to pretend he doesn't notice, but I can understand why he wants to be alone. He'll never admit it, I think affectionately, but I suspect he needs a break from awkwardness.

More than anything else, he probably needs a break from me. Right now, I'm queen of awkward. Secret awkward. Reminder of heartbreak awkward. Superfluous awkward.

Maybe what we all need is an awkwardness reset. Time and distance for the dust to settle.

Perspective time and Atlantic ocean distance.

I sneak a glance at Malcolm. I hate the thought of

leaving him, leaving either of them, but it's for the best. Last night, I deluded myself that maybe it would actually be easier after Ian and I lied, once the idea of being related was no longer an obstacle between us. Now the lie hangs between us and the idea of being alone with Malcolm fills my stomach with worms and Large Blue butterflies and all kinds of squirmy things.

Malcolm
Declaration

The nurses in the cardiac care unit all come to say goodbye as Izzy and I leave my father, and when we tell them we'll stop back to visit, I can see they don't believe us. Some of the off-duty nurses are still hovering in the corridor nearby, pretending they aren't there whilst they whisper together about the final letters. Mrs. Mittal, Panya, and Laksha are there, too, standing outside the waiting room door, and Laksha stops Izzy and holds out a small package wrapped in yellow embroidered silk.

"What's this?" Izzy asks.

"Open it." Laksha smiles shyly, her hands extending again in a graceful offering gesture.

Panya nods. "From all of us."

There are eight red glass bangles in the package. Izzy holds them up and joy pours into her face. Pure, radiant, and light-filled joy that shines from every pore as though she has swallowed up the sun. That's Izzy, that ability to feel so much. My heart swells, because love makes it do that and because there is so much generosity in the world.

"The bracelets are traditional," Mrs. Mittal says. "To go with bare arms on a special occasion is considered to be inauspicious."

Izzy sways forward then back again. I can see she wants to hug the Mittals but she's afraid of doing the wrong thing, so she stops herself. "Thank you," she says instead, her voice full to overflowing. "You shouldn't have, but I'll always treasure them."

Laksha steps forward and holds her arms wide. Izzy hugs her back.

We walk away a few moments later, and Izzy does her best not to cry. I draw her into the stairwell where it's quiet and pull her to me on the landing midway between floors.

"I'm fine." Her voice is fierce, and she pushes away from me, her beautiful wild hair tossing around her shoulders like a dark cloud against the pale beige wall. "Don't feel sorry for me. I'm only crying because I wanted to do something nice for the Mittals and now if I bring them something, they'll think I'm just doing it out of obligation."

"They wouldn't think that—and even if they did, they wouldn't care."

She fights to pull herself together. It's hard to watch her so upset when all I feel is relief and joy that she isn't my sister. But then I remember what she's lost. She must feel as though the last piece of her family has died all over again, and she's been brilliant about that all morning, putting on a brave front for Dad. I wish she didn't feel she needed to be quite so brave.

"You're not really upset about the Mittals," I say. "Talk to me, Iz. You can be honest."

She's half-turned away and she whips toward me. "Don't you dare tell me what I feel. You don't even know me!" Her eyes are wildcat wounded and afraid, and if I let her, I suspect she will cut and run—if not physically, then at least emotionally. I can't let her do that.

Catching her chin in my hand, I tip it up until her eyes meet mine. "I know everything about you that matters, and all I want is time to know the rest. Don't push me away. Not being related should make things easier, not more difficult."

"I don't belong." The words are a whisper in the dark, far away and full of longing.

I wet my lips, because my mouth is dry with the ache of her loneliness. I consider telling her what I did this morning when she excused herself to the restroom after my father broke the news. I won't tell her yet, though. Knowing would only make the waiting harder

"You do belong," I say instead. "With me. With Dad. You've even managed to make me feel like I belong with him again. I hope you feel the same way about me that I feel about you, but if you don't—or if it's too soon for you to admit it yet—then at least give us time to work things out."

She's pale, lost, and beautiful. "You can't be sure it would work out."

"I love you. I think I have since that first moment I saw your Shakespeare T-shirt and heard you talk about Walpole and serendipity. You woke me up and made my life catch fire, but at the same time, you've given me peace within myself. No one's ever given me that."

I pause and take a deep breath, feeling as if I've torn off all my clothes in the middle of a Halford tour and I stand before her naked. Her eyes have turned the color of honey in the sunlight, full of surprise and wonder and confusion, and I search for joy in the depths of them, and it isn't there. Not yet. Belatedly, I realize my fingers are still cradling her chin, and more than anything I want to bend my head and kiss her. I force myself to wait. Releasing my grip, I start to pull away, but she catches my fingers in her own, and her other hand brushes my cheek in a light, trembling stroke.

"I'm sorry. I need time to think. Can you understand that?" she asks so gently it's like a knife plunged into my throat. "I thought this would all be simple, and but my heart is all tangled up with feelings, and I don't have the right words to sort them yet. I don't know what I want to say."

Izzy
Reunions

There are supposed to be five stages of grief and loss, as if it's a progression. As if there's only one right way to grieve. That's another misconception, though. I'm living through the fine print. The stages can come in any order and there's no prescription for how long they take. The problem is that denial comes first, and it makes you numb enough to withstand the initial shock. It also lets your mind trick you in hundreds of other ways.

I grieved for my mother, but I think I put it on hold by fixating on her letters. On finding Ian. On finding the truth. Now the letters are finished, and there's no truth coming. Not for me. There's nothing to fixate on except reality.

Loss hits me all over again while Malcolm's talking, a sense of loss so deep I'm not sure it has a bottom. I felt bad right after Ian and I played out our charade with the blood types, and I excused myself and sat in the restroom with my face buried in my knees, trying not to sob out loud. Now it's even worse.

I think I love Malcolm, I know I do, but what if it's for all the wrong reasons? Is he just my next fixation, a human connection to replace the one I've lost?

I don't think so, but how do I trust myself? I have to be careful not to hurt him.

I already have, though. Just now. By not saying what he wants to hear. There's a frozen stiff-upper-lipness to his face that tells me so.

My hand goes up to cover the one he's pulling away from my chin. I link my fingers through his, trying to keep him from withdrawing into himself, withdrawing from me. His shoulders hunch into curves of pain like a hedgehog drawing in to armor itself in swords and pride. I brace myself. I know the next thing he says will slice me raw.

"Take all the time you need," he says without any inflection to his voice at all.

He's spent his whole life keeping his emotions locked inside him. Partly that's British, and partly it comes of growing up a Halford, I think. When I look at him, though, I see the scared, lost boy who went through the same grief I'm feeling now, except that he was only twelve. And he was even younger when he lost his twin.

The thought brings me a fresh wash of shame. But I can't—I won't—make things worse for him. I won't begin another generation of letter writing, failure, and heartache by saying things I can't live up to. Not aloud.

Thoughts and emotions are blunted weapons until they're defined in words. After that they can't be taken back. They can only build or destroy.

I press my hand to Malcolm's cheek, and I stand on my toes to kiss him. I mean it to be a quick kiss, a placeholder kiss. But our lips touch and it turns to something else.

He draws me closer, his hands fierce and hot against my back. My shirt separates from my waistband and I feel rough skin graze mine, drawing goosebumps. I let my own fingers burrow into the firm ropes of his muscles, and his heart beats thick and fast. I want to savor every moment of this kiss as if it's the last one I'll ever have. Just in case it is.

You can't replace love if you lose it. Mom and Ian are the perfect example of that. I suspect they'd both have given anything to be able to love someone else, someone easier. But maybe the once-in-a-lifetime kind of love isn't meant to be easy. Maybe that's the price it demands.

Reckless

We arrive at the Subhash Bazaar near the Red Fort railway station, and I'm still reeling, still feeling too much. The bazaar is the perfect place to recover from that. The newness of it flies at me insistently from every direction so I don't have to worry about what I feel. I think Malcolm is having the same reaction. Both of us pretend everything is normal between us.

I buy gifts for everyone I know—two silk *sarees* and glass bangles for Elli and another *saree* for her mother. Finding something for the Mittals and Mahadevi and the nurses is harder, but I finally settle on silk purses and gorgeous silk shawls, each embroidered with motifs that remind me of them.

The bazaar is the oldest one in Agra, and as I spot the same people over and over among the tight press of crowded individual shops, I picture Khurram and Mumtaz Mahal catching sight of each other and beginning their lifelong love affair. Maybe that's why my breath catches every time I spot Malcolm as the two of us prowl through the dozens of bookshops. He buys a half dozen leather-bound books that look like the thousands they already have at Halford. These are Indian history and epic poetry, though. Meanwhile, I pick up an Indian novel in English that won the Pulitzer and two that won the Booker Prize, and then I find a shop where stonecutters make the incredible *parchin kari* in the same way they did when the marble of the Taj Mahal was inlaid with precious gems. I can't resist buying a beautiful box to hold my mother's letters. It's as close as I can come to giving her a part of the honeymoon trip to the Taj Mahal that she never had the chance to take with Ian.

Everywhere we go, the bazaar smells of indefinable, delicious spices and leather and people. Too many people, all swirling in their bright colors and hand-fluttering, rapid chatter.

Vendors offer us everything, and it's hard to refuse. I desperately want to try the *dalmoth*, a dry savory snack made of fried lentils, nuts, and spices.

"It probably isn't safe for you yet," Malcolm says. "You're still not used to the bacteria."

"I want to live dangerously," I say.

"Maybe not that dangerously."

He smiles and shakes his head at the vendor, and we wander on to the next stall with my stomach growling. By the time we move on to the Sadar Bazaar an hour later, I'm too hungry to keep resisting. I wait until Malcolm's distracted and buy some *petha*, the soft, translucent candy made from white pumpkin, and some *gajak*, which is a sesame seed brittle that lingers on the tongue long after it has melted in your mouth. He watches me eat a piece, then he sighs and laughs and holds out his hand.

We share a bag between us while we fight temptation all the way down the *chaat wali gali*, the snack street, where the street food vendors offer dozens of vegetarian options that entice us to want to sample everything.

Chai *wallahs* have become one of my favorite things in India, the way they turn the making of tea into performance art. I stop and watch an old woman in a royal blue *saree* who looks as if she's dancing while she cooks. She's the only female chai *wallah* I've seen, and she offers me the first cup from the new batch, and I'm not sure whether she's made it better than the other versions of chai I've tried here or whether my taste buds have adjusted to the more subtle, complex sweetness of the non-Starbucks version. But it's delicious.

It may have been a mistake, though. Or more likely, it was the *petha* or the *gajak* or something else. I have to admit that, finally, at one in the morning when I dive out of bed and race to the bathroom the first of countless times. Eventually, I stop going back to bed in between throwing up, and everything—all the nausea and regret and grief and confusion and fear and sadness of the day—all roil together in my stomach. I feel bad enough that everything finally overwhelms me.

That's where I am when Malcolm finds me, huddled in a miserable heap by the toilet. "I thought I heard something," he says. "Poor you."

He unwraps my arms and lifts my head, and then he lifts me up in a single motion. I'm not sure if I'm holding him or if he's holding me. We're simply holding on to each other.

It isn't just Mom I'm crying for, or Ian, or Malcolm,

or even me. I recognize that. I think I'm crying my heart out for all the possibilities that never happened, for the Ian I will never get to claim, the one I somehow managed to fall in love with almost as much as I love Malcolm. I'm crying for both the real flesh-and-blood Ian and the one that was in my mother's letters. I'm crying for what they didn't have, and I'm crying for the years their love cost Malcolm, who gave up so much of his childhood to anger.

"I guess it's a good thing we didn't try any more of the *chaat*," Malcolm says.

I wipe my nose with some toilet paper. "I'm not crying because I'm sick."

"I know. You lost a father today. But we can share. I'll share my father and anything else with you."

He tries to pull me from the bathroom, but I'm not ready yet, and I slump back down to the floor and he sits down beside me, his head resting against the wall. His fingers lace through mine, which is brave of him considering where my fingers have been.

"It's been a lot for you, hasn't it?" he says.

He turns and my forehead falls onto his, and we sit like that, not moving. Breathing. Ugh. *Trying* not to breathe on him.

I slide my knees beneath me so that I can kneel

beside him. "I don't want to hurt you by saying things I can't live up to."

"Don't make senseless sacrifices. Just talk to me. That's all I want. Tell me how you feel."

He's as good as Elli at picking up on exactly what I need. How do they do that? It's uncanny and scary and wonderful. Except he's wrong about one thing.

"Sometimes sacrifices make more and more sense the longer you think about them," I say. Then my stomach turns over and I dive for the toilet again, and Malcolm holds my hair back while I throw up emptiness from my stomach.

For most of the rest of the night, he alternates between handing me wads of toilet paper and bringing me coconut water so that I don't shrivel up into a dehydrated husk. The sun has already risen when he finally puts me to bed with a cool washcloth folded over my hot forehead, and he sits beside me, smoothing my hair back as I drift off to sleep.

That kind of a guy is worth whatever sacrifice.

Surprise

It's past noon before I even get up. I've missed breakfast, and I'm in no mood for lunch. Even the distant smell of coffee drifting under my door threatens to make me head back to the bathroom, so I just sip more of the coconut water Malcolm left for me and pad into the bathroom to take a long, hot shower.

I refuse to be embarrassed over the fact that Malcolm watched me throw up at least a dozen times. On the other hand, he watched me throw up at least a dozen times.

It has to be really hard being Prince Charming in the modern age. There aren't many external dragons they can slay to prove they love someone, and if they so much as hold a door open, they can't be sure whether they're going to get a thank-you or a dirty look. All the things their grandparents knew are gone, all those romantic notions in novels and movies. The whole idea of the alpha hero who sweeps a girl off her feet is totally suspect. These days, even Disney princesses save themselves.

But holding a girl's hair while she throws up, and still being willing to hold her hand? That's a modern dragon.

I brush my teeth very carefully, and I dress in my second favorite Oscar Wilde T-shirt. Then I go forth to do battle with my own inner snarling, fire-breathing wild thing. I don't want to be too afraid to reach for something beautiful. Malcolm is beautiful. If I let him slip through my fingers because I'm afraid, then the rest of my life will be asplendorious.

BEHIND EVERY *exquisite* THING THAT *existed, there* WAS SOMETHING *tragic.*

Brass rings, baby. You can't catch them if you never try.

He looks up from the sofa as I open my bedroom door. "Feeling better?" he asks. "I figured I should let you sleep as long as you could."

I crawl up on the sofa beside him, and I kiss him until we are both breathing fire. He looks bemused as he pulls away for a second and searches my face, then he sighs and smiles and swoops in for a second helping. This time, it's what kisses are supposed to be, not desperation or sorrow or goodbye or nerves. Just asking and giving and the exchanging of breath and heartbeat.

"What brought this on?" he asks when we come up for air.

"I wanted to pave the way for the words," I say. "Words matter. Are you listening?"

He smiles. "Intently."

"Okay, here goes. I love you. I loved you when I wasn't supposed to love you, and I loved you when it was okay to love you but I was too scared to let myself. I loved you when I wasn't sure if I loved you for the right reasons, and even then I loved you enough not to want to tell you if the reasons weren't right."

"Love doesn't need reasons."

"There are always reasons."

"Reasons change. For instance, right now I love you because you kiss me before you say 'good morning' and yesterday I loved you because you bought up half the bazaar for other people, and the only things you bought for yourself were other people's words and a container to hold your mother's thoughts. Tomorrow, I'll love you for an entirely different reason."

I kiss him all over again for that, and by the time we get back to the hospital it's nearly mid-afternoon. We have armloads of gifts to distribute, so we do that, too, before we go in search of his father's room. By which time, it's really impossibly late.

A grim-faced nurse gives us the room number and points us down the corridor. And I'm slow to pick up the clues.

Gifts

First, there's a voice that spills out of an open door-way, and then there's the shape of someone sitting beside Ian's bed. Someone with long lavender hair and a hot pink shirt.

I'm so, so glad to see Elli, I squeal aloud. I didn't even know how much I needed her until she's got her arms around me and we're bouncing together in the middle of the room. That probably seems ridiculous to Ian, but I don't care.

"What are you doing here?" I ask when the springs on our feet have gone still again. "How did you get here?"

Elli nods toward the door where Malcolm is standing. "Prince Charming called me yesterday after Ian told you he wasn't your father. He figured you might need me to cheer you up. It was after midnight my time, but he and Ian gave me the number for someone in London who made all the arrangements, and I was on a flight to New Delhi at six in the morning. They even arranged a private plane to get me here from Delhi. Well, not all the way here. Ohmygod, those roads! People should get medals here just for arriving at their intended destination. But meanwhile Mr. Chandra was a superhero, and he got me here from the airport."

I'm looking at Malcolm, who's trying to look nonchalant, and I realize he must have used my phone while I was sobbing in the bathroom.

So that is dragon number two.

My prince in invisible armor. And Ian, too, because he had to be in on it. I walk over to the bed and kiss him on the forehead.

"Thank you," I whisper. Then I raise my voice. "Thank you both."

"It was purely a selfish impulse on my part," Malcolm says. "I wanted to meet her."

I raise my eyebrows at him, but it's Ian who explains. "He's lying. We were both worried you might bolt for home, so we brought home here for you. Elli's meant to try to help us convince you to come to Halford for the rest of the summer. She's even agreed to come with you."

"It was a hard sell, let me tell you," Elli says solemnly. "High-pressure tactics, arm twisting, water boarding, the whole nine yards. I mean, who wants to stay at a gorgeous English estate? Not me."

It's scary how easily Elli manages to put things into perspective.

Or maybe it's scarier that I'm so slow to see the same things for myself.

"Also," Elli continues, "I was looking up Oxford. Did you know Oscar Wilde went there? And J.K. Rowling wanted to go? Also J.R.R. Tolkien went and T.E. Lawrence, T.S. Eliot—"

"Are initials mandatory?" I ask.

"Of course not." Elli glares me into submission. "There was also Jonathan Swift, Lewis Carroll, Diana Wynne Jones, Dorothy L. Sayers, Harper Lee did a program, and John Donne, Sir Walter Raleigh, John LeCarré, William Golding, Tina Brown, not to mention

Emma Watson and Indira Gandhi. We could apply together for next year. Did you know they have an entire Environmental Change Institute?"

"You found this all out since they called you?"

"Are you kidding? I've been planning it since you said you were going to India with them."

"You're slightly insane," I say, because there are so many—too many—other things to say and I'll start bawling if I say any of them.

Where before I felt empty and alone, I'm suddenly full to overflowing, and even though I'd already reached the same conclusions without Elli's help, having her here, knowing she'll be right beside me, is wonderful.

Malcolm and I and Elli sit shoulder to shoulder while we talk and keep Ian entertained for the rest of the afternoon. I have to resist the urge to keep telling Malcolm how grateful I am that he's done this every time Elli says something that makes us laugh. Instead, I just squeeze his hand. He smiles, and I can see he gets it. That's what makes me know that he's worth any amount of risk. Words are magic, but maybe the most important ones never need to be said aloud.

Pillow Talk

Elli lies beside me on the enormous bed, her arms

crossed behind her head and her feet up on the headboard. I'm leaning back against the pillows as I finish telling her about Ian and Malcolm and my mom.

"Wow," she says. "I'm not sure if that's wonderful or awful. Both. But you can't ever tell him, you know that, right? However much you're tempted to get it off your chest."

"I know."

"Because I'm pretty sure Malcolm is William in *A Knight's Tale*. He wouldn't try to save himself when his secret is revealed. He'd try to find whoever was supposed to be the next Earl of Mortimer—even if in the end it turns out he was the one who was meant to have the title all along. And it's not like it's cheating, really. He is a Halford, and his mother was married to Ian when he was born."

"He'll take good care of Halford—he loves it."

"That's my point," Elli says. "And Ian loves him. Anyway, this is the only thing that puts the universe back in balance for what your mom and Ian went through. Otherwise, everything they sacrificed would have been for nothing."

"I know."

She stares at me hard. "How do you feel?"

I stare up at the ceiling. "I'm fine."

"No, you're not. I meant about your relationship with Ian."

"Still fine."

"Iz. Hello. You went nuts every time you had to wait to get back an English paper on the fractional chance you might get an A- instead of an A. How are you going to stand not knowing if he's your father?"

"But I do know. At least I think I do."

I climb off the bed and pad over to the chair where I've left my purse, and I pull the folded piece of Hotel George V letterhead out of the pocket in my wallet. "Ian's kept it all these years," I say. "He gave it to me, and it was what first made me realize Malcolm wasn't his. I was so focused on that, I didn't see the rest of it until much later. People reuse phrases they like, don't they? And Mom liked to repeat her jokes, but I think this is different."

Elli screws her face into concentration and starts to read. She reads the letter twice before looking up. "You mean the part about 'a string of long good nights'—that's what she told you about your father, isn't it?"

"Yeah. But maybe it's wishful thinking."

Elli bounces off the bed and hugs me. "See? I told you I was right. He's your father. He has to be. Have you told him yet?"

I shake my head before she even finishes her sentence, because I'm still not sure I should. "It's not conclusive, and anyway, why risk it? He'd only feel more guilty about what he's asking me to do."

"Izzy!" Elli studies me and sighs. "Well, I hate to

admit it, but you aren't wrong. I've known him five minutes, and I can tell he's a good guy. The kind of guy who's so busy trying to do the right thing that the universe can sneak up behind him and knock him cold. He and Malcolm are both like that, so maybe it's up to you to save them from themselves. Save them so they can save their little corner of the world." She smiles then, and it's a little forced but a definite A for effort. "At least you know. That's what counts. And you still get to spend time at Halford. Plus when you marry Malcolm, you'll be a real-life Disney princess."

"Assumption much? Also, I'm not the one with delusions of grandeur."

She flops back onto the bed and folds her arms beneath her head looking smug. "Some are born to princess and some have princess thrust upon them. And you're wrong about assumptions. It shines out of Malcolm when he looks at you. And you when you look at him. But I get to pick my own bridesmaid's dress whenever you get married. Just saying."

This is Elli. She takes things I think are complicated and makes them simple.

She yawns, which is contagious, so I find myself yawning, too. We should both have been asleep hours ago.

"I'm glad you're here," I say, slipping into bed beside her and pulling up the blanket. "Good night, El."

"Good night. And dream about Oxford, okay? I'm serious. We could totally own that place."

"What about your parents? And working in the lab?"

"You're more important than the lab, and my parents have Ethan and Owen and there are planes and phones. Anyway, I'll borrow Ian, too. You borrowed my dad, so that's only fair."

"As long as you find your own Prince Charming."

"Maybe I'll put an ad in the Oxford paper."

Knowing Elli, I wouldn't be surprised. I can see it now:

WANTED
Bona fide Prince Charming,
true love mandatory,
armor and dragon-slaying optional.

Auspicious

I've seen the Taj Mahal from a distance so many times now that I thought I was prepared for the reality. But early in the morning on the day after Ian is released from the hospital, the hotel golf cart takes us the few hundred yards from the hotel down to the entrance. And I am not prepared.

The fairy-tale perfection comes from the setting as much as from the white marble that floats lavender in the hazeless dawn. It's more than the physical artistry and the romance of the story that make it special. The true miracle is that something so fragile can have survived through war and famine and human greed for all these centuries. Everything about it is beautiful, and its existence makes it a tribute to the timeless pull of love.

Everyone I've met in India so far seems to be in love with the idea of love. The very fact that we're all here at dawn is a conspiracy between closet romantics. Mr. Singh at the hotel insisted on bringing us personally, and now he rushes off to speak to a young woman—Mrs. Sharma—who emerges, beaming, from the building with the tickets. She accompanies us up the short drive to the main entrance and whisks us through the snaking security line.

With his air of quiet dignity, Ian holds the inlaid marble box containing my mother's letters on his lap. He's still too weak to walk very far, much less to navigate the crowds and heat later in the day. Already, the air is thick and shimmering, and the line at the entrance winds halfway back to the ticket office.

Mrs. Sharma beams at him as if he's Shah Rukh Khan himself straight from the Bollywood silver screen. Mr. Singh maneuvers the cart past a small tour group of elderly Japanese tourists and across the forecourt toward the gatehouse. Calligraphy inlaid into the red sandstone around the doorway invites visitors into the gardens of paradise, and through the arched gate, the central mausoleum of the Taj is outlined in perfect symmetry.

Again, I'm unprepared. Certain things, and certain people, are too much for the eye and mind to wrap around all the facets of them. Their beauty can only be captured by the heart.

"We're all so arrogant these days, aren't we?" Elli says. "With all our skyscrapers and in-your-face modern cities that make us feel so superior. Then you see something like this and you realize that it's been perfect for the last five hundred years."

"A perfection that won't ever happen again," Malcolm says. "It couldn't."

"It shouldn't, given how the people who built it

were treated." I look down at the box of letters that Ian's holding, and I can't help wondering how much of the money I paid for it actually got to the person who made it. How much is art worth? And how do we pay for it?

Maybe that's exactly why we need places like this and like Halford. They're monuments both to our arrogance and our mortality, built on the backs of the people who came before us. But they preserve our sense of wonder for those who will stand here centuries after we are gone.

Malcolm and I each take one of Ian's elbows and help him up the steps. At the entrance, we all pause and stand without speaking, and Ian shakes off our support and walks forward with the box of letters clutched against his chest. Malcolm offers me his hand. Our fingers tangle together, and we watch each other as we step through the gate. Navigating the still-thin crowds, we wait to take our turn at the place where lovers take their photographs, the most romantic spot in the entire world.

"Stand over there, Dad." Malcolm waits until Ian reaches the apex of the pool, and Ian waits alone beside the water with the remnants of the love my mother carried in secret for twenty years stowed away in an inlaid box. Malcolm snaps a photo, documenting the moment when Mom and Ian are finally here together at the Taj Mahal.

Together after all these years.

The thought brings a fresh rush of sorrow, but the tears that fall are gentle, peaceful. And while Ian's own eyes are red and wounded, his shoulders relax as if coming has brought him peace as well.

Malcolm uses his thumb to wipe the moisture from my cheek.

"This is what they wanted," he says. "Not quite a honeymoon but as close as we can make it."

The sun clears the horizon at just that moment, dusting the white marble in pink and gold and turning it translucent. My chest swells with the vastness and the loveliness.

Malcolm smiles, that beautiful grin that makes my heart beat faster. "I'd say that's definitely an auspicious sign."

He kisses me then, because he can—because *we* can—and Elli snaps another photo. We turn to her, laughing, at the sound of the click. I feel like the luckiest girl in the entire world for getting to be there with them all.

"Tell us the story," Elli says.

"What story?" Ian asks.

"The Izzy version of Ian and Marcella," Elli answers. "Would you mind? Or would that be too painful?"

Ian smiles, bemused. Elli has that effect on people. "No," he says. "I'd very much like to hear it."

Magic

I rub my thumb over the jasper, jade, and carnelian inlaid into the marble of the box Ian holds beside me. Like the delicate work in the Taj itself, the seams are perfect and undetectable.

The four of us move farther down along the reflecting pool, and I begin.

Once upon a time, I say, *a medical student fell in love with a musician when he heard her play from a fourth-row seat at the ceremonial hall in Oxford. Two days later, she went into the hospital with appendicitis, and they met in person. He brought her a book to read while she recuperated and a poem from Omar Khayyam as an invitation to a picnic when she was well:*

> *A book of verse, underneath the bough,*
> *A jug of wine, a loaf of bread—and thou*
> *Beside me singing in the wilderness—*
> *Ah, wilderness were paradise now!*

They became inseparable after that, spending every moment they could together. Two years later, the doctor proposed to her in that same garden, and swept up in love and hope and wine, she believed that love was all they needed. They agreed to marry and begin their life together on a wedding trip to the Taj Mahal, where a long-ago emperor had built a monument to love that had lasted through five centuries. But the doctor had an obligation to his family and the musician was destined to become one of the world's greatest pianists. The doctor told her he couldn't leave the house that had become the legacy of his forefathers, and she told herself that if she stayed, her legacy of music would die before it ever lived.

She left him.

For years, she hoped to find love somewhere else. She waited for it. She searched for it. She saw love in every pair of pale green eyes that reminded her of the doctor's and in every man whose thick, dark brows were winged in a similar shape. Then one day, when she had given up hope of finding love again, they met in Paris and the old love sparked back into a fire. For a single day, they lived a dream, a time outside of time. Then it was over, and they both returned to their lives and obligations. The doctor had his family to think about, and after a while, the musician, too, had a child of her own. They each poured all of their love into their children.

The children grew. The musician was the best mother any child could wish for. And for the child and for herself and for the sake of love, she gave the world the gift of music, an exotic world full of beauty and paintings and moonlight. The doctor cared for his patients and his son and his home, and he grounded himself in thoughts of ancestors and future generations and almost never thought of himself at all.

Most days, the musician was happy, though in the small hours of the night, she would come down to where her piano sat in the still moonlight that flooded through the windows of her music room to write letters to the doctor she had left behind but never forgotten. She wrote to him of her fears and hopes and dreams, and though she never mailed the letters, in her heart she dreamed that they would be together again someday. She searched for him in the audience when she played in London or Edinburgh or Paris. And because he, too, hoped that someday they would be together again, he was often in the audience watching. When he was alone, he played her music. When he closed his eyes, he could almost feel her there beside him.

Years passed. Their paths took them in different directions, but love has a will of its own. When the musician died, her letters brought them together again for one sunrise at the Taj Mahal, where love exists forever within the moonlit gates of paradise and the fiery sun reflects the domes and minarets of an emperor's monument to immortal love. They came together again, and, having found each other there, they couldn't be separated again by time or distance or responsibility. What they couldn't have in life, they would have for eternity.

I'm not sure where to look as I finish speaking, so I crouch and run my hand through the water of the reflecting pool. When I finally glance up, Malcolm nods at me, smiling. Tears glisten on Ian's cheeks, but I think they are happy tears. He looks stronger, less bent, his shoulders broader.

I pull my fingers from the water. Droplets rain

back to the surface, the tempo as quicksilver as one of my mother's arpeggios. The impression is so strong, I can almost hear her playing.

My heart squeezes with longing, love, and hope at the sound. Then a dry leaf appears from nowhere in the air and falls into the reflecting pool, rocking gently on the surface.

"That's odd," Malcolm says as the leaf floats away. "Where'd that come from?"

"It's magic." A shiver rolls through me, and the sound of music swells. "The best kind of magic."

And it is.

That leaf, here, is as magical as my mother. As magical as India and Halford and this cobbled-together family I have found. As magical as what I feel when Malcolm smiles at me, and as magical as the calm certainty that, though he and I are only just beginning, for us there will be the happiest of ever afters coming. A happily ever after with enough love to fill two lifetimes.

Acknowledgments

The debts of gratitude I owe for this book are legion.

Thanks from the bottom of my heart to Kate Brauning for an editorial eye that is exquisitely insightful, sensitive, and exacting. Kate, I hoped you would get this book, but you saw more in it than I knew was there and helped me pull it out. Which is pretty much the dream definition of an editor.

Busloads of thanks to the fabulous authors who read the manuscript and provided their insight, brilliance, and advice. Jodi Meadows, thanks for the countless smart (and often late night) discussions, your patient ear, your incredible generosity, and your beautiful calligraphy. Erin Cashman, as always, thank you for being the perfect barometer of character perspectives and reactions. Victoria Scott, thank you for the title. Liza Wiemer, thank you for text message and creep factor advice. And Sabina Fidahic, thank you for being my Malcolm guinea pig and for making me work for the perfect ending.

A heartfelt thank-you also to Riya Mehta Saran for reading, alleviating my nerves, and affirming my decision about Ian and the ending. And to Roopal Saran, happy anniversary! There aren't enough measures of respect or thanks I can give to you and all the folks at the Literacy Council of Northern Virginia for the wonderful things you do.

Much gratitude to Kalen O'Donnell for a wonderful cover, to Jennifer Harris and Linda Au for making the copy better than I could, and to everyone under the Mayfair umbrella for design, editorial, formatting, marketing, and all the myriad things that go into getting a book out to readers.

Huge thanks to Sarah Kershaw for the gorgeous limited edition art card, the other beautiful artwork, and for her patience and flexibility.

And thank you to One More Page books and Lelia Nebeker for the early order incentive. Even among a long list of fabulous indie bookstores, One More Page is truly special.

Finally, thank you to my fabulous early reader team—especially Sandra Bright for being first in and making me tear up, and Elizabeth Nyreen and Georgia Parker for their sharp eyes and careful attention—and to every reader who is kind enough to give this book a chance.

You all make my heart sing.

About Martina Boone

Martina Boone is the award-winning author of the romantic Southern Gothic Heirs of Watson Island series for young adults, including *Compulsion*, *Persuasion*, and *Illusion* from Simon & Schuster, Simon Pulse, and of heartwarming contemporary novels for adult readers interwoven with romance, history, and legend beginning with *Lake of Destiny*.

She lives in Virginia with her husband, children, a too-smart-for-his-own-good Sheltie, and a lopsided cat, and she enjoys writing books set in the sorts of magical places she loves to visit. When she isn't writing, she's addicted to travel, horses, skiing, chocolate-flavored tea, and anything with Nutella on it.

More Information:
Website: http://www.martinaboone.com/
Twitter: @MartinaABoone
Facebook: https://www.facebook.com/martina.boone/

Made in the USA
Middletown, DE
01 April 2019